Darsham's Tower

Darsham's Tower

a novel by
Harriet Esmond

DELACORTE PRESS / NEW YORK

Copyright © 1973 by Harriet Esmond
All rights reserved.
No part of this book may be reproduced
in any form or by any means
without the prior written permission of the Publisher,
excepting brief quotes used in connection with
reviews written specifically for
inclusion in a magazine or newspaper.
Manufactured in the United States of America
First printing

Designed by Ann Spinelli

Library of Congress Cataloging in Publication Data

Esmond, Harriet.
Darsham's tower.
I. Title.
PZ4.E763Dar   [PR6055.S5]   823'.9'14   73-4725

The head does not know what
the heart is after.

— MARQUIS DE VAUVENARGUES

Darsham's Tower

Chapter One

The hammering at the door took some time to reach Kate Quantrill in the depths of sleep. For three nights the northeast wind had rattled her window and shaken a loose trap door in the stable. The roar of waves on the shingle struck echoes between the cottages. They were familiar sounds: stormy and thunderous, but without the note of real danger which every man, woman, and child on this coast could recognize in every bone and muscle.

At first the knocking could have been just another theme in the whole wild serenade. Then its insistence added a new rhythm.

Kate turned drowsily over. There was no more than a thin line of gray light down one edge of the heavy chenille curtains. Dawn would be a long time coming.

Footsteps thumped down the stairs. She heard the door

open, and the mutter of men's voices. Her brother's slow baritone growl was easily identifiable. The other was lighter, quicker, more urgent.

Kate slid out of bed, reaching for her tartan shawl to pull over her shoulders. The windowpane was icy cold as she pressed her forehead to it.

She was in time to see a man cross the yard. Wall and gate were shadowy under the cloud-raked moon, but though she couldn't watch his departure she did hear the faint jingle of harness and a clop of hooves as he turned what must have been a small trap and trotted off up the road.

A brighter light moved into the yard. Daniel carried a lantern toward the stable.

Kate began to open the window, to call down to him; but the wind tugged wildly at the frame and howled about her head. A conversation carried on from here wouldn't get very far.

She drew the shawl tighter about her, lit a candle, and went downstairs.

Daniel came back into the kitchen, the cat leaping skittishly past him. He was in his middle twenties, clean-shaven, but the flickering shadows cast by his lantern and Kate's candle gave him, for a moment, the ghost of a heavy beard. It was the first time she had ever observed the close resemblance to their father. For that brief instant it was as though Captain Josiah had stumped back in unannounced, home from the sea as huge and boisterous as ever.

Then Daniel set down the wagon lamps he had brought in, the lines of his face settled into their usual pattern, and the illusion fled.

"You're not going out at this time of night?" said Kate.

"It's for Mr. Darsham."

That was enough of an answer. What the Darshams

asked, Senwich folk were accustomed to give. But Kate, still only half-awake, persisted. "At this time of night?"

They both glanced at the kitchen clock, plodding its steady beat against the swirling background of wind and rattling doors. It was five o'clock in the morning.

The cat sat in front of the cold grate, washing itself and looking around occasionally, marveling that it should have been let in from the yard this early.

"Got to take some luggage to the morning train," Daniel explained.

"A fine time to decide to go away!"

"Only her ladyship. And only her luggage, 'cause she's gone already, so Emberson says."

Kate stooped over the kindling box by the grate. "You'll need something hot before you go."

"Time I get there, get loaded up, and then to the station, it'll be a near thing. Reckon I'd best get started."

Sheverton, the nearest station on the Great Eastern line through Suffolk, was a good ten miles inland, with a gentle but long climb over the heath. At least, thought Kate wryly, Daniel would have a good following wind this morning.

She shook herself into wakefulness, still puzzled by the suddenness of it all. "Lady Charlotte must have left in no end of a hurry."

Daniel shrugged. The goings-on up at the big house were no concern of his. If they needed a carrier, he'd be there, and he'd get paid; and that would be that. "All Emberson says was the master wouldn't have her things in the place a day longer. Had to be rid of them this very morning, and no later."

"You'll have to eat as you go." While he filled the lamps, pulled on an extra jersey, and took down his caped coat, Kate hastily wrapped a cloth around a hunk of bread of her own baking, some butter, and a slab of cheese. At the last minute she took the lantern to the smokehouse to fetch him a couple of herring.

It was impossible to go back to bed after the cart had rumbled off up the road toward the Darsham gates, tempting as the thought might be.

The house was chill. The backhouse boy did not begin work until half-past six, so there was no hot water yet in the copper for washing, and no fire in the grate.

When Tommy did appear he was horrified to find her fully dressed, eating an early breakfast, with the kettle swinging over a blazing fire. He shot a fearful glance at the clock.

Kate laughed. "It's all right, Tommy. Mr. Daniel had to set off early, and I couldn't sleep, so I started the day's work just to keep warm."

The lad breathed a sigh of relief and applied himself with a will to cleaning the knives, making a great show of it to impress his audience. It was such a distracting performance that after a while Kate made him stop and stoke himself up on tea and salt pork. When it was daylight he went out to chop more kindling and fill the coal scuttles.

The February dawn came gray and reluctant. But at least with its coming there was a slackening of the wind. When Kate walked into the village in the middle of the morning, the gale had almost died away. Only on a corner of the lane above the creek did fretful gusts still whip her cheeks, stirring the hem of her woolen cloak and trying to pluck the hat from her thick black hair.

It was straight hair, long and coarse and coal-black rather than the gleaming blue-black of a raven's wing. If Kate ran a hand through it first thing in the morning, it crackled against her fingers. Even now, as she touched the end of her hatpin to test that it was secure, a few strands tickled harshly under her palm. It was unfair: two of her brothers had natural dark curls, and although Daniel's hair was as straight as her own it was positively silky. Even her father's thick mop, exposed to the salt winds of the seven seas, was softer to the touch.

She emerged from the warren of streets which made up the heart of Senwich and came out on the hard above the beach.

This cobbled stretch was a truer center for the village than the more sheltered marketplace. Here you got an uninterrupted view of the sea; and since nearly everything in Senwich depended on the sea, living or dying by reason of the sea, this was the place to meet and talk . . . and watch. Here you learned the changes and portents of wind and weather. Here you knew fear, waiting for an overdue fishing boat which might never return. Here you prophesied good seasons and bad ones, happiness or disaster.

Now that the wind had dropped, an opal mist engulfed the water a few yards from the shore. There was no horizon. Ripples of water shimmered away into a rippling haze, hurting the eyes with a distillation of pale but penetrating winter sunshine.

The usual groups were here: women shopping, three men smoking pipes before resuming work on an upturned boat dragged clear of the tide, a cluster of older women who had converged from their accustomed places on their front doorsteps, where they would squat by the hour weaving or repairing nets.

A girl's voice was raised indignantly.

"As good as thrown out with the luggage, I was. As though it was my fault. As though it was me what put her up to it."

"Didn't need no putting up to it, that one," said an older woman.

There was a dry rustle of agreement, like wind in the marram grass. At the same time another of the group edged back to her doorstep and bowed her head once more over a net, carefully not listening. For her it wasn't right to gossip about the Darshams.

For everyone else it was a golden opportunity. In these parts gossip was a commodity nearly as precious as fish. Sour critics from neighboring parishes declared that if you sneezed on Senwich dike you'd have the ague by the time you reached the parish pump.

"And now what am I to do?" the girl was lamenting. "Brought me all the way from Norwich, and very good references I had, too." Full of self-pity, she meant to make the most of the drama while it lasted. "Brought me all this way, and nobody can say I didn't do what I had to do, and never a word against me, and now what am I going to do?"

Kate recognized the girl as Lady Charlotte's maid. She was pert and artful-eyed, accustomed to think of herself as a cut above the ordinary domestic. Most girls wanting to go into service had to travel some way from home, and it took years to save up for a wedding dot while still sending what they could to their parents. A lady's maid did better than most. But a lady's maid thrown brusquely out of the house had farther to fall than most.

"And it was supposed to be one of *his* friends!"

Kate made a show of paying no attention but had to confess to herself that she was fascinated.

"One of Mr. Darsham's own friends. Or he was, at the start. Connections at court, I heard. Oh, there's a lot I heard." It was doubtful if she had known quite as much as the arch wagging of her head indicated. But this was her last fling, making up for what she had just been deprived of. "Knowing me lady, I could have told you which way it'd go. Seen it before, though it never got this far before. Always talking about people they knew, and how lovely it'd be dropping in on this one and that one, and the subscription balls and the races and heaven knows what else. And then . . ."

Her audience was spellbound.

"And then," she cried, "off she goes with her young officer. Such a to-do. The way he went on at her—the master, I mean. Such a clash-ma-dang I never did hear."

One of the women muttered a question. The girl nodded vigorously. "Oh, yes, they was always having rows, her and the master. Long before this one came. She was a spoilt one, and she didn't like him not bothering with her. If you take my meaning." They were not sure they did, but wanted to hear more. Grudgingly the girl conceded, "She was always good to me, I'm not saying she wasn't. But she didn't belong here. That I'll swear to."

Kate's own recollections of Lady Charlotte were vague. As a child she had been puzzled by Mr. Darsham's wife being a Lady Charlotte Darsham instead of plain Mrs. Or perhaps it was the other way around that was funny: if she was Lady Charlotte, why wasn't he Sir Oliver or something? Once she had seen something in the Sheverton newspaper about her having been Lady Charlotte Finch-Howard before she married, but that hadn't helped her to understand.

The lady had been as remote and puzzling as her name. She rarely appeared in the village, and when she did so, seemed determined to keep her face shielded not only from wind and sun but also from other people's gaze. Kate retained the merest impression of wide blue eyes in a pale, heart-shaped face; eyes contemptuous beneath a lace bonnet trimmed with silk and flowers. Sometimes there would be friends from London. The carriage would rumble into the village, and the visitors would descend while Lady Charlotte leaned from within, pointing out the curiosities

of the place with long, satin-gloved fingers. On the few
occasions when she herself took a few paces along the
street, she protected both hands in a muff.

She had presented her husband with one daughter and
no more. Somehow it was just what the locals would have
expected of her.

Of Mr. Darsham himself, it seemed they never knew
quite what to expect. Kate had heard hushed accounts of
his outbursts of rage, and of spells of brooding silence
when there was no sense to be got out of him. She was
half-amused, half-indignant that his men should be so
ready to shift the blame onto a woman, all of them reck-
oning it was her ladyship who made him that way.

"The wind hadn't made up its mind when they two
met," Captain Josiah Quantrill had once said. It was the
nearest thing to a criticism that Kate had ever heard her
father utter of his employer. "That was a bit late when he
found which way that wind *did* blow."

Kate moved away from the group to the edge of the
cobbles and peered into the frostily dazzling haze.

A whiff of shag swirled pungently about her on a flurry
of wind. Old Dodd—usually known as Hodmedod, the
local name for a snail, because of his slow dragging gait—
stood to windward, puffing his pipe and nodding at her.

"They don't make this tide," he said, "they'll have to
stand off till nightfall."

He knew who she was waiting for. If you stood on this
hard long enough, you came to know everything about
everybody.

Senwich lay on a shallow hillside above a Suffolk creek,
opening into the river Wilding. Once upon a time it had
been a port and harbor of some consequence, and there
were still proud records of its having long ago maintained

six galleys in the king's service. Coastal erosion in the early eighteenth century had undermined a large part of it, dragging houses and churches down into a watery grave and silting up the estuary. Now only two decrepit quays remained, one close to the harbor entrance and one in the shelter of the creek. The narrow channel in and out of the harbor was navigable for only an hour on each tide.

Still, most of the local men scraped a living from fishing. When they couldn't put out or when the season was poor, they managed with what they might make from eel-spearing in the reed-rustling marshes all around, or from seasonal gang work on the farms. A few turned their backs altogether on the treacherous waters and committed themselves to farming or to service with the Darshams. The family gave employment on its land to a number of hedgers and ditchers, and allowed gathering of reeds for sale to thatchers. Younger men worked the tide mill down the coast, and some lads went to work on the Darsham quays in Ipswich, twenty miles away. Once there, they rarely came back to settle.

Kate blinked and turned to rest her eyes on the green marshes.

Seen from here the reedy expanse was broken by two towers beyond the northern end of the village. One was the flinty gray tower of the church. The other was a high, spindly column in dulled red brick, with mullioned windows and a castellated battlement at the top.

This was Darsham's Folly.

It had stood there for nigh on two hundred years. There was a tale that the Darsham who built it, thwarted in other ambitions and turning to commerce, had wanted a high lookout from which to catch first glimpse of his returning merchantmen. There were other tales: of a haunting, of rebellious daughters locked away in upper rooms, of

strange half-human scaly creatures lurking in the cellars—
stories which the tellers themselves didn't really believe but
which were in keeping with the soaring, senseless pillar.

The founder had grandly named it Darsham's Tower.

From the day of its completion it had been known to
the locals as Darsham's Folly.

Kate could distinguish the iron cresset in which a
beacon light was kindled for shipping in bad weather. The
windows, piled up in threes to the fifth narrow story,
stared blankly back at her. She wondered whether Mr.
Darsham was raging through that gaunt building from
room to room, floor to floor, cursing the names of his wife
and her lover; or sitting at a window, brooding over the
vista of unchanging yet ever-changing sea.

All at once the windows seemed, in a faint shift of the
light, to come alive. Kate looked hastily away, back into
the mist.

Right ahead of her appeared a darker patch. As she
watched, a ghostly shape solidified and pushed its way
through the hazy curtain. The darkness glowed a deep red
and became the spread canvas of a spritsail barge. She let
out a gasp of relief. Not that she had ever doubted they
would come safely home. Not really doubted. But it was
always good to be sure that they were well and truly
back.

John had almost brailed up the mainsail, but had left
enough topsail to catch the spasmodic wind above the
harbor wall. The barge shuddered. Her bowsprit came
around and jutted toward the entrance, apparently lined
up on the northern groin.

"That go nicely," said old Hodmedod approvingly.

Kate walked from the hard to the lumpy path by the
groin. The barge was slowing into the channel. She looked
down on Abel at the wheel, and he waved. John also

waved, and shouted. Unable to hear, she bent precariously over the bank.

"Hot buns!" he yelled.

She nodded acknowledgment and began to run back to the pastry cook's in the marketplace. Then she forced herself to slow down. There was ample time to buy the spicy buns her brothers loved. She could pace her progress to the shop, up the lane, and down the slope to the house, just as accurately as they could time their tack into the creek and their tying up at the jetty.

And her father's words still resounded in her head. She could still see his expression when he returned from China that last time.

He had watched her run to welcome him, her skirts tucked up above her knees. She had been wading in the shallows with two little village boys who called her Auntie Kate and were always at the kitchen door asking if she had time to tell them a story or come out to play. Her father had laughed when he saw her, and she had laughed back and run into his arms. But after hugging her and rubbing his beard against her cheek as he always did, his laughter had unexpectedly died. He held her away from him and the smile was gone, and he said ponderously, "It's time you walked. A bit less running. You're not a child anymore."

She was taken aback. He would often roar at her as he roared at the boys, and she was used to his wrath. This time there was something different, something inexplicable. Gruffly he added, "You're nineteen. And a young woman shouldn't expose herself in that fashion."

With three older brothers, she had never been treated as a younger sister. She had been just another of them—a tomboy, and happy with it. Now she nearly laughed out loud, but saw that her father wouldn't enjoy a laugh. Later she told Daniel about it and hoped they could share the silliness of it. All that happened was that Daniel reddened and said: "Yes . . . well . . . yes, you're nineteen."

So now she restrained herself from running impetuously and walked to the shop as though—she thought with a flash of irritation—Lady Charlotte or one of her precious friends might be studying her and waiting for some crude error in her deportment.

It was not until she had left the huddle of the village for the lane curving around to the creek that she sensed she was indeed being studied.

She looked back, catching Darsham's Folly from a different angle.

A fresh figure had been added to the landscape in the last ten minutes or so. It was one which could hardly be mistaken.

Even standing still, Oliver Darsham showed his lameness in the way he slumped slightly to one side. His right leg took the weight. His shoulders were hunched within his Norfolk jacket, the right shoulder pushing forward. He had set himself on a hummock in the uneven, tussocky ground between his house and the church, as though assessing the bounds of his property. But he was paying little attention to the walls and hedges. Nor was he reading the sea for its threats and promises, as they all compulsively did at all times of day.

He was gazing straight at Kate.

Even from this distance his deeply etched features were clear. The gash of his mouth, the lowered head, the crouch of his shoulders—all spoke of a seething anger.

Anger . . . at her? It was absurd. Although his head was turned in her direction, he was surely not even aware of her existence. He was seeing somebody else, someone far away, the mere thought of whom lashed him into an inner turmoil.

Kate quickened her pace. Then she slowed again.

If he were just conceivably watching her, in whatever mood, by whatever chance, she must let him see her as her father would wish her to be seen.

At the top of the lane she glanced back just once.

Oliver Darsham still stood there. Only his head had moved, had turned a fraction to follow her.

Chapter Two

On Sunday morning the remaining Darshams did not flinch. Their carriage drew up at the lych-gate its customary five minutes before service. Last Sunday four members of the family had sat in the box pew on the south aisle. Today there were only three. The heads of two of them were as erect as ever. Only the thirteen-year-old daughter, for once without her mother beside her, sat slumped forward until tapped on the shoulder by her grandmother and made to straighten up.

Old Mrs. Darsham was her usual somber self beneath the whiteness of her late husband's marble memorial. She wore a jet-trimmed jacket over a black taffeta dress, and her bonnet gleamed darkly with jet beads. The only bright touch was a gay cluster of feathers at the front of the bonnet.

Lettering on the plaque between two sorrowing angels told of the long and virtuous life of Robert Hubert Darsham, devoted husband of Letitia and beloved father of Elizabeth and Alice. In conclusion it thanked God for the gift of a son, Oliver Alexander, only a few months before he departed this vale of tears.

Beside the aging widow sat that same son, grown up and head of the household now, staring rigidly ahead.

Kate was several pews back on the other side of the aisle, accompanied by her brothers and the girl Daniel was soon to marry. At intervals during the service she found herself stealing a glance at what she could make out of Oliver Darsham's craggy profile.

Like Mrs. Darsham, he was dressed in black. His dark brown hair descended into luxuriant sideburns, curling in across both cheeks so that the livid scar on the left was partially concealed. It could be regarded as a cruel face, or perhaps as a mask contrived to hide another self.

Kate let herself muse about that other self. The real one, perhaps. How would he stand up to the affront he had just suffered? Would the mask harden and take over completely, or one day crack in despair?

She shook herself. The gloating gossip of the village was bad enough. This private guessing about a man so remote from her was out-and-out silly.

In the pulpit stood his cousin, to whom had been presented the living of the parish. Alive or dead, the Darshams looked after their own. On all sides were testimonies to the departed: back over the generations, back through grandparents and great-grandparents to the time when there was a Lord Darsham of Blackshore instead of merely a Mr. Darsham of Darsham's Folly. There were the names of many a lady, too, added to their husbands' inscriptions.

With Lady Charlotte gone, was Oliver Darsham
doomed, alive and dead, to lie alone?

Kate's attention was distracted by a warmer note in the
Reverend Godfrey Hartest's thin voice. He was looking
down at their pew and smiling benignly.

He called the banns for the marriage of Daniel Quantrill
to Sarah Abigail Tooke.

Heads turned. There were echoing smiles.

Only the Darshams did not look around.

At the end of the service Mr. Darsham escorted his
mother and daughter with ceremonial slowness from their
pew to the door. His lowering eyebrows concealed whatever expression might burn in those deep-set eyes. As light
from a window fell on his cheek, the whiteness of the scar
became the outline of a claw, groping out from his hair.

Everyone knew he had been pitched from a horse when
small, and that his flesh had been torn open by the jagged
end of a branch. Still there were those who whispered of it
as the devil's handiwork, or the mark of the phantom
black dog of the marshes dragging him from his saddle.
Another curse to add to that of the hip twisted at birth.

From close range this time Kate saw the anger in his
features, in the tight set of that large mouth which was
surely made for generosity rather than resentment.

The slightest jerk of his head turned his gaze full on
her.

His slow progress along the aisle did not falter. But he
tensed, and his eyes seemed to ask a question—of himself
or of her?

Then they had passed and gone out into the cold bright-
ness.

Friends came up to talk to Daniel and Sarah as they
crossed the churchyard. Kate fell back a few paces and
idly surveyed the scene.

Clusters of primroses had sprung up around the graves,

and below the shelter of the wall was a swaying line of daffodils. Beyond the wall, in the shadow of the elms, Sunday bonnets bobbed away toward the village.

"They'll make a handsome couple," a woman was saying, close behind Kate.

"Put his sister's nose out of joint a bit, though."

Then there was a startled little "Oh" as they realized who was within earshot, and the hasty shuffle of footsteps back around the tower.

Dominating everything on this side was the Darsham mausoleum, a great stone hulk against the churchyard wall nearest Darsham's Tower, a burial chamber almost as grandiose a folly as the house itself. Surrounded by ornamental iron fencing commissioned by Mr. Oliver some years ago, it held the bodies of all the Darshams save those who had been lost at sea or in battle abroad, or who had died of the plague in seventeenth-century London. At each corner stood a vast stone urn, and Latin lettering formed a frieze all around.

Kate preferred the simplicity of the stone beneath which her mother lay, garnished with posies of the flowers she had loved.

Three days later Kate came to the church again, in company with Sarah's mother.

Miss Hartest was waiting for them.

"I'm sorry my brother isn't here. He has been called to the bedside of one of his parishioners."

"We'll get along better without the men." Mrs. Tooke, a plump woman with a red-apple complexion, did not lower her cheerful voice even a fraction simply because she was in church.

Miss Hartest said sharply, "People always expect him to be everywhere at once."

Her abruptness could reduce many of the village women

to nervous silence. Others called her a dry old stick, a born spinster. But she was not much over thirty, and Kate was prepared to believe it was only shyness which gave her such a prickly manner.

"As long as he's at the ceremony!" chuckled Mrs. Tooke.

"He's far too conscientious in his duties."

Flora Hartest looked after the diffident parson with as fierce a devotion as any wife could have shown.

Kate said, "Daniel asks me to—"

"To represent his interests?" Miss Hartest barked a short laugh. "Yes, I suppose Mrs. Tooke is right. We shall get along better without their intervention."

When it was a matter of arranging for weddings, christenings, or funerals, Miss Hartest came into her own. Of course they would want the organ. Was there any special music the bride or bridegroom favored? "Well," said Mrs. Tooke, "there's that hymn she's always liked, you know . . . the one that . . ." She tried to hum, with unrecognizable results, and burst into an infectious giggle. Kate thought of Daniel's reaction if consulted on what music he would like, and found it just as amusing.

Miss Hartest clucked her tongue impatiently, but was obviously glad to be made responsible for the final selection.

"And, of course, the flowers . . ."

She had it all so clear in her mind that there was little for Kate and Mrs. Tooke to do but nod agreement.

When they had almost finished, Mrs. Tooke said to Kate, "And it'll be your turn soon, I shouldn't wonder?"

"I've no plans," said Kate awkwardly.

"High time you thought about it."

"There's . . . nobody particular."

"Doesn't do to be too particular."

At that moment the heavy ring of the latch grated against the door of the south porch. Miss Hartest turned, alert for a new face, fresh problems.

Oliver Darsham emerged from the cool shadow of the porch.

"Godfrey is not about?"

"He's ridden over to Markmill. Somebody there is afflicted."

"Yes. Old Rogers. I've told the doctor he must have whatever he needs. And I'm sending food over. I doubt if he'll last, though."

Mrs. Tooke was studying the window embrasures as though visualizing them rich with vases of spring flowers. Kate found herself staring straight at the newcomer as he approached.

Miss Hartest said, "Cousin Oliver, I think you know the Quantrills."

"I do."

"This is Miss Quantrill. Miss Kate Quantrill."

He put out his hand. It was sinewy and possessive as it closed on Kate's.

"Captain Josiah's daughter," he said.

Some perverse impulse almost drove her to say that she was not merely Captain Josiah's daughter but Kate Quantrill in her own right. She restrained it. As he looked so intently into her face, she sensed full well that he saw her as a person in her own right.

His hand slowly relinquished hers.

"Your father will be home for the ceremony?"

"We're hoping so. Daniel and Sarah waited for a message from the mail packet before choosing the date. Father should make Ipswich—"

"One week from Tuesday next," Mr. Darsham finished for her. He nodded. "Captain Josiah's dependability is a watchword on my wharves. It would be a foolhardy sea god who tried to hold him back."

Miss Hartest, deciding it was her duty to rescue him from this polite condescension, said, "Is there a message I can give Godfrey when he returns?"

"Hm?" Mr. Darsham appeared to have forgotten what had brought him here. "Oh, no, no." He waved it aside. "It will wait. Miss Quantrill, you've had a considerable responsibility, all these years, with so many menfolk to look after."

"I haven't found it too arduous."

"No." He looked her up and down as he might have done a horse, appraising its physical capabilities. "When your brother is married, it may not be so easy."

"My Sarah will do her share," contributed Mrs. Tooke eagerly.

"Quite so. Two women in one kitchen!" For the first time the deep pools of Mr. Darsham's eyes twinkled. "I'm sorry," he said with mock gravity, "for the backhouse boy, with two mistresses to serve."

Miss Hartest said, "Well, I think there's nothing further we need discuss at this stage."

Mr. Darsham did not move. He said, "Strange, Miss Quantrill, how time has gone by since I last saw you. Quite a tomboy, as I recall."

"We do not all stay the same forever," said Kate with a touch of defiance. The steadiness of his gaze was disconcerting.

"A pity," he said. "It's no disgrace to play the hoyden." And then, in an abrupt, muted, but breathtaking fury, "To allow oneself to be pampered, and to give nothing in return, is a far less pretty conceit."

Miss Hartest gave an involuntary little cluck of disapproval. The weal on his cheek burned with a whiter heat.

He turned on his heel and limped down the aisle. His head came up only as he passed a group of memorial plaques, to which he nodded as though owing each one a ritual courtesy.

Kate bristled. There were plenty of Quantrills, too, lying in the good earth outside these flinty walls. They had no great tombs or ornate monuments, no lavishly carved tributes and no fine flowers of marble poetry. But they were as much the bones and blood of this land as were the Darshams.

Captain Josiah had fathered three strapping sons before Kate arrived. It was taken for granted that the boys would go to sea in some capacity or other. John and Abel worked on a boomie, a coastal barge, carrying steam coal from Wales to the east coast until they could afford to run their own. Oliver Darsham had come to their aid: he put up a large part of the money for them to have a spritsail barge built in an Essex boatyard on the understanding that they would contract half their trade through his Ipswich company. Mainly they carried grain. And it was when delivering to the maltings at the highest navigable reach of the river Wilding that they met the girl who was to marry into the family—not to wed either of them, but their brother Daniel.

Daniel had not gone to sea. To his mother's relief, he had set up as a carrier, working from their large sprawling home above the creek. Captain Josiah made a great fuss at the time, but really he admired a lad who could tackle a job so different from his own and make a success of it.

Told jokingly of the maltster's beautiful daughter, Daniel made excuses to branch off the Sheverton road and down to the river in search of custom. After a while he ceased bothering with excuses. John and Abel denounced him, a landlubber, for courting their beautiful girl while they were away at sea; but neither of them truly wanted to marry yet, and Daniel most assuredly did.

The transom ribbons of the barge carried, within a fine surround of gilded scrollwork, the name *Mary Matilda*. The real Mary Matilda died of a marsh fever when Kate was fifteen, and she had to come back from her school in Beccles to take over the running of the household.

She had been sent there on her mother's insistence. Mary Matilda never raised her voice and always deferred to Captain Josiah's wishes, even when he was oceans away and would not know whether she followed them or not. But over this one matter she was gently determined to prevail. The boys had attended the National School off and on, but had been in a hurry to escape. Boys ought to be out earning their keep. Kate, said her mother, was going to be treated differently.

"I want something better for her than just going into service till she marries some farmer or fisherman. Or worse—some clipper captain she'll see once every few years, when he takes it into his head to call."

Her husband had boomed indignation and she had retaliated with a pretense of tantrums. Both of them soon dissolved into affectionate laughter.

Kate lodged with an aunt in Beccles, attended Miss Pringle's school during the week, and came home Sundays. She enjoyed her lessons and picked up more than she was officially taught, for the faded Miss Pringle was more concerned with money to keep a roof over her head than with pushing much knowledge into her pupils' heads. What Kate least enjoyed was the exile from Senwich itself. There were pleasant enough saunters along the river and in the colorful streets of this little town, but they were not to be compared with her village and its empire of sea, marsh, and heath. She longed to be home of a Sunday. Away from the rich air and great skies of the coast, she felt stifled.

It was a sad homecoming when her mother died. But out of her new responsibilities Kate shaped a new pattern which suited her. Its threads were erratic, but she loved them: Captain Josiah's unpredictable comings and goings, John and Abel making up their timetable as they went along, Daniel working from home and closest to her.

And now Daniel was to be married and would be bringing his bride into the house which Kate had ruled for four years.

He was busy. On top of his usual commissions there were personal things to be attended to. Furniture had to be carried from Sheverton. He bought paint to freshen the neglected west wing of the house, and wood for repairing a rotted window frame in what would be their bedroom. The decorating was done in his spare time, which meant, on the whole, late at night.

One evening he was late back from collecting a consignment of provisions and some bolts of cloth from Sheverton station.

"I saw our Mr. Darsham getting off the London train," he commented, appreciatively sniffing the soup Kate had been keeping hot for him over the fire.

"Most likely he got on at Ipswich."

"Looked more like he'd come all the way. He had a London newspaper with him. And there was a sort of look about him."

"A sort of look?"

"He was still far away. In a kind of daze, you could say. Only he was all tightened up, and yet he was laughing with it. Not the kind of laugh you'd like to hear."

"Something to do with business," she hazarded.

"And somebody got the worst of it, I reckon."

Daniel applied his spoon vigorously to his bowl of soup, and said no more.

On the day of the wedding the sun shone and the frosty air was still. Gulls bobbed up and down like tiny skiffs on the smoothly undulating water, instead of swooping and screeching about the rooftops.

Captain Josiah was home.

"You grow larger every time I see you," Kate had laughed as he swaggered into the house, hugged her, and lifted her exuberantly off her feet. "What do you do out east—eat the natives alive?"

He did indeed seem more massive on each visit. He filled the house with his presence—his voice, his mane of hair and his beard, his broad shoulders, and his rolling gait. Yet in church, as his son and Sarah made their vows, there was a stillness about him and a gentleness in his smile which dimmed the resplendent glitter of his uniform and gleaming buttons.

Kate found her eyes straying every now and then to the vacant Darsham pew. The marriage of Oliver Darsham and Lady Charlotte Finch-Howard must have been more dazzling than this, but the promises had been the same, the words of the service the same; and now the words had been defied, the promises shattered.

"Forsaking all other . . ."

Mrs. Tooke began to weep joyfully.

"To have and to hold from this day forward . . ."

Captain Josiah rubbed his right eye with his knuckles, and endeavored to disguise the movement by tugging at his beard.

"Those whom God hath joined together, let no man put asunder."

Sarah, a sturdy girl with sparkling gray eyes and a complexion as rosy as her mother's, was playing an ethereal role for just one day. Her wedding dress of flimsy white tarlatan, trimmed with ribbons and flowers from her mother's wedding dress, swept into a train at the back, imposing on her a dignity which she hadn't known before and would soon learn to forget.

Beside her, Daniel was clearly wishing the whole awful ceremonial over and done with.

When at last he stepped from the church door with his new beaver hat on his head and Sarah on his arm, his gasp of relief sounded, said his father, "like a squall fit to bring the topgallants down."

In the house were cold chicken and a great side of roast beef and four large rabbit pies. There were bowls of frumenty, its tangy smell drifting into every corner and every fold of curtain in the parlor, and bottles of blackberry wine arrayed on the sideboard below the oval portraits of the Queen and her late consort.

For those who could find no space indoors or who preferred in any case to move about in the open, John and Abel had set up trestles on the green before the house. The landlord of the Darsham Arms had racked up two barrels of ale on a trodden patch of ground, and for the children there were homemade cordials.

Nobody felt the afternoon cold. Food and drink fought off the chill.

A clatter of wheels on the stony lane did not penetrate the hubbub until the gig was level with the green. Then voices faltered. One youth went on talking unsteadily, but finally sagged into a half-respectful, half-uneasy hush.

The backhouse boy hurried across to stand by the horse's head.

Oliver Darsham got down from the gig.

It was said that since his childhood fall he had never bestridden a horse again—not from fear, but because of the pain and awkwardness of his movement.

Kate was on her way from the scullery with some clean tankards, along the stone-flagged passage to the front door. She emerged as Mr. Darsham halted before the bride and bridegroom.

He had already sent them a tea service in brightly flowered china. It was the standard gift from the big house on such occasions and, like so many of its predecessors, would be kept in a glass-fronted cupboard in the parlor and taken out only to be dusted or to impress visiting relations.

Now he gave a stiff little bow. "I would esteem it a privilege to drink to the health of Mr. and Mrs. Daniel Quantrill."

Kate set down the tankards on the end of the trestle table. "I'll fetch a glass of wine."

"Please, Miss Quantrill, you are not to put yourself out." He moved closer to her father, who was holding the quart pot that hung from a hook in the pantry during his absence and was touched by no one but himself. "Like the captain, I think our local ale is as fine a tribute as one may drink."

A tankard was filled for him. He raised it toward Daniel and Sarah, and his deformity was overcome by the graceful flourish of the gesture.

It was taken as a signal by the hired fiddler, who began to play a lively jig.

Someone started to sing. Half a dozen boys and girls danced into a ring, which speedily widened. The man was a good player and a tireless one: he would need to be, with the afternoon and evening hours ahead of him.

Kate allowed herself a moment's respite and reached for the cider jug.

Her father and Mr. Darsham drew apart from the rest, as she had often seen men do—men who derived greater pleasure from talking their common business than from social chatter.

"New Zealand?" she heard her father boom. He was frowning.

Mr. Darsham began earnestly to explain something. Captain Josiah shook his head.

"All these years in the tea trade . . ."

"Lost . . ."

Music drowned their conversation. Kate turned her attention to some children whose boisterous games threatened to send cups and plates flying.

At last Sarah's brother arrived with the trap in which he would drive Daniel and Sarah to Sheverton station. When they had been put on the train, on their way to spend four days somewhere whose name they refused to divulge, he would return with the trap to pick up his parents and take them home.

Sarah was lifted, struggling and laughing, by John and Abel. From the heart of her bouquet she plucked a cluster of marsh marigolds and tossed it into the air.

Kate tensed instinctively, sprang . . . and caught the butter-yellow posy in midair. Sarah waved; a red-haired girl let out a moan of disappointment; and Kate felt all at once young and clumsy and ridiculous.

Close by her elbow, Mr. Darsham said gently, "You take it as an omen, Miss Quantrill?"

"I am not so romantic."

"Very wise of you." His lips tightened. "There is too much pain in it."

She felt her face redden. Felt her hand about to tighten and crush the flowers. Felt gawky and undesirable; and wondered why it should be so humiliating, since it mat-

tered not what the warped, disdainful Mr. Darsham
thought of her.

Her father was a few steps away, moving to join them.
Mr. Darsham said to him, "You have three fine boys."

"God has been generous."

"And a fine young woman this one has married."

"I'm happy for him."

"They'll produce a good crop of grandsons for you."

Captain Josiah guffawed. "You have them started early,
sir!"

The trap was turning. The young men and girls chased
it, trotted beside it, keeping pace until the wheels were
spinning too fast and they had to drop back.

Sarah moved. Everyone waved.

"Sons," mused Mr. Darsham aloud. "Boys. It is in your
destiny, Captain. You are one of the fortunate ones."

Despite herself Kate burst out, "I'm sorry you think so
ill of daughters, Mr. Darsham."

It jolted him. He was literally caught off balance, startled, twisting all his weight onto the painful leg and hip.

"Discourteous of me," he said after a reflective pause.
"After all"—his mouth wrenched with an inner anguish—
"without a woman, how shall a man have sons?"

He was steady now, in control of himself. And on his
face was a look such as she had seen once in her life
before, on an utterly different face. A drunken trawlerman
on Senwich hard had watched her come ashore from
Abel's little longshore fishing boat when she was just six-
teen, her wet clothes clinging to her breasts and haunches.
In a matter of seconds she had realized what the twist of
her body could do to a man's appetite. She had been glad
to have her brother with her.

Now she saw it again. Not in the bleary features of a
drunkard, but in the autocratic eyes of Oliver Darsham.

He did not move from where he stood, or permit the flicker of one muscle in that distorted cheek. Yet he was all the more frightening for that.

The fiddler struck up a wilder tune.

Its leaping cadences danced through her blood until she longed to turn and run and shut herself away indoors. But even with every door and window tightly shut against the sound and against the naked greed in Oliver Darsham's face, she knew the pulse would continue to beat.

Chapter Three

Kate crossed the kitchen and reached for the poker. The fire was damped down and needed livening before she could use the oven.

"Ooh, Miss Kate, I wouldn't!"

Florence, the maid, was coming in from the yard with a load of clean washing in a wicker basket.

"But I want to make a cake."

"So does Mrs. Daniel. A fruit cake. And it's already in the oven, doing nicely."

Kate shrugged to show it was of no consequence, and made a point of ignoring the girl's saucy grin.

Sarah was quick, competent, and full of energy. She was more than willing to take much of the burden of running the house off Kate's shoulders. Too willing: Kate found she was being robbed, with the best will in the world, of a large part of her day's work. To complain would be absurd. Daniel was her senior and had a greater claim on the house. His wife was entitled, if she chose, to a greater say in its running.

Not that Sarah would assert such a right. She made a point of fitting in tactfully, deferring to Kate in most things. She brought her own special treasures with her, including the patchwork quilt which she had made from vivid silks and brocades brought by Daniel's brothers from Holland without too many questions asked, and strips of cloth of silver brought from the East by Captain Josiah. This, naturally, belonged in the bedroom in the west wing that Daniel had decorated, and her other possessions went into the room adjoining. Nothing in the rest of the house was to be altered by her coming.

But how could it help but be altered?

The kitchen was the center of Kate's daily life. It was a large kitchen, but with another woman in it the space had contracted.

Florence was carefully spreading out one of Sarah's frilled petticoats, ready for the goffering iron. Kate leaned over it, admired it, and then was left with nothing to do. The furniture in the parlor had been polished. Florence would do the dusting upstairs later on. The backhouse boy had scrubbed down the floors and the passage. Daniel had mucked out the stable before setting off this morning. The oven was in use. The pantry was well stocked.

Kate wandered aimlessly out into the yard.

She reached the gate as her father came pacing around the house from the front.

His head was back, he was sniffing the wind. These last few days he had been positively surly. Three weeks had passed since he came home, and for him that was too long. He felt the urge to be away again.

They exchanged a sheepish, conspiratorial grin.

"Do you need a cook on your next voyage?" asked Kate.

"Not going to risk bad luck by taking a woman aboard. Besides"—he tugged her arm through his, and they strolled toward the creek—"I've still got my Chinese boy. You're nearly as good as he is, but you've still got a bit of a way to go."

It was the nearest thing to a compliment she was likely to get from him.

She squeezed his arm. "Did you enjoy yourself in Ipswich yesterday?"

"Enjoy myself? Shuffling about the docks advising on new wharfage—what kind of task is that for a seafaring man?"

"I'm sure Mr. Darsham wouldn't have consulted you if he didn't value your opinion."

"I'm a lot better value to him fetching the stuff to *fill* his warehouses." They stopped by the jetty. The mudbank where the creek met the river was exposed, glistening with a slime like fish scales. "I'm to go up and see him this morning, an hour from now." His restlessness was that of a craft straining at its moorings. "Don't know what he'll have to tell me."

"Something special?"

"There's no way, ever, of being rightly sure what's in his mind. Sometimes I think he makes a decision the way the mood takes him. And then sometimes you get to understand it's all part of something too big for any one other person to see. He don't let on, any more'n he lets on about knowing the name and position of every man jack who works for him, and all about their families. But he *does* know. Knows where everything rightly belongs." Captain Josiah stared across the shallows at a gull picking its way daintily along the edge of the mud. "And you?" It came as an abrupt challenge.

"Me, Father?"

"High time you were away. Why don't you find yourself a likely young fellow?"

She flared up. "It's not for me to go searching."

"No? Without you search, there's nothing much around here. You've done enough for the rest of us, girl. Time you cast off."

Kate stamped her way back up the slope, too confused to answer. With the best part of an hour to fill, her father headed toward the inn. She debated whether or not to go back indoors, and chose the heath instead. Alone, unobserved, she could forget rules of poise and decorum, and stride over the springy ground, running if she felt like it or standing for untold minutes in silent contemplation if she felt like it.

Sarah's presence had at least made this possible. She had free time once more. Learning how to use it once more would be quite a task.

White violets glimmered on the bend of an old cart track. Above a brackish ditch was a glow of primroses. Kate sauntered past. When they had sunk below a barrier of bracken, she stepped out more vigorously.

The road from Senwich to Sheverton turned back on itself below this ridge, forming a loop around a barrow whose contents had been variously described by successive generations as the bones of three witches, an East Anglian king who would one day wake up and set sail for a land beyond the world's end, or victims of the Black Death heaped into a communal mound. Whatever the forgotten truth, nobody would set foot on the mound, and no path would ever be driven across it.

Ahead was a crossroads, where a lane cut north past a decoy pond to an isolated farm.

Usually there was silence here—the hundred-voiced silence of the countryside, rustling with insects in the gorse, pierced by the high shrill of a lark, stirred by the breeze through stunted bushes. Today there was a strange throb which she had never heard before, and gusts of a harsh, throaty breathing.

Kate climbed a rise and came out above the crossroads.

A spluttering monster was rolling toward the junction. A hot, metallic smell drifted up the bank. Pacing solemnly ahead was a man with a red flag. He looked back and waved a caution as the traction engine neared the cross-roads. The clanking note changed. The vast wheels slowed. The man with the flag ventured a couple of feet out into the road and peered both ways.

From her vantage point Kate could see a donkey and trap jogging along toward Senwich. A girl was driving. Even from here her tenseness was obvious. She, too, slowed as she approached the crossing.

Now Kate recognized her. She was the daughter of Lady Charlotte and Mr. Darsham.

As the little trap rolled safely past the man with the red flag, he raised it and flicked a signal to the juggernaut behind him.

The engine let off a hiss of steam. The chain drive jangled as it took the strain.

Braying in terror, the donkey tried to rear up. The girl was tipped sideways, dragging on one rein. This slewed the donkey around. The girl screamed and clung to the side of the trap as it tilted. Then donkey and trap were away toward Senwich, careening madly from side to side, the wheels jarring and skidding from lumpy grass to flinty road.

For an instant Kate was frozen where she stood. Then she began to run. Stumbling down the slope, she cut an angle across the uneven turf toward the long loop of the road. There was a glimpse of the donkey's head and a flutter of the girl's golden hair before both were wrenched out of sight under the curve of the bank.

It would be a miracle if the animal didn't charge straight into the mound. And a miracle if the trap didn't fly off at the turn.

Panting, Kate reached the tightest twist of the loop. She was just in time. The inside wheel grated hideously as the trap came around, scattering dust and jagged fragments of stone. The girl was making no attempt to control the runaway animal: one arm was up over her eyes, while her other hand gripped the rail. At any moment she could well be tossed bodily out.

The turn had slowed the donkey in spite of its panic. Its hooves scrabbled for a purchase, and it brayed again, straining to increase speed.

Kate jumped.

She got her left arm around the animal's neck. It fought to be free, turning and twisting its smooth, hard head. A leg flailed wildly. Her feet were dragged cruelly along the ground.

They rocked perilously in toward the low bank. The donkey kept trying to kick her, but in kicking it was losing momentum.

Kate's right shoulder was plunged through overhanging brambles. She was sure she was about to be crushed. Something tore. Spiky fingernails seemed to slash across her throat and chest. Still she held on, and the donkey slowed and stumbled, and gave in. They jolted to a halt.

The girl was sobbing. Kate steadied herself, testing the ground and the solidity of her own ankles. Warily she relaxed her grip on the donkey, and walked slowly around its head.

"It's all right now," she said, though the breath scouring her throat made it difficult to speak.

The girl was crumpling forward. Kate stepped up and put an arm over her shoulders. Convulsive tremors ran through the girl's whole body.

Soothingly Kate said, "I don't think I know your name."

The shoulders writhed under her hand.

"You'd better tell me who you are," said Kate. "I don't know your name. Mine's Kate Quantrill."

The shuddering continued, but with an effort the girl raised her head. Her eyes were wet, her hair tousled. Without the tears, the terror, and the dishevelment, she would have been in every respect a miniature of her mother.

"I'm Verena Darsham," she whispered.

"Of course. Verena. And now I think we'd better be on our way, don't you?"

The girl seized her arm. "Oh, I don't want . . . I can't . . . couldn't you get someone to come and . . ."

"We'll be all right now."

Kate took the reins and coaxed the donkey into motion, avoiding any sudden movement or command which might goad it into another frenzy.

The stump of Darsham's Folly thrust up above the ridge like a marker guiding them homeward. It dwarfed the church, dominated the land, defied the sea.

On the outskirts of the village a boy was bowling an iron hoop proudly from one side of the road to the other. The donkey veered, twitching again. Kate reined it in and beckoned the lad closer.

"Run and tell Dr. Cawdron that Miss Darsham's had an accident. Miss Darsham—you've got that? Tell him I'm taking her to the Tower."

It was the first time she had ever had cause to drive in between the two stone pillars of the gateway. Each was topped by a prancing stone dog, and as she slowed on the

drive before the main door, it was to see another weird
beast carved into the lintel.

Verena got down shakily and turned the ornate iron
knob. The great door creaked open.

The hall echoed with the solemn tick-tock of a grand-
father clock. A sickly yellow painted moon was sinking
below the minute hand, leering at Kate as it went. Immediately within the door was a suit of armor, the left arm
bearing an emblazoned shield, again with a dog, and em-
bossed with arrows.

A stooped but vigorous woman in gray bombazine, with
a trim white cap on her sparse hair, hurried from a side
door like a guard dog alarmed by intruders.

"Miss Verena!"

"Mrs. Jenkyn, I've . . . oh, that *awful* donkey!"

The girl was on the verge of dashing toward the woman
and throwing herself into her arms. But shaken as she was,
some stubborn pride of her own fashioning kept her in
check.

Kate said, "I found Miss Darsham in some trouble.
She's had rather an upset."

"And you too, miss, by the looks of you."

The housekeeper was used to making decisions. She
took Verena's arm and indicated to Kate with a gentle but
firm little nod that they should accompany her through the
baize-lined door.

At the foot of the staircase curving down from a balus-
traded landing was another, more darkly polished door. It
opened suddenly. Framed against a background of book-
shelves and cigar smoke, Mr. Darsham said, "What is
happening?"

Verena would not run even to her father. She shrank
into herself as he crossed the floor, one foot striking a
louder resonance than the other.

"She's had a bit of an upset, sir," said Mrs. Jenkyn. "This young lady brought her home."

"Ah. Miss Quantrill."

Kate had been unconscious of her own state until now. Glancing down, she realized that her dress had been torn away from her shoulder. The scratches of the brambles stung her throat. Thickening spots of blood spattered the whiteness of her breast.

Instinctively she groped the ragged flap of wool back into place.

Behind Mr. Darsham, her father loomed in the doorway.

"That donkey!" Verena cried. "It bolted. It tried to kill me. I told you it would. Papa, I told you."

Kate explained, "The animal was frightened by one of those traction engine things. I was near enough to get it under control."

"I'm indebted to you, Miss Quantrill. But the child should have been capable of controlling it herself."

"She was scared."

"She's scared of so many things." Mr. Darsham swung upon his daughter. "You can't handle even a donkey? With all I've tried to—"

"Sir!" Kate was outraged. "After your own accident as a child, I'd have thought you could find room to sympathize with your own daughter in danger."

Mrs. Jenkyn gulped. Captain Josiah tugged at his beard. She waited for him to thunder at her, but was saved by the tinkle of a bell in some far recess of the house.

"That'll be the doctor," she said thankfully.

"A doctor—to cure cowardice . . . ?"

Mr. Darsham checked himself as Mrs. Jenkyn opened the front door to reveal Dr. Cawdron on the step.

He was a small, businesslike man in his forties, with a

neat sandy moustache and neat, stubby hands. "Mr. Darsham," he said in respectful greeting, but swiftly sized up the situation and addressed his main questions to Kate. When she had answered, he put one arm around Verena and led her toward the stairs.

"Perhaps we can get you to lie down comfortably, hmm, while I have a look at the damage?"

Verena hesitated on the second stair and held out a trembling hand. Not to her father, not to Mrs. Jenkyn, but mutely to Kate.

"It would do her good," said Mr. Darsham, "to go straight out and back into the trap."

"Most unwise," said Dr. Cawdron. For all his deference, he was a man of caliber in his own field.

He conducted Verena up the staircase, below the rich hues of a large stained-glass window. Kate followed, with Mrs. Jenkyn close behind.

Verena's room had frilled curtains, and a row of dolls with pretty china faces sat stiff-legged on a rosewood chest of drawers; but it was all unreasonably tidy. The doctor pulled back the plain dark blue counterpane of the bed, and Verena stretched out.

"A bruise on the arm. The elbow—hmm, nothing serious, though it'll probably ache a bit tomorrow. A few grazes." Dr. Cawdron straightened up. "She has the tremors. I think a warm drink, Mrs. Jenkyn."

"I'll fetch one."

"And perhaps some hot water as well. I fancy Miss Quantrill is the one in greater need of attention."

"A few scratches," said Kate. "As soon as I'm home . . ."

But Mrs. Jenkyn was already hurrying away. She returned so quickly that one might have supposed her to have some secret means of issuing advance commands to the scullery.

Dr. Cawdron bathed Kate's scratches and inspected the deepest gouge in her throat. "You were lucky, young lady. That could have been an ugly one. I suggest you follow Miss Darsham's example: as soon as you reach home, lie down for a while."

Mrs. Jenkyn had also brought a short cape, draped over her arm. She unfolded it to reveal a beautifully embroidered hem.

"This will see you home, miss." She fastened it across Kate's throat. "You can return it whensoever."

The door opened without ceremony. Mr. Darsham came in. "Miss Quantrill, I wished to inquire after . . ." The words faltered. He was looking at the cape. "But where . . . ?"

Mrs. Jenkyn said, "I'm lending it to Miss Quantrill, sir, to see her on her way."

"I was under the impression that I'd given orders that nothing, absolutely nothing, was to remain . . ."

"Her Ladyship presented it to me three years ago, sir."

"Did she, indeed? I've never seen you wear it."

"Not about the house, sir, no."

"Very well, Mrs. Jenkyn. Thank you."

"I'll see the young lady out, then."

"No." He waved at the bed. "I leave you to deal with the invalid. I shall take Miss Quantrill down."

Outside the door, they turned right. Kate, strange to the house, was not sure which way they had approached the girl's bedroom, but had an idea that they must now be going in quite a different direction.

Mr. Darsham held open a door and ushered her through.

Certainly she had not come along this gallery before.

On one wall was a rank of paintings. Light from the windows overlooking the village gleamed on varnished faces as she walked slowly toward the far end—slowly, because of the funereal pace Mr. Darsham was setting.

"A solemn assembly, Miss Quantrill."

She read the names at the foot of the gilded frames. Hugh Percival, Fifth Lord Darsham of Blackshore . . . Henry William Herbert, Sixth Lord . . . Hugh Alexander . . .

"No portrait of the first earl, I'm afraid. Or his immediate successors. All too busy to have their portraits painted. That sort of vanity came later."

His laugh implied that none of it was to be taken seriously. Yet if that were so, why were all these earnest faces preserved; and why had he wished her to pace devoutly beside them?

"This is the one who got us into trouble by supporting Lady Jane Grey."

Kate was lost. Miss Pringle's lessons had included little history, and that consisting only of some scattered dates and a few royal names.

"My ancestors were a quarrelsome lot. We won our way back into favor many times, only to blunder our way out again."

Standing before the last picture in the row, he was more real and substantial than any of them. Close to him, she was disturbed by the seething inner intensity of the man. His words were of less importance than the vibrant undertone which was somehow telling a much more significant story.

The final painting bore the name of Robert Hubert Darsham, 1771–1838. Between it and the end of the gallery were two vacant spaces.

"And it all comes to an end with me," said Oliver Darsham. "Unless . . ."

He sought solace from the remaining patch of blank

wall. Perhaps its very existence was an encouraging omen. Then he opened the door at this end and led Kate around a corner and onto the staircase.

Her father was standing in the middle of the hall, as indomitable as the suit of armor. Mr. Darsham led Kate to him with the formality of one returning a dancing partner to her chaperon.

"I apologize for keeping you, Captain. But we are agreed?"

"Aye, sir, it's settled." Captain Josiah's way of putting it did not altogether express agreement. To Kate he said bluntly, "Australia for me this time. And maybe New Zealand, if things go as they're supposed to."

"In your hands," said Mr. Darsham, "they'll go as they're supposed to."

Kate's father must have had time to turn things over in his mind while waiting for her. "Maybe you'd care for a passage out to those parts?"

Taken aback, she could see it only as a clumsy joke. "A woman to bring you bad luck, first time on a new run?"

"Going out light, we'll be taking some emigrants. Likely there'll be a few women among them."

"And paying passengers aren't so unlucky?"

"You'd have no objections?" Captain Josiah asked his employer.

It was clear from the flush which spread up through his taut features that Mr. Darsham did have objections. But, taken as much by surprise as Kate had been, he was speechless for a moment.

"There's a surplus of good young men out there," her father went on. "Wouldn't be hard to find yourself one who's striking it rich."

For the second time in a few hours she answered him hotly back. "I'll not be the one to go seeking."

"Quite right." Mr. Darsham had found his voice. "I'm not authorizing you to trade your daughter, Captain."

"Sir!" Captain Josiah's ready anger matched his own.

Kate put her hand on his rough sleeve. She didn't want the hall to become a battlefield, with herself as the provocation.

In a more reasonable tone Mr. Darsham said, "I fancy it would be a mistake to take your daughter away."

"I'll be letting her say what she thinks," said Captain Josiah.

But not here and now, thought Kate dazedly. She needed time, wasn't prepared to be an item on his bill of lading, to be ticked off on the spot without more ado.

Abruptly Mr. Darsham said, "Miss Quantrill, would you care to work for *me*?"

She was numbed by this senseless onslaught from both sides at once.

"Work for you?"

"Looking after my daughter." He could surely have conjured this up only on the spur of the moment. "She's too much alone. Needs companionship. Guidance."

"I . . . I have no qualifications," she fumbled.

"I fancy you have the very ones needed. I'm not asking for a nursemaid or a personal maid. No foolish notions and vanities."

Like her mother's—was that what he left unsaid?

"In any case," he hurried on, "I'd not insult you by offering such a position. My daughter studies with Miss Hartest, who I'm sure is admirable. But she needs more than indoor tuition. I want her out in the open much more. Taught to handle the trap, to get used to horses, to be given confidence—by the right person. The company of someone maturer, someone active rather than academic, and of spirit. I have no taste for timidity. Tell her about the land, Miss Quantrill. Take her riding, walking. She is to understand her inheritance." He was warming to his own plan now. "To *understand* it, not to see it only as a slipway from which to launch herself into the fripperies of London."

Her father gruffly cleared his throat. "It's a remarkable opportunity, girl."

"What time of day," she ventured, "would I be required to come?"

"You mistake me. I prefer you to reside on the premises. There are more than enough rooms to spare: you shall have a suitable one. Perhaps you may enjoy attending my daughter's lessons with her. It will be good for Verena to share in this way—and you yourself may profit."

"There's precious little for you to do at home these days." Kate was not sure whether her father was over-anxious to please his employer, after that near-outburst, or whether he genuinely felt it would mean advancement of some kind for her. Perhaps a mixture of both.

She thought of the house without him. There was always a wrench when he went away—a pang of parting which told her what it must have been like, so many times, for her mother. Now Abel and John were more often away than at home, and Daniel had his Sarah and needed no one else.

She said, "If you think I can contribute to your daughter's happiness, sir, I'm willing to be given a trial."

Mr. Darsham let out a strange little sigh. "Thank you." He held out his hand. Again she was imprisoned in that domineering grasp. "And thank you for your courage today. If there's any way in which I can . . ."

"You can be gentler with Miss Darsham," Kate dared.

Her fingers slid from his. He bowed stiffly.

"If you'll both wait while I call the carriage . . ."

"We shall walk, thank you, sir," said Captain Josiah.

"Miss Quantrill needs some consideration."

"To walk home will ease some of my aches," she said.

He did not argue, but bowed again respectfully and let them out on to the drive.

As they walked toward the gates, Captain Josiah growled, "You're too insolent, my girl. If you answer back like that while you're working for him, you'll soon be taught your place."

"He's a bully."

"Not so. Not wholly so."

"He speaks of consideration. It would do him no harm to be more thoughtful in many other ways."

"Being alone, he's got nothing to think about. Nothing he wants to think about, I reckon, but business. And that maybe means he makes more business than is there to be made."

"You're not happy," she said gently, "about this Australia run?"

"We'll see."

"It's something new?"

"Not for a start. Wool first. And then there's talk of frozen meat."

"From that distance?" said Kate incredulously.

"It's said it can be done."

"But the wheat shipments haven't helped farmers hereabouts. If it's meat next, what's *that* going to mean to them?"

"One thing I can tell you," said Captain Josiah weightily. "Once he's set his mind on something—well, maybe he won't get it. But he won't ever give up. Not him."

Kate said she could very well walk up to Darsham's Tower. Daniel said she could do no such thing. She was his sister, and she should be driven up to the front door, and he would then deliver her luggage to the servants' entrance.

Kate protested. Daniel showed himself more masterful than she had known him. Perhaps having a wife had brought out some willful traits in him.

They drove between the gates again, this time with Daniel holding the reins.

And stopped before that same door, beneath the lintel with the twisted animal trying to fight its way out of the stone.

She rang the bell and stepped back, peering up.

Was there still time to change her mind?

The tower of Darsham's Folly reeled dizzily against scudding clouds. She longed to call after Daniel as he went on his way around to the back of the house, to leap up beside him and urge the horse homeward before it was too late.

The tower leaned ever more ominously out from the sky, threatening to topple forward and crush her.

Chapter Four

The spring tides built up a rampart of water and shattered it on to the shores and inlets of eastern England. Kate prayed that John and Abel were lying safe in Harwich or Ipswich and not braving the turmoil of the estuary.

After excursions over the heath and along the shore, she and Verena were virtually confined indoors, while the wind howled through twisted elms and set Darsham's Folly shuddering.

True to her instructions, Kate had walked the girl many a mile. She was surprised by her own unwitting knowledge, soaked up over the years. Things which she had always taken for granted were new to Verena. At first it was hard to tell whether their newness pleased: Verena was sullen and unresponsive, doing as she was told merely because it was what she had been told. But sparks of curiosity were kindled, some to a small flame.

They found cuttlefish bones, and the twisted strands and blobs of wrack. Kate pointed out the sand martins' shallow holes in the dunes. It amazed her that Verena could not identify the pale lilac petals of lady's-smock, the swaying catkins in the hedgerows, or the birds returning to England after their winter in warmer climes.

One afternoon, her attention caught by a great spread of black sail rounding the spur of the bay, the girl said, "That's a nice barge."

"Not a barge," said Kate sharply. "It's a wherry."

From Verena's hurt expression, Kate realized that she had been making a shy advance, trying to say something appreciative because she knew Kate's brothers worked a barge. Hastily Kate began to explain the differences, but Verena made a show of being no longer interested.

When they took the trap out, Kate drove. Verena sat rigid beside her, every muscle tense. Each jolt over a stone or rut made her wince. It was only gradually that she allowed herself to relax, until the day when Kate decided it was time to take a more positive step in breaking down her fears.

Harnessing the donkey, she talked to it and to Verena as though the whole procedure were the most natural thing in the world. Then, as they climbed up, she said casually, "No, no. You drive this time."

Verena at once sprang backward and edged away from the trap.

"Come on," Kate coaxed. "Up you come."

"I can't."

"Of course you can. All you have to do is—"

"Don't try to make it sound easy, because it isn't. Just because you saved my life—"

"I don't think that's anywhere near true. You'd soon have got control again that day. Just as you will now, once we've started."

"You saved my life," Verena persisted, "but that doesn't give you the right to make me risk it again. I don't want to drive. And I don't want to have anything to do with awful beasts like that one."

"It's only a little dickie."

"A little what?"

"That's what everyone in the village calls a donkey."

"Well, I don't live in the village, and it's not what *I* call a donkey," said Verena pettishly. "If a lot of stupid people who don't know any better . . ." A tear glistened in her eye. "I'm sorry," she said unexpectedly. "Miss Quantrill, I'm sorry. I shouldn't have said that. It didn't mean . . ."

"It didn't mean anything," said Kate.

Verena looked guiltily away. She looked at the step, and covertly at the reins. Then she sprang up. The trap rocked, the donkey took a tentative step forward; and with a little squeak of apprehension, Verena guided it out of the stableyard and around the side of the house.

It was Verena herself who chose to head for the crossroads where she had had such a fright. Kate said nothing. It was an encouraging sign.

Three miles toward Sheverton she suggested they might take a side lane bringing them around in a long arc past the farm and the decoy pond. On the turn, the donkey slipped on some loose flints and shied toward the opposite verge. Verena whimpered. Kate nearly made a grab for the reins, then sat quite still. Verena seemed about to throw up her hands in despair, but gave the gentlest tug on the rein, and they steadied and went ahead.

Near the farm there was a flicker of movement from a slope some two hundred yards off the lane. It was a lonely spot, with three mounds as mysterious and little fre-

quented as the one which twisted the Sheverton road out
of true. A dark shape, like that of a crouching dog, was
grubbing away at the base of one hummock.

The clatter of wheels disturbed it. It reared up on two
legs.

And proved to be Mr. Darsham.

Kate said, "There's your father. Wave to him."

Verena refused to let go of the reins.

"He'll be pleased," said Kate, "to see you doing so well.
It's just what he wanted."

"He doesn't really want anything of me," said Verena.
"He just wishes I wasn't here."

"I'm sure you're wrong." Kate spoke with as much conviction as she could muster.

She did not know whether to be relieved or disappointed
that in these first few weeks she had so rarely set eyes on
Mr. Darsham, and then mainly from a distance.

Now the gales had blown them indoors. Instead of taking
Verena "out of herself"—Mr. Darsham's phrase in the
brief interview she had had with him on her arrival—she
became the one to be drawn into Verena's everyday routine.

Each morning Miss Hartest came up from the rectory
and settled with them in the schoolroom. Lunch was
brought in every day except Sunday, when Kate was free
to spend the day at home.

With outdoor activities suspended, Verena read books
which she declared she had read a hundred times before;
or sewed; or sulked.

"Perhaps," Kate suggested one afternoon, "you could
show me around the house."

"It's horrible. I wish I could live with Aunt Alice. She'd
love to have me—and she's got a *nice* house."

"You wouldn't like to show me your hiding places, and where you've made up special games, and everything?"

"You don't have to stay with me all day. No one'll stop you looking around. You'll never meet anyone."

It seemed true. There were plenty of people within these walls—more below stairs than above—yet the place did not feel lived in. Spacious rooms were empty. Corridors and galleries, longer and airier than one would have thought from the outside view of the tower, remained untrodden. There were sequences of doors through which no guests ever passed; half-landings with shadowy bronze statuettes of nymphs and game birds; framed, yellowing diagrams of forgotten castles.

And windows.

From the north, a vista of the saltings and the curve of the bay. From the west, the heath and occasional plumes of cloud which might just possibly be smoke above the distant railway. South lay the village.

The Senwich habit was always to look east. The sea gave, and the sea took away.

Kate, exploring the echoing labyrinth of the second floor, stopped at a window looking down on the garden. By standing close to the glass, she could just see the narrow terrace immediately below. Its steps were cracked, and tilted alarmingly. What must once have been a large lawn sloped to an abrupt halt against a blackthorn hedge. Beyond, half-sunk in wet ground, were fragmented remains of a stone wall. Incursions of salt water had given birth to a colony of reeds on the far side of the hedge, while marsh flowers intruded to the very edge of the remaining formal flowerbeds.

"It's not the same." A woman's voice spoke close to Kate's right ear. "Never been the same since Jenkyn went."

Kate gasped.

Mrs. Jenkyn said, "Sorry I startled you, miss."

Kate got her breath back. "There . . . isn't much garden left, is there?"

"Not what it was." There was a hint that Mrs. Jenkyn's late husband had better qualifications than King Canute for holding back the waves. "Not what it was when Jenkyn brought me here—from Lincolnshire, that's where I came from."

"He was gardener here—I think I just remember him."

"Head gardener," said Mrs. Jenkyn reverently. "I was just a housemaid. The gardens was worth his attention then. Lord knows what he'd say if he was to see them now."

"Things indoors," Kate flattered her, "are better kept than those outside nowadays."

Mrs. Jenkyn preened herself. "It was Mr. Oliver. He was the one. Known me since he was little, and he was the one who told his mother she had to make me housekeeper. And when he got an idea into his head, there was no arguing with him."

"He hasn't altered," said Kate dryly.

"Cook left, and the still-room maid said she wouldn't work under the likes of me. Went off in quite a storm. But here I am. Which," said Mrs. Jenkyn, "just goes to show, doesn't it?"

They stood side by side, watching the newly budding branches thrash in the grip of the relentless wind.

"And you?" asked Mrs. Jenkyn. "Are you having any little troubles with Miss Verena?"

"We're growing more friendly, I think."

"She looks a little better, I'll say that."

Kate said, "She never mentions her mother."

"Nor she won't."

"I wonder how much she misses her."

"Her Ladyship wasn't that easy to get on with. Maybe she doesn't miss her that much. Or maybe more than she'll admit. Hard to say, with Miss Verena. But she'd get no sympathy admitting anything. None. Not from the master."

"If only he could be more at ease with her!" Kate felt that this was something she could say to the housekeeper.

Mrs. Jenkyn's nod confirmed it. "But that's the way he is. Never did take life easy. With a beginning like his, you'd find it hard to blame him. A wonder he's here at all, really."

"His accident, you mean?"

"Just getting born in the first place. That was worry enough. Him that sickly, and brought out twisted as he was. And then his mother having that fever right after. A fine kettle of fish if they'd lost him. Only those two older sisters, and *they* don't count for anything."

"They visit often?" Kate thought of the empty rooms, waiting for movement and gaiety and family chatter.

"Mr. Robert didn't like having them about the place. And Mr. Oliver's no better."

They fell into step along the corridor. At the end, Kate said, "I haven't seen Mrs. Darsham since I've been here, except in church."

"She keeps to the fourth floor mostly. Keeps herself to herself."

"It's a long way up for an old lady, isn't it—getting up and down the stairs?"

"Better that way," said Mrs. Jenkyn cryptically.

She moved to one side, leaving Kate's only route the descending stairs. Along the next passage was a subdued glow on the carpet, suggesting another stained-glass window just out of sight at the far end.

"What's along there?"

"The master bedroom, and her La . . . the private suite."

A floorboard creaked, emphasizing the silence.

"Mr. Darsham's away?" said Kate.

"Been gone these four days now."

Kate started down the stairs. As they passed a cupboard door on the half-landing, Mrs. Jenkyn began, "I'd never have been surprised if . . ."

"Yes?"

Mrs. Jenkyn changed her tune. "What do they say in the village?"

"About her Ladyship?"

"Yes."

"Just that she ran off," said Kate. They reached the first landing, and she paused, waiting for Mrs. Jenkyn to come level. "Why? She *did* run off, didn't she?"

"Oh, she ran, all right. But what happened to her: where is she now?"

"Well . . . with *him,* I suppose. The young man."

"Sometimes I think it'd have been more like him—the master, I mean—to have gone right after her and killed her that very day."

"Mrs. Jenkyn!"

"No, I've no right to say that," said Mrs. Jenkyn agitatedly. "Forget what I said." But she herself couldn't forget. It was a notion she must have wrestled with many times since. "He's not a man to let go easily," she said. "Not to let anyone get away like that. But if there was anything . . . if . . . no, we'd have heard."

She began to urge Kate toward the final flight. Kate shivered as she went. "I don't understand how people can be married, and share so much, and then . . ."

"Such a splendid couple, you'd have said." The words dropped on Kate's head as she descended. "To see them together, I mean. She was too lovely for him—whatever she was like inside, she looked wonderful when she set herself to it. And she had a way of making *him* look . . .

well, less hunched in. Lovely," said Mrs. Jenkyn. It was accusation rather than praise.

They reached the ground floor. Mrs. Jenkyn invited Kate to have a cup of tea and muffins with her in the housekeeper's room. There, attempting to blur her recent indiscretions, she asked about Kate's brothers and about Sarah, whose family she knew slightly, and about her father's voyages. It was a snug little room, as shipshape as the cabin of a pernickety sea captain. Kate sat back and enjoyed the respite, feeling her family drawing closer around her once more as she talked about them.

Her own room, close to Verena's, overlooked a small plantation with a few flickers of road visible through the trees. Its furnishings were less spartan than Verena's. The bed was comfortable, there was a sagging but still serviceable chaise longue which must have been brought up from one of the reception rooms during some rearrangement, and a capacious window seat. In the lee of the sea wind, it was quieter than much of the house—a trifle too remote, even.

That night Kate was preparing for bed when she heard a faint but familiar rasp and rumble down the road. She could not mistake the sound of Daniel's wagon. It was an odd time for it to be coming this way.

Odd, too, that it should crunch up the drive instead of heading for the yard. Only when escorting her here had Daniel ever defiantly driven up to the front door.

Kate put her hairbrush down and went quietly out into the passage. She chided herself for being so inquisitive; but that did not stop her from going to the top of the flight and tiptoeing far enough down to see over the balustrade of the second-floor landing.

From this angle she had a distorted picture of Daniel helping Mr. Darsham across the hall, their heads close together.

Mr. Darsham sank onto an oak settle and waved at a bell pull. "I'd be obliged if you'd give that a tug, Quantrill."

Kate was tempted to hurry downstairs. But it was not her place to do so. A moment later a maid appeared, with Mrs. Jenkyn not far behind.

"Fly came off the road," grunted Mr. Darsham. He said a few more things Kate did not catch, and the maid scuttled off. "Bank given way . . . a wheel off . . ." More unintelligible murmuring.

"Those tides haven't done us any good." Daniel was audible enough.

"You'll collect that confounded vehicle first thing in the morning?"

"You can rely on me, sir."

"I'm glad you were to be relied on tonight."

"I'd take good care of that leg, sir." Daniel's growl was his instinctive reaction to a compliment. "That's a sprain, as like as not. Don't want to dash about too soon."

But two days later, limping far worse than usual, Mr. Darsham was off again. In spite of his outspoken scorn for the frivolities of London, he did not seem averse to spending much of his time there—if, indeed, it was London each time. Daniel had once described the look on his face when returning. Business triumphs . . . or women?

Miss Hartest occasionally made use of the rectory donkey cart, but her brother had more frequent need of it. This involved her in trudging to and from the Tower in all weathers. Kate, incensed by the indifference of anyone in the house to this, suggested one damp day in the schoolroom that she and Verena could perfectly well drive down to the rectory for some lessons: the spell of fresh air, however tumultuous, would be good for Verena.

Miss Hartest demurred.

Verena pouted that she didn't want to go out in the cold and wet.

Kate caught Mr. Darsham at his library door one late afternoon, and put it to him. It took a few seconds for him to come back from the throes of whatever problem was engaging him just then; one hand on the doorknob, he contemplated her as though she were a complete stranger, pondered, and then said, "I have no objections at all. I am quite happy to accept your decisions on such matters."

He went on into the library. As she turned away, just before the door closed behind him, Kate glimpsed a weird, dark-eyed head on a tall tripod table. It was a skull, with other shadowy, jagged hollows in it.

Verena's objections to the new system were quenched after one visit to the rectory.

The reason was a cottage piano, set against one wall of the parlor in which Miss Hartest now gave many of her lessons.

Today they were supposed to be studying Latin. Miss Hartest herself had never had tuition in it, but her brother loved the language, and she had gleaned a few fundamentals from him. "It helps you to enjoy so many other things," he claimed; and dutifully Miss Hartest tried to transmit as much as she had been able to grasp. She was not making an especially good job of it. Verena fidgeted, and her eyes strayed toward the closed lid of the piano, and finally she could contain herself no longer.

"Aunt Alice has a piano, only it's nicer than that. She lets me play it when I go there."

Miss Hartest bridled. "Your father's given no instructions about piano lessons."

"I used to have them. When . . ." Verena faltered. "Before it was put away upstairs." Her lips trembled.

It was obvious to Kate that neither Latin nor arithmetic would win Verena's attention today. She caught Miss Hartest's eye. As if against her better judgment, Miss Hartest said, "You'll find some music in the piano bench. I'll make some tea. Miss Quantrill and I will enjoy the break."

Her reward was a radiant smile. Verena rushed to the bench and dug out two or three albums. She eagerly riffled through the pages. At the door, Miss Hartest indicated with a discreet nod that Kate should follow.

From the kitchen they heard a stumbling sequence of notes which steadied, grew in confidence, and swelled like a stream freeing itself from rocky twists and turns into full spate.

Kate said, "She's very talented, surely?"

"I'm afraid so."

"Afraid?"

"I'm not sure I should allow this. Her mother played the piano. That's why the instrument has been relegated to the storeroom."

"Lady Charlotte was an accomplished pianist?"

"A pleasant amateur. Pleasant enough in the drawing room, provided she wasn't too greatly taxed."

The phrases from the parlor, though muffled, fell limpidly on the ears.

"Verena has real ability," said Miss Hartest. "What good can it do her? It will merely anger her father, and be of little use to her when she marries."

"Save that in the drawing room she'll be more than a pleasant amateur."

"Few husbands wish their wives to be more than that."

When the tea tray was ready, they went back into the parlor. Verena said over her shoulder, "It's by Mendelssohn," defying them to stop her, and danced on to a graceful concluding cadence.

"Very nice," said Miss Hartest crisply. "Now, after we've had tea and a biscuit . . ."

"Ten minutes is no good," wailed Verena. "I need lots of practice. All the time."

"It was a mistake," said Miss Hartest to Kate.

Knowing that as a matter of discipline she ought to support the other woman, Kate nevertheless could not resist saying, "I have some tapestry work I'd like to collect from home while I'm down here. Perhaps we could allow Verena half an hour more, provided"—she tried to make it suitably stern—"she'll promise to concentrate on her other work afterward."

Miss Hartest had little choice but to agree, though she made no attempt to hide her disapproval.

A cascade of joyful notes followed Kate as she left the rectory and made for the sprawling house which, in its tangle of rooms and passages, its busy routine and laughter and argument, was so different from the bleakness of Darsham's Tower.

Today it still echoed with all that exuberance, although only Sarah was there. They chatted for a few minutes, Kate inspected three of the cat's new litter—"There's another one somewhere, he's already a bit of a wanderer," said Sarah—and then she collected her tapestry and retraced her steps toward the rectory.

At the corner of the lane she heard a plaintive mew above her head.

The wandering kitten had wandered too far. It was a ball of brindled fluff, stuck like a burr to a branch, scared to go on and scared to scrabble back.

The tree was one which Kate had climbed many a time in years gone by. She set her roll of tapestry on the stile, hitched up her skirts, and clambered onto the top rail of the fence. Each maneuver came as naturally as the piano keys falling into place under Verena's fingers. She stretched up for a handhold, set her right foot against the trunk, pushed up and away from the fence, and heaved herself up on the knotty shoulder of a branch.

The kitten miaouled more desperately as a cluster of twigs swayed and scraped its back.

Kate tested her weight on two intertwined branches, and reached out. Her fingers brushed the kitten. It tried to edge away. She grabbed a handful of fur and drew it toward her. Tiny claws stabbed through the fabric of her sleeve.

The descent was going to be more difficult. She kept her face to the trunk and probed with one foot for the top of the fence. At last she found it. She braced herself, holding the writhing kitten and preparing to push away from the tree and leap down.

There was a movement in the corner of her eye.

Already letting go, she glanced down. A man was looking up at her, laughing, his arms spread wide. She gasped, clutched the kitten even more tightly, and fell.

Her right knee jarred against the fence. She flung out one arm to save herself. Then two arms were securely around her, and she was being set upright on the grassy verge of the lane.

The arms remained locked about her. The man's face was close to hers.

"I . . . thank you . . . I'm safe now," she spluttered.

The kitten clawed itself free, sprang to the ground, and bounced off down the lane like an outsized tuft of thistledown.

One arm still held her tight. The other came free, and his hand pushed a tendril of hair from her brow.

"Please, I must ask you . . . I am perfectly all right now. . . ."

"You must forgive me, ma'am." There was an alien lilt in his amused, leisurely drawl. "I'm newly come from where all the girls have flaxen heads. Nigh on all of them, I do declare. Makes a mighty refreshing change to see one so dark. And so fascinating."

He was young, lank, rangy, and far too sure of himself. His light brown jacket had a check too bright for this part of the world, though his high collar was severe enough. His glossy stovepipe hat was set at a rakish angle on his head—though, to be fair, Kate might have knocked it that way in her fall.

She said, "Thank you for catching me."

"What I'd call a fine catch." He grinned.

"You're very forward, sir."

"When I'm to spend some time in a place, I like to make myself known right away. Don't often get an opportunity like this one, though."

"I'm afraid it will prove no great opportunity," said Kate frigidly.

"No? I'd say that in a place of this size, we'd be liable to meet again pretty soon."

"I would think not. Thank you for your assistance. Good day."

"Good day, ma'am."

She did not look back, because she was sure he was laughing at her, laughing after her.

Late in the afternoon Mrs. Jenkyn came to the nursery to say, "Miss Verena is to sit up to dinner."

"But I don't want to," Verena protested. "I want to go to bed early."

"First time I've known that," said Mrs. Jenkyn.

"To think. And to practice—in my head."

Mrs. Jenkyn made no attempt to unravel this one. "There's a guest. The master thinks it will do Miss Verena good to hear the problems they're discussing."

Kate felt a tingle of warmth toward Mr. Darsham. So he was making an effort to draw his daughter closer!

"She is to join them in the library when she's ready," said Mrs. Jenkyn. "Not later than seven o'clock."

Kate helped Verena to get ready, and was touched by the bright, shy little picture in frilled white muslin with its lilac sash.

"Will you walk down with me?" Verena pleaded.

"You're not frightened of going on your own? You look such a grown-up lady now."

Verena smiled wistfully. "I don't feel like one."

Kate went down with her. The wind was abating, but there was still a sad, moaning draft in the hall. She tapped on the library door.

Mr. Darsham's deep voice answered.

This time she saw the library whole. Its far wall was a great array of books, piled rank upon rank to the ceiling. The skull grimaced at her, its cranium and jaw as gashed and splintered as its grin. Near her, as she advanced, was a glass case in which she thought she glimpsed fragments of bone.

Mr. Darsham stood with his guest before the crackling log fire, its ponderous overmantel carved with heraldic shields.

"Miss Quantrill." The smile was frank and welcoming, perhaps warmed by the whiskey they were drinking. "Let me introduce you, my dear Rouse. If you are to spend any time here, you're likely to bump into Miss Quantrill now and then."

"Just how I figured it would be," said Mr. Rouse, his hand outstretched.

He was the brash young man who had treated her so boldly by the stile.

Chapter Five

Mr. Matthew Rouse was very much in evidence during the following weeks. Whenever Kate and Verena went driving or walking, or were on their way between house and rectory, they seemed to encounter him. He paced out distances from one corner of the village to another; leaned hazardously over dikes to study the movement of the water; and made copious notes in a small notebook he carried always with him. At the sight of Kate he would raise his hat with a provocative flourish.

"Miss Quantrill," Verena said as they returned from an exploratory saunter along the beach, "*you* don't think we'll be swept away, do you?"

"Swept away?"

"The sea, coming in the way it has been. It couldn't really get around us and carry us all off, could it?"

Kate conjured up a grim picture of all the churches and houses of old Senwich which now lay out there under the water, their stones engulfed in mud, the fish swimming in and out of gaping windows.

She said, "Where've you been hearing such tales?"

"It was all they talked about, that night I sat up to dinner." Verena grimaced. "It was all so dull, really. I don't know why Papa bothered to have me there."

"I expect he thinks you're old enough to hear about the things that have to be done on the estate."

"Well, it was dull. But frightening as well. Papa was telling Mr. Rouse about the ground giving way, and unsafe roads, and flood levels, and I didn't understand half of it, and I didn't like what I *did*."

The spring tides had certainly wreaked some damage. It had taken Mr. Darsham's own accident to awaken him to the full realization of the way the very foundations of the village were being undermined.

Kate, going home for Sunday, found the path from the Quantrill house to the creek gradually sinking beneath a thick sludge. The bank below the church had weakened, and some of the gravestones in the southeast corner were tilting and working free from the sodden ground.

The Darshams had regularly employed local men to maintain the earthen seawall and to repair breaks and clear inlets of silt and weed. But each fresh onslaught demolished their work so easily that they had grown pessimistic.

The arrival of the purposeful Mr. Rouse met with scant welcome.

"Don't much fancy bein' told how to do our jobs," said one ditcher in Kate's hearing. "Least of all by a furriner."

A Norfolk or Essex man, or one from the black fens beyond the Suffolk border, was foreigner enough. Matthew Rouse was ten times so. He was American, and known to be newly come from a year in Holland. So what had he got to do with Senwich and with Senwich ways? One or two of the girls appraised him hopefully. His answer was a raised, flirtatious eyebrow. His breezy self-confidence did nothing to commend him to the older folk, who grumbled that he'd work no miracles here. When the sea was good and ready to come in, then that would come, whatever Mr. Darsham and his hired engineer might set up in opposition.

"That's the way ut has always bin, and that's the way ut will always be."

A number of men were allocated to Mr. Rouse. They accepted his commands respectfully; did their work skeptically; and, although their own lives and livelihood were at stake, assured one another that it would all be of no use in the long run.

Nevertheless he drove them on. Ditches had to be cleared and widened. To the wonderment of all, he opened a breach in the seawall. It was like doing the invader's job for him. But with a free run, with room to expand over a large area of unfarmed, long-abandoned levels, the pressure of the tides nearest the village was relieved. Mr. Rouse wanted the creek dredged and new piers built for the collapsing jetty. The groin at the harbor entrance must be doubled in thickness. Over the next two years, he decreed, at least twenty breakwaters must be set up along the shore, stretching out at least forty feet.

And he wanted a drainage channel cut between the churchyard wall and the wall of Darsham's Folly, on this side only a few yards from the Tower itself.

"You reckon he knows what he's doing?" Daniel asked Kate, after news of this had been muttered derisively about the village. "There's both walls leaning over, fair to collapse, and he wants to dig the gap even deeper. I'd say that'd certain for sure bring the whole lot down."

"He's supposed to be an expert," was all Kate could offer.

"Nice enough feller, in himself."

Kate refused to commit herself on this. She preferred to say nothing about Mr. Rouse and to have nothing to do with him. He was too forward for her tastes. Busy as he was, he lost no opportunity of smiling at her, sprightly and inviting, as though sooner or later she would inevitably smile back. She had no intention of encouraging him.

After the first week he had taken up lodging in the rectory. Whether this was Mr. Darsham's tactful way of putting rent into the pockets of his none too wealthy cousins, or simply that he did not care to have a mere hired craftsman under his roof for more than a brief introductory period, there was no way of telling.

One afternoon when she and Verena reached the rectory for one of those piano practices which Kate was allowing to grow longer and longer, in defiance of what she guessed her employer's wishes would have been, they found Matthew Rouse there explaining some point to the rector.

The Reverend Godfrey Hartest could not have been more than ten years older than his lodger, but looked three times that. He was sallow and cadaverous, with a gentle smile prone to flicker out into feebleness. His voice was a drowning alto, sounding eerie and impressive from the pulpit but mannered in everyday conversation. He was a kind, unworldly man, and his habit of blinking faster and faster when someone was speaking to him gave him an appearance of chronic bewilderment.

"I've been hard at it trying to impress on Mr. Darsham," Rouse was saying, "that there's a whole lot more to it than just shoring up the seawall near the village. The Tower itself is in danger. He's approved most of my other plans—studied them with great care, I'll grant him that—but he just won't hear of including his own home in one allover scheme."

"My cousin is a practical man. I'm sure he would make no decision without a sound foundation."

"A sound foundation is just what we don't have. The rise the house stands on is spongy with seepage from the marsh. Instead of draining away, the water goes on working in there all the time."

The rector greeted Verena and Kate with more than his usual courtesy, manifestly thankful for a respite.

Matthew Rouse smiled at Kate, but was still caught up in what he had been saying. "There are times when I get the feeling your Mr. Darsham regards himself as immune to trouble just because he *is* Mr. Darsham. Because the old world has lasted this long, it's going to go on lasting."

"We may pray that it is so."

"We may indeed. And meanwhile I'll help those prayers along with some muscle power."

He went out.

This afternoon Kate and Verena had walked down. On the return journey they chose a roundabout route. Somewhere a plover was hoarsely whistling its insistent tune. Bluebells made a secret, dusky lake in the heart of a coppice. At the end of the bushes and saplings was a pool which sometimes brimmed with water, sometimes sank to little more than a puddle. A shelduck, startled by their approach, rose from the reeds in a long parabola, drifting slowly toward the coppice and then rising again, a wheeling speck against the sky.

Verena caught Kate's arm. "It's like music!"

It was the greatest compliment she could pay. Watching the speck soar and dwindle against the sky, Kate could feel and hear the music of it; and all at once was furious with Mr. Darsham and his callousness in punishing Verena for her mother's misdeeds.

She began to quicken their homeward pace, the taste of the afternoon soured by her irritation.

When the maid brought tea up to the schoolroom as usual, Kate asked, "Is Mr. Darsham at home?"

"Yes, miss. He's been working in the library all day."

When the girl had gone, Verena said, "Why did you want to know about Papa?"

"I must speak to him on a certain matter."

"He hates interruptions when he's shut away in there."

Full of high resolve, Kate went to her room, washed and tidied herself, and came downstairs again. The late-afternoon sun was pale through the stained glass. In one pane a demure maiden was playing a keyboard instrument of some kind. "A dulcimer," Verena had said a few days ago. "Don't you love the sound of it?" Kate had had to confess that she had never heard the instrument. "No, the *word*, I mean," said Verena dreamily. "Just the word, 'dulcimer.' Only perhaps that isn't a dulcimer after all— but I shall go on thinking it is."

Kate reached the foot of the staircase. Trying to suppress the flutter in her throat, she went to the library door and knocked.

Mr. Darsham was standing at his desk, leaning over some shards of what looked like chipped slate spread out before him, and a magnifying glass close to his right hand.

He was displeased by the interruption; but the displeasure faded when he saw who it was.

There was no indirect way of broaching the subject. Kate said, "I'd like to consult you about Verena."

"I've told you, Miss Quantrill, you have my full confidence. I'm happy to let you make whatever decisions you think best."

Kate said, "I've heard there's a piano stored somewhere in the house."

He rested his hands on the desk. His shoulders hunched, his eyes went as steely as a horizon threatening some far-off storm.

"You play, then, Miss Quantrill?"

"I have heard Verena play."

"Where, may I ask?"

"At the rectory."

"I don't recall music lessons as part of the curriculum which Miss Hartest and I evolved."

"Verena wished to try the piano. I encouraged her."

"Did you?" Without softening, he conceded frostily, "I suppose we must accept it as one of a young woman's permissible accomplishments nowadays, provided it is not overdone."

"She needs to practice regularly at home if she's to make real progress."

"I prefer her not to make progress in that direction."

"It means so much to her," Kate burst out.

"I will not have the sound of it in my house."

Kate trembled. The skull gaped at her. Raw edges of bone and black hollows reflected from the glass doors of a bookcase. She stood her ground.

"I believe she's very gifted."

"There was enough of that kind of vanity here before."

"Sir, I see no vanity in her wish to play the piano, and to play it well."

"You're growing too heated, Miss Quantrill."

"You once said you had no taste for timidity."

There was the twitch of a wry, appreciative smile. "I stand corrected."

"You also said, only a few minutes ago, that I was to make what decisions I thought best. If I had arranged for the piano to be restored to its old place without consulting you—"

"But you did no such thing. Your own good taste told you how wrong that would have been."

"So I must know by instinct, sir, what you will consider is right and what is wrong? I have freedom to decide—but must always guess what you wish me to decide . . . and always guess correctly? You avoid your daughter, you never trouble to ask whether she is happy, whether her work is making good progress. You stay far away from her, and from me—"

"Because I dare not come too close!"

It was torn from him on a sob that flailed across her like the most savage, agonized oath.

The walls of the library closed in. The skull was grinning hideously; the reflections from glass on this side and that side shook and menaced her with new, distorted glints and patterns.

"I have sworn to be patient. I have no right, no right . . . not yet." The cry had crumpled to a whisper, still as piercing and still as tormented. "We must wait." Like the walls and lights and shadows, he seemed to be leaning toward her. "Wait," he said. "Be patient."

His sheer physical, animal presence was overwhelming. She wanted to run from him, wanted even more to run toward him.

He breathed, "Kate, I promise—"

There was a sharp rap at the door.

Mrs. Jenkyn came in without waiting for a summons, and stopped short. "I'm sorry, sir, I didn't know you had someone with you."

He pushed himself up and away from the desk, the storm looming again, gray and ever closer.

Hastily she handed him an envelope. "I'm sorry, sir. But Emberson was given this when he was in Sheverton. It was a special delivery, and I thought it might be urgent."

"Thank you, Mrs. Jenkyn."

She went out.

Mr. Darsham looked blankly at the writing on the envelope. He might have tossed it on his desk and left it. Kate took a step backward. He paid no attention. "Kate," he had called her. Her name seemed still to quiver in the air. But now she might as well not have been here. He reached for a paper knife, slit the envelope, and took out one sheet of paper.

As he read it, his face flamed with exultation. He looked up unseeingly at Kate, read the letter again, and then said, "Thank you . . . Miss Quantrill."

Leaving the room, she was "Miss Quantrill" again. Had Mrs. Jenkyn's arrival saved him from making a fool of himself; was he at this very moment thanking his lucky stars for that intrusion?

Mrs. Jenkyn was still in the hall, moving about and fingering the armor and the settle as though to check the dusting efficiency of the maids—or waiting for Kate?

She said, "Well. Well, I declare. Maybe there's more of his father in him than I'd thought."

"I don't think I quite—"

"The way he was looking, when I came into that room unexpected like."

"We were talking about Miss Darsham," said Kate.

"I dare say. But it's the first time I ever did see him look like that." Mrs. Jenkyn uttered a crackly laugh. "You'll have to be nippy on your feet, same as I used to be."

"Mrs. Jenkyn!"

The housekeeper held open the baize-padded door, and automatically Kate went through. They both came to a halt by the side window overlooking the terrace and garden.

"Old Mr. Robert," said Mrs. Jenkyn, "was a terror. Not a girl was safe once he'd taken a fancy to her."

"I've never heard a word of anything like that before."

"Oh, he wasn't too bad in the village. That I will say for him. What he couldn't find right here in his own home, he'd go farther afield for. There was plenty of young 'uns who . . ." She shook her head. "Young 'uns. But they won't be young no more, will they? All be growed up by now."

She stared wonderingly out at what was left of the garden, seeing time eating into her memories the way the storms had eaten into the shifting land.

Kate said, "You really are mistaken about what you . . . what you thought you saw."

"It's not natural. Not natural," said Mrs. Jenkyn, "for a man to be on his own, without a woman. A man like him, in this house, and his life the way it is."

We must wait. Be patient.

Kate lay awake that night, stumbling and jerking on the edge of confused dreams.

Kate, I promise . . .

What promise could Oliver Darsham possibly have considered making to her?

She groped through shadows, still tossing and turning in bed, yet somehow in London—a grotesque London of her own imagining. There was a gutter, and Lady Charlotte was dead in it.

The shock jarred her back into wakefulness.

If it were possible, if she were patient, if he would mellow and let her teach him to enjoy his daughter's company, to accept life and not to shut himself away . . .

There must be a way of reaching him. Was he not imploring her to do so; wasn't that what he had been trying to say?

She sank into a drowsy whirlpool and was rocked, spun slowly around and around. And it became a lulling, coaxing embrace. Became more intense, warmer, and more ecstatic, until she was fighting back against an animal savagery which at the same time she longed to accept.

If she had been Mrs. Darsham. No Lady Charlotte, Lady Kate—simply Mrs. Darsham.

To give him a son.

She was drenched in sweat, drenched in shame. The spring dawn sang its jubilant chorus; a mad melody sang in her veins.

She tried to struggle free from these appalling fantasies.

I have sworn . . . I promise . . . Be patient.

Patient for how long? Until he had swept what impediments aside?

Kate, I promise . . .

Chapter Six

Verena fidgeted. The sun scorched through the window; the air was somnolent with a hum of bees. It was no day for formal lessons, but Miss Hartest was plodding on with what Kate found an odd choice of subject.

"The First Earl Darsham of Blackshore was created, you know, by William the Conqueror."

"Yes," said Verena pettishly, "I do know."

"It was a reward for services during the Norman invasion. He was granted a castle outside St. Edmundsbury, and also built himself a fortified manor in old Senwich. Unfortunately, the fourth earl joined the rebel barons against Henry the Second, and lost the castle and all his estates."

Kate waited for this family history to lead into some more general historical topic, which was what she supposed Miss Hartest had in mind. Instead, the string of Darsham names and exploits continued. She began to lose the thread. Verena grew more and more rebellious, and made a great show of yawning. "Cousin Flora, I *know* all this."

"Charles the First restored the coastal estates, but not the title." For some reason Miss Hartest ignored Verena's justifiable complaint. "But after the Civil War, Charles the Second gave the manor on Senwich heath to the brother of a Cambridge lady he was fond of at the time. It burned down soon after."

"And then," said Kate helpfully, "Darsham's Fo . . . Darsham's Tower was built?"

"And ever since," cried Verena, "the family's been fussing to get the earldom back. All Papa's work in Ipswich— you think he hopes to be made a baron, the way the brewers and moneylenders are being made barons?"

"Verena!"

"Or perhaps that's what those lectures to the Royal Society are about. He thinks the Queen will remember Prince Albert's interest in science and hear about Papa and decide he's wonderful. But she won't. She just shuts herself away and grumbles, and we'll never be noble again."

"Where have you heard such dreadful talk, child?"

"It's what Mama . . . ."

Verena faltered and stopped. Then, without warning, she sprang up and rushed out of the door. Kate rose to follow, but Miss Hartest said, "Leave her, Miss Quantrill. These tantrums of hers are not uncommon."

There was an uncomfortable pause.

"I trust you won't take it amiss," Kate ventured, "if I ask why, when Verena knows her family history off by heart, she has to hear it all again?"

"Those are my instructions from Cousin Oliver."

"But surely—"

"The lessons are not exclusively for Verena's benefit. It appears to be hoped that you, also, will learn."

Kate was taken aback. Was she considered, then, too ill-schooled for Mr. Darsham's daughter; or was there some deeper, more complex reasoning behind it all?

She paced, discomfited, to the window. Verena was perched moodily on a tree stump at the end of the garden.

"It's the first time I've heard her mention her mother."

"She is very like her mother, in many little ways."

"I hope she'll learn to be happier."

"You mustn't think Charlotte was unhappy." Miss Hartest turned the idea over in her mind. "Her . . . wayward-ness . . . was all part of her. Part of what Cousin Oliver, as much as anyone, saw in her. She had the manner—the style, you know. No man could resist her."

"So I've gathered." Kate watched a finger of sunlight touch the forlorn figure in the dappled shadows, flicking sparks from the golden hair.

"Men marry for beauty," said Miss Hartest, "or for money. For both, if they can have both. They will not be happy where there is neither."

Alarmed, Kate turned to glance at her. The bitterness was too naked for a stranger's eyes. She returned to the prospect of the garden, to see Verena making her slow way back toward the house.

"I wouldn't envy any woman," said Miss Hartest, "who tried to step into Charlotte's shoes."

When Verena came indoors, she was so subdued that for once she made no plea to stay and play the piano. She and Kate walked back to the Tower in silence.

The door of the small drawing room, at the foot of the stairs, was open. It was so unusual for it to be left like this that they both glanced in.

Verena let out a gasp of disbelief.

The grand piano standing between the two windows was far more impressive than the Hartests' upright. Its walnut lid was inlaid with a mother-of-pearl rim, and the brass candle-holders gleamed from a recent polishing.

Kate was left in the doorway as Verena rushed to the stool and, in a wild desire to prove it was no illusion, began to play.

It was a Chopin nocturne. Verena knew it off by heart. So did Kate, by now. She had listened to it day after day, hearing the difficulties being overcome, the wrong notes surrendering at last.

The library door opened. Mr. Darsham came to stand by Kate's shoulder.

When Verena saw him, she stopped in mid-phrase and ran to him. "Oh, Papa." She clung to him. "Thank you, it's wonderful, it's . . . oh, thank you."

Absently he patted her head. "Since Miss Quantrill wished it."

"It was Verena who wished it," said Kate.

He released the girl. She smiled up at him, with a tinge of the old uncertainty creeping back, then hurried to the piano keyboard again, to confirm its reality.

Oliver Darsham closed the door. A heavy curtain fell upon the sound. He nodded to Kate, went back into the library, and put another door between him and the music.

The excursion trains carried summer visitors up the coast. John and Abel reported the arrival of a stentorian German band in Yarmouth. A few hardy souls brought their coaches through Senwich and went disdainfully on their way. Chedstowe was reported, according to Daniel, who had it from a man in Sheverton who managed a troupe of minstrels in Lowestoft, to be constructing a new pier to cope with the growing influx of holidaymakers and with pleasure boats which, it was said, would be setting out regularly from the Thames next year.

Senwich had no pier, no minstrels, no circulating library. There were no bathing machines on its beach, no reading room or lecture hall for penny readings, no sea-front hotels.

"Nor wanting for it," said Daniel.

"After the Horse Fair," Verena told Kate, "Papa says I may go to stay two or three weeks with Aunt Alice. Will you take a holiday, Miss Quantrill? Where will you go?" Before Kate could frame an answer, she bubbled on, "And the Horse Fair—you're to come with us, you know."

"You'll have to ask your father about that," said Kate. "He'll hardly want me with you on a family outing."

"But he does. He's the one who suggested it."

"That was . . . kind of him."

"He'll have such a lot of people to talk to, and someone will have to keep an eye on me, and Grandmama's too slow on her pins, as Mrs. Jenkyn says."

"I see."

It was wiser to take what Verena said at its face value than to recall yet again the other things Mrs. Jenkyn had said—let alone what Miss Hartest and Mr. Darsham himself had let slip.

She assumed that on the day of the fair she would take Verena in the trap and meet Mr. Darsham there when it suited him. But he would have none of this. Traffic would be heavy, and with every inn crowded to its doors, more erratic as the day wore on. They would all three journey there in comfort.

They set out in the barouche, drawn by two mettlesome bays, at eight o'clock on a warm, tranquil morning. Dust rose from the dry road. A fallen tree trunk gleamed with dew. In the ripples of the creek a group of turnstones, bright in their chestnut and black plumage, waded and dipped their bills, nudging splinters and pebbles aside. The air was filled with a sharp, eager, summery twittering.

"You have such a pretty hat, Miss Quantrill," said Verena.

Her father nodded and smiled, as though this had already occurred to him.

Kate sat imperiously upright, making the most of her plum-colored felt with its plunging brim, and the ostrich feather sweeping back over the crown. All the world around seemed to smile at her.

As they approached Sheverton, conveyances of all kinds joined them from side roads and farm tracks. There were a few carriages as gleaming as the Darshams' own. Drivers saluted with their whips; a squire here, a sumptuously bedecked young woman there leaned out to wave. And there were gigs and traps and dog carts, and a number of tradesmen's vans.

The closer they drew to the town, the thicker the traffic and the slower their pace.

Mr. Darsham said, "We have a lunch hamper beneath the seat. I fancy we shall be starting on the cold chicken before we reach Sheverton."

Verena had been sitting beside Kate. Now she pushed herself over from one seat to the other, and slid in beside her father.

Put your arm around her, Kate mutely implored him.

But he edged a fraction of an inch away, unsure of himself—unready, thought Kate miserably, to let his own daughter into his life.

At a crossroads the congestion was so bad that the coachman reined in to the side. They sat for a few minutes looking out over the fields toward the distant railway embankment.

Along the field immediately beyond the hedge, a gang of

men and women were cutting back an invasion of nettles. Occasionally a man would straighten up and cast an insolent glance at the slow-moving procession on the road, then stoop drearily to his work again.

A young woman, slatternly but with an alluring olive complexion and dark eyes, came close to the hedge and unashamedly allowed herself a rest. She surveyed the row of coaches, and her gypsy eyes grew bolder.

Kate leaned out. A little way ahead of them was halted a dray from Senwich. Five or six men on it were drinking from a beer cask they had brought from the inn.

One of them was Matthew Rouse.

He seemed engrossed in the boisterous exchanges of his cronies. But when he caught the glance of the girl in the field, he braced himself against the cask and stared greedily back at her.

Oliver Darsham said amiably, "I'm glad Rouse has an eye for something other than flood levels and soakaways. I began to fear he was too stern a taskmaster, with himself as the hardest driven slave."

"Rather than a slave," said Kate, "I'd say he was far too free and easy."

"Free? Yes. And easy—so much that is easy for him."

His ironic melancholy struck a chill through the heat of the morning. Was he so envious of Matthew Rouse's freedom to choose where he would, when he would, or not to choose at all?

Kate said, "I fancy him as light in his affections."

"A young man far from home has no need to be too scrupulous. In Holland, or in Senwich."

"What has Mr. Rouse been *doing*?" Verena demanded.

The coach lurched forward, conveniently putting an end to the conversation, and passed the dray. They began the descent into Sheverton.

So Mr. Darsham wished to play the philanderer? To

take lightly, and lightly discard, as he supposed the younger man to do? Was that what he really wanted of Kate; what he was clumsily leading up to, with his father's appetites but less of his father's bravado?

At last they reached the meadow.

The coaches of the gentry were drawn up in the best places. Smaller vans and traps were marshaled along the muddy edge of the stream. Farmers in their best velveteen coats and high-crowned hard hats stumped to and fro, bellowing greetings and covertly studying the horses that were being assembled.

Horse copers ran their wares along one side of the meadow to demonstrate their paces. Verena clung to Kate's hand as a mischief-maker cracked his whip loudly to alarm the horses, so that one or two broke loose and had to be pursued through the yelling crowd.

Coconut throw-stands had been set up in one corner. Verena tugged toward a printed notice announcing a donkey race in the afternoon, and a "Grand Race with Barrows." A prize of a new hat was offered to anyone who could climb a greasy pole.

"Daniel, you'll win a new hat for me?"

Kate, laughing, watched Sarah try to drag her husband away from the animals on display in a roped-off square at the center of the meadow.

"I'm here to replace old Bessie," retorted Daniel, "not to make a greasy fool of myself."

For the main reason for being here, after all, was the buying and selling of horses.

Dealers from all over the country came to Sheverton in August. There was an insatiable demand for the great Suffolk Punches in particular, scornful of all rivals when it came to pulling wagons from the docks of London, Liverpool, or Hull. Between demonstrations and auctions there was plenty of time for drinking, dipping for oranges,

watching the Punch and Judy, urging on a tipsy friend in
the blindfold race. But instinct told the men when a good
horse was about to be shown. They would all be there,
alert, when the drawing and backing tests took place.

"Oliver, my dear fellow!"

A local squire bumped into Mr. Darsham, and there
was a flurry of greetings. His sister, an auburn-haired
young woman in a peacock-blue dress, twirled her parasol
to produce roguish shadows across her face as Mr. Darsham drew Verena forward.

"But it's an age since we last met." Her hand on Verena's shoulder turned Verena this way and that. She dim-
pled and cooed. Verena wriggled. The lady's smile did not
falter. "See how she grows!"

"What brings you here, old man? Heard you were more
interested in dead meat than live meat these days."

Kate had seen the squire before, riding to hounds from
his estate south of the heath. He was one of those who put
on a fine show of disdain for such as kept up their estab-
lishments on the fruits of vulgar commerce. But his sister
knew how comfortably one might live by such debase-
ment. She was setting her cap at Mr. Darsham, thought
Kate, shocked by the brazenness with which the girl's arm
slipped through his. She was apparently unperturbed by
the continuing existence, somewhere, of Lady Charlotte.

Kate was jostled away from the group by a movement
of the crowd. She was tempted to go and join her brother
for a brief spell, but for the first time felt it would be an
intrusion. They were standing close together: the two of
them, belonging together, married, content, and with
Sarah happily thickening at the waist and moving more
heavily with the child growing within.

A hand touched her elbow.

Matthew Rouse said, "I think you're now permitted a
few minutes' diversion, Miss Kate."

"I'm well diverted, thank you."

"What shall I do for you—climb the greasy pole, run a race for you, win a scarf or a shawl for you?"

"Thank you, Mr. Rouse, but I don't wish you to exert yourself on my behalf."

"A labor of love," he said.

"Love?" She was angered by so cheap and airy a use of the word. "You're too free with your sayings."

"It *is* only a saying. A turn of phrase. And now, may we indulge in a stroll about the meadow? With my strong right arm to protect you."

"I need no protection, thank you."

She was immediately proved wrong. A group of youths who must have spent the morning so far in the nearest inn came reeling over the grass, cannoning into Kate and knocking her even farther away from Verena and Mr. Darsham. Rouse caught her with one arm and raised the other threateningly. One youth swore, then ducked and hurried off.

The protective arm remained where it was.

Kate said, "Please, Mr. Rouse . . ."

"I'm called 'Matthew.' "

"We are not so forward in this country."

"No." His hazel eyes twinkled with little green flecks. "Where I come from, it's no crime to be friendly."

"Nor here. But such haste is foreign to us."

It sounded stuffy as she said it, and drew an easy laugh from him. "Oh, now, Miss Kate. Foreign? My father is of good English stock—taken over from Bristol when he was so high—and my mother's folk are Dutch, which I guess could be said of many hereabouts. Does that make me so foreign?"

"So that's how you came to be in Holland." Somehow it was impossible not to respond to him.

"You've been checking on me? I begin to hope."

"It's common enough talk in the village."

"My father's a drainage engineer, way down in the Mississippi flood basin. My mother's cousins got me the chance to study in Holland, having a look at their methods of flood control. And now I'm here."

"Having learned all they can teach you in Holland?"

"That's a sharp tongue you have there, Miss Kate. No, I came here because there are different aspects to study in England. And then I met Mr. Darsham, and he offered me a challenge."

"And you can't resist a challenge?"

He grinned. It was an infectious grin. But she wasn't going to let herself be infected. He thought it was all so easy. And Mr. Darsham thought it of him. Kate thought otherwise.

Yet, still, despite herself, she wanted to smile.

"Over here," he said, "you've got yourself on the defensive, just shoring up what you've already got. Way out where I come from, we're making things over, making them new. Building, not just preserving. I'd like to show Mr. Darsham more than he knows about his own land."

Kate began to feel dizzy in the crush. Elbows dug into her ribs. A heavy boot stamped on her toes. A young couple, pressed together, blundered into her, giggling, pawing each other.

And Matthew Rouse's arm was still around her as he shouldered a way toward a less congested area.

Mr. Darsham watched them emerge, and frowned. He must be seeing the two of them, thought Kate, as just another feckless couple in the middle of the rowdy throng. After what she had said in the carriage about young Mr. Rouse . . . here she was, being hugged closely to him.

Rouse made an exaggerated bow. "One lost lady, safely returned."

A train let out a shrill whistle from the embankment

above the meadow, and there was a clatter of wheels as it slowed into Sheverton station and hissed to a standstill. A few children chased up the field toward it.

Dealers were waiting as a swarthy man with a red and white handkerchief knotted around his neck led a massive Suffolk Punch into the demonstration space. A twenty-foot length of thick tree bole had been laid at the edge of the clearing. The man hitched the horse to it with a long pair of traces, and then flicked his whip.

The barrel-chested sorrel took the strain, and heaved.

Nobody expected it to budge the tree; but all waited for it to show its lineage by sinking to its knees in the gallant attempt.

The sorrel stayed upright, its feet scrabbling.

Its breeder swore.

One attentive dealer shook his head. If a horse would not get down to the task, it would not be bought.

The whip cracked. The horse braced itself again, rested, and pulled.

Oliver Darsham watched, his features immobile: a thoroughbred watching a thoroughbred—sympathetic toward its failure so far, or contemptuous of the flaw?

There was a mutter of protest from the audience. The man had snatched up a stick and was beating the Punch on the inside of his knees until he began to sag. "You'll see!" he shouted to the dealers, who wagged their heads dubiously. "Look—you'll see!" He slashed the horse over the wallows until he was fully down to his knees, then made coaxing noises, and cracked his whip explosively. The horse began to draw, then slackened.

The stick rose again.

Suddenly Mr. Darsham broke from the crowd, limping into a run and grabbing the man's arm in midair.

"If your horse can't show its paces without that," he thundered, "he'll be no use to a civilized master."

"Damn you, let me go."

"Not until—"

Mr. Darsham's words were cut short as the stick came around and thrashed him across the cheek. He hunched away from the blow, and floundered to one side.

Matthew Rouse appeared at his side; was past him, snatching the stick through the man's palm until he yelled at the pain, and tossing it far across the grass. One twist, and Matthew had sent him to join it.

Oliver Darsham regained his balance and brushed the sleeve of his jacket as though it had been contaminated.

"You're all right, sir?" Matthew held out a hand to steady him.

"How else should I be?" They confronted each other more as opponents than as allies. Mr. Darsham's rage had not spent itself; it had to splash out over somebody. "There was absolutely no need for you to . . ."

His voice trailed away. He was looking past Matthew, past the heads of the nearer spectators.

Kate turned.

A lady in a black-and-gold dress, with a white-and-gold bonnet fastened under her chin, was walking down a grassy aisle between two sections of the crowd. She was haggard, her once-wide eyes puckering in on themselves; but she walked with the arrogantly stepping grace which nothing could rob her of.

It was Lady Charlotte.

Her husband's face was as drained and pallid as her own. Once, just once, his eyes sought Kate's. She read in them a wild, unutterable appeal. Then Lady Charlotte reached him, and he laughed once, harshly, and color flooded back into his face and filled it with blazing, uncontrollable triumph.

Kate was close enough to hear Lady Charlotte say, "I thought to have engaged a fly at the station. It seems they are all taken today." The languid movement of her head took in the whole meadow, the sound and turmoil of it all. "Perhaps you can find me a seat when you're ready to . . . to go home."

There was a sob of joy. Verena threw herself at her mother and hugged her, and wouldn't let go.

Over the girl's head Lady Charlotte looked steadily at her husband. She might have been asking whether, with so many present who knew them both, he would take his revenge by spurning her.

He said, "I don't think we shall want to stay much longer. If you're tired from the journey, we may leave as soon as you wish."

She made the faintest inclination of her head.

"Miss Quantrill"—with an effort he recognized her existence again—"if you'll come with us now . . ."

But she knew that in these first minutes, these first hours, there was no place for her. Verena still clung to her mother. Mr. Darsham could not keep his eyes from her: he stared, piercingly, as though to gouge each last little secret out of her.

Father, mother, and daughter; Kate's excuses to them provoked no more than an incurious nod of acceptance from Lady Charlotte. She hurried off to find Daniel and his Sarah, to drive home in their company.

The journey seemed interminable.

Chapter Seven

Daniel's wagon rumbled again to Sheverton a few days later, this time drawn by his sturdy new chestnut, its glossy brow gashed by a white blaze. He collected Lady Charlotte's trunks from the station and delivered them to the Tower.

"Not nigh on as much stuff as she took away with her," he observed to Kate.

Everybody knew about it, and everybody had a shred of guesswork to contribute. Her paramour had deserted her. Or she had stormed out on him and sunk into squalor amidst the dregs of London. She had sold her jewelry to maintain them both in idle luxury. They had starved. He had gone abroad, been killed. She had ceased to love him and yearned for her daughter. A corn factor from Ipswich passed on a story from his nephew working in London

who had met someone who swore that Mr. Darsham had
been to London to have a fight with the young officer. No;
he had gone to London to plead, not to fight.

Guesswork it remained. There had been no ceremonial
announcement of Lady Charlotte's departure; there was
none of her return. On Sunday morning four Darshams
appeared in church as before. Again Mr. Darsham stonily
outfaced his little world.

"She won't be choosing a maid from town," Mrs. Jenkyn
confided to Kate with a sparkle of malice. "Mr. Oliver's
engaged one from up Blackshore. Nice tidy little thing."

There was a lapse in Verena's lessons, her walks, her
schoolroom lunches. She did not go for the promised holiday with her aunt, but stayed possessively close to her
mother. Kate heard their voices far away along corridors,
muffled behind closed doors. The piano sometimes gave
out Verena's recognizable accentuations; at other times,
Lady Charlotte must have been at the keyboard, with a
quite different touch—different and, thought Kate, with
less conviction. When they strolled in the garden, Verena
looked fixedly up at her mother and chattered unendingly,
presumably pouring out all that had happened, and perhaps what she wanted to happen from now on. Lady Charlotte nodded, looking continually around her as though to
get her bearings again.

And when she and her husband were alone together—
not merely shut away from the world within Darsham's
Folly, but shut away in the closer intimacy of those rooms
upstairs in the southwest corner—what then? How did
Oliver Darsham think then, and speak and behave then,
with his beautiful, reclaimed wife?

Kate was conscious not only of Lady Charlotte's elusive
voice in the house, but of other cadences—ghostly laughter, a chuckling and gossiping in the beams and floor-
boards, mockery whispering under the doors, some de-

risive spirit cackling away to itself. All scoffing at the daydreams she had never openly admitted to herself and was now stricken to discover lurking there.

He had implored her to be patient. This was a strange reward for patience.

She had only one thing to be glad of: whatever fantasies might have shaped those daydreams, she had confessed them aloud to no one.

Mrs. Jenkyn, finding Kate wandering purposelessly between her room and the deserted schoolroom, invited her down for a midmorning taste of freshly baked bread and her own quince preserve. She was above gossiping with the staff, but regarded Kate as being on a different level. Her curiosity was keen but good-natured.

Kate was glad of someone to talk to, but wary of saying too much.

"Things seem to be settling down," Mrs. Jenkyn prompted.

"Not for me."

"You haven't been dismissed?"

"Not yet."

"No, I wouldn't have thought so," said Mrs. Jenkyn comfortably.

"But there's nothing for me to do."

"Hold you hard. You're there when the master wants you."

"So I'm to fritter the days away, holding myself in readiness, doing nothing whatsoever until . . ."

Until what?

"Same as for the rest of us," said Mrs. Jenkyn.

But it wasn't the same at all. There was nothing now that could make any sense for Kate. She must leave. Leave of her own accord. Back home. But there, too, she would simply be waiting—until, as her mother would regretfully have predicted, she married some farmer or fisherman. Or a clipper captain who'd be away most of their married life.

"There's many a girl would count herself lucky to be where you are," said Mrs. Jenkyn.

But I don't *know*—Kate was too cautious to utter it aloud—where I am.

Then Lady Charlotte sent for her.

The interview was in a room which Kate had not known existed—a small, very feminine sitting room on the second floor, looking out over the village and the sea.

Lady Charlotte sat with her back to the window. "Sit over there, Miss Quantrill, otherwise the light will be in your eyes." Her shoulders squirmed their distaste. "I find it too harsh. And I cannot bear to look at the sea. I hate the sight of the sea."

Kate sat on a lacquered chair almost too dainty for use.

"I felt we must have a little talk about Verena," said Lady Charlotte.

"I've seen little of her just lately, madam."

"But a great deal before . . . in recent months." Lady Charlotte laced her fingers together in her lap and said, "I'm most grateful for all you've done, Miss Quantrill. The child has obviously learned much from you. She has more confidence than when I . . . went away." Voice and fingers were tight, defying even a breath of criticism. "But now we shall have to rearrange a few things, naturally."

"Naturally, madam."

"As I've said, I'm grateful to you for bringing her out. But perhaps she should not be let out too frequently? She is, after all, a young lady, not a country lad."

"We tried to preserve a proper balance," said Kate defensively.

"Please don't be offended. I wouldn't for a moment

suggest you had let her run wild, or overstepped your instructions. I hope Verena can continue to rely on you for many things. It's simply that from now on we may have to alter the emphasis somewhat." The effort of saying even this much seemed to fatigue her. The long fingers went limp; her voice dropped into a vague drawl. "Sooner or later Verena will have to face the Season, and display talents more suited to the salon than the open countryside. For one thing, she must not neglect the pianoforte."

Kate was taken aback. Nobody, apparently, had told Lady Charlotte how the piano came to be where it was. Did she take it for granted that it had remained there during her entire absence?

"Now, Mr. Darsham and I are seeking a governess."

"I understood Miss Hartest—"

"Flora is an admirable woman. It is time, however, that some of the responsibility was taken from her. And Verena needs someone with . . . well, shall we say with rather more knowledge of the world. Senwich and its surroundings"—she allowed herself a swift glance over her shoulder at the window, and a delicate shudder—"are not to be her entire life."

"You're saying, madam, that you have no further use for my services?"

"Miss Quantrill, I've already assured you that that is not the case. There are many different facets to be considered in my daughter's upbringing—different but complementary. My duty is to see that the balance is correctly established and properly maintained until she comes out."

And waits, thought Kate wryly, not for a farmer or a fisherman but for a viscount, a colonial administrator or, at the very least, a country squire in good standing.

"My duty," Lady Charlotte repeated with an odd little catch in her throat.

There was a rap at the door.

Mr. Darsham came in. He was about to apologize for the interruption when his wife said, "I have been discussing Verena's future with Miss Quantrill."

"I'm glad Miss Quantrill is being consulted."

Lady Charlotte stiffened almost imperceptibly at the idea of consultation. "I was *telling* Miss Quantrill"—the emphasis was light but unmistakable—"of our plans for a governess, but not in any way to supplant what Miss Quantrill can contribute."

"There is no question of anyone supplanting Miss Quantrill," said Oliver Darsham levelly.

The disquieting thing was that neither of them now looked at the other.

Mr. Darsham went on, "I came to tell you that I've accepted an invitation for us to dine with Harry Martindale next Wednesday."

"I don't care to see the Martindales. Not so soon."

"I've accepted. Eleanor will drive over to see you in a day or two, and you may decide times and suchlike between you."

His eyes dwelt fleetingly on Kate, and he was gone.

Lady Charlotte's fingers crooked like fine talons. Then she said with icy calm, "We must have another chat soon, Miss Quantrill."

Her mind was already elsewhere.

The dinner engagements multiplied. Kate found herself once more walking with Verena—an inattentive Verena, chafing at her mother's two-day absence with friends near Bury St. Edmunds so that they might all attend a subscription ball there. Another couple were invited from far across Norfolk to stay at Darsham's Tower for several nights.

Mr. Darsham was showing his friends and acquaintances that his wife had returned, parading her so that there should be no doubt left in anyone's mind.

Kate saw for herself the truth of what Mrs. Jenkyn and Miss Hartest had said of them. They made a strikingly handsome, well-matched couple.

Yet their faces were so cold. She could imagine the fine picture they would present at a ball or at dinner. But it was unreal: they trod a stately pavane, somehow without hearing the real music.

Lady Charlotte sent for her again, one afternoon when the curtains were drawn against the sunlight. Verena sat at her feet, a sheet of music open. Kate had the impression that Lady Charlotte had been paying little attention to what Verena had been telling her, and that Verena was aware of this.

"Verena has asked, Miss Quantrill, if she may go for a walk with you."

Kate held out a hand toward Verena, who got to her feet.

"Apparently," said Lady Charlotte, "my company begins to bore her."

"But, Mama, you weren't even listening! It wasn't me who was bored, it—"

"A walk," said Lady Charlotte. "Nothing too vigorous. I'd prefer her not to return with a red face and mud up to her knees."

Kate took Verena away. Both of them instinctively adopted a stately tread as they walked down the drive, but as they reached the gates, Verena giggled. "It's nice to be out again, isn't it?"

"You seem to have managed very well without me." It came out more sharply than Kate had intended. She was appalled by her own pettiness, and covered it with a laugh.

Verena said, "Not all that well."

They went on, and gradually the awkward silence turned into a companionable one.

An hour later they had turned and were heading back toward Senwich along the river towpath. Along the road to the north came the rattle of wheels and a coachman's brisk encouragement to his horses.

"Mama," said Verena, "setting out to issue her invitations."

"Another dinner party?"

"The Harvest Ball. It is to be two weeks from now."

"I've never heard of one before."

"There hasn't been one before. Papa is very angry," Verena added inconsequentially.

"If it makes him angry, why have it?"

"Well, something funny must have happened. I mean, I know he told Mama there would be this ball, and she was talking to all those friends of theirs. And then one of them said she was giving a special party for her daughter's engagement on the same day—it was to be a surprise, only of course everybody was told about it so they could be sure of being there—and Harvest Homes were for tenants and those sort of people, so they weren't really interested."

"But your mother is still driving off to invite them?"

"Papa's very angry," Verena repeated. "He says he will give his Harvest Ball for those who deserve it—his farmers and bailiffs, and his managers from Ipswich. There's to be a special train to bring them to Sheverton, and Mama is seeing the tenants' wives."

So instead of the usual Harvest Home in the great barn, with food and drink and bawdy jokes and a boisterous cacophony of uninhibited singing, there was to be a grand occasion in Darsham's Folly itself.

Kate thought of the reactions throughout the county. The idea would not go down at all well. The gentry mixed with their tenants on the hunting field and in the back room of the inn on market day. They talked man to man when it suited them. But there were places where they did not meet. Hunting, yes; shooting, no. A visit to the barn to make a few jokes after the harvest and graciously accept a toast from the tenantry; but not an invitation to them to roister in the big house itself.

"You'll be coming, won't you?" said Verena as they skirted the village and came back full circle to the gates.

"As your chaperon?" Kate tried to make light of it in spite of her misgivings.

"As yourself."

"I'll have to wait until I see if I'm on your mother's list."

"Papa will ask you."

Perhaps he had been watching their approach from one of the upper windows. Perhaps there was some fated pattern to it all. In any case, there he was, in the open doorway, as they reached the house.

"Papa, I was telling Miss Quantrill about the Harvest Ball."

"At which we hope to see you, Miss Quantrill."

"I'm afraid I'll prove a poor dancer, sir."

His right hand reached toward her, then fell back to his side. "We shall find you a suitable partner, Miss Quantrill."

By the following morning there began a great scurrying and twittering in and beyond the parish boundaries. Wives and daughters descended upon Sheverton, whose two dressmakers kept the girls in their workrooms sitting up late. Lady Charlotte took Verena to Norwich. The wife of the Senwich chandler was startled by a sudden, increased, urgent demand on her services. She was a seamstress, trained in a fashionable London establishment. After a year of working eighteen hours a day at the mercy of petulant ladies of good family, she had come home to marry the boy who had never looked at anyone else and who was ready, with her beside him, to take over his ailing father's business. She still worked long hours, in the shop and at her journeywoman's stitching and sewing, but looked younger now than she had done when she came home five years ago. With the aid of fashion plates retained from her London days, and some magazines which a friend sent her regularly, she rose to the latest challenge.

"Won't *be* no harvest, if we don't have a bit more work and a bit less tittle-tattle," grumbled one farmer, as hostile to the whole notion as the county squires were when news of Darsham's latest eccentricity reached them.

Kate resorted to the chest in which she kept treasures her father had brought back at one time and another from his travels. She knew what she was looking for, and found it as rich and radiant as when he had presented it. She had shaken her head then, not seeing how it could ever be used in Senwich.

It was a length of lime-green silk, glinting with mysterious shadows when light fell one way upon a fold, transformed to the shimmer of moist spring foliage by the slightest movement of the fabric.

Mrs. Doy added a darker green velvet ribbon, and offset the straight front with an overskirt looped to fullness at the back. There was a frilled bodice, and the skirt hem was a ripple of little puckered frills. At the last minute she produced, with a few deft turns of her stumpy fingers, a huge velvet bow which she stitched into the sash, just above the gracefully sweeping train.

"There you are, my dear. There won't be many to match you."

Mrs. Jenkyn stood with her back to the double doors and looked down the polished expanse of ballroom floor to the overhang of the minstrels' gallery.

"I've never seen this room opened up since his father's day." She was hushed, almost reverent.

Two intricate porcelain candelabra hung from the molded ceiling, their candles sprouting from the ends of willowy branches supported by dreamy-eyed dryads. Colors were blurred here and there by an accumulation of old, yellowed wax droppings.

Evening sunshine was reflected from the polished floor to do battle with the pale flicker of the candles.

Traps and gigs began to arrive. The coaches meeting the train at Sheverton came in a cluster, and the room filled up with a multicolored tide. Girls were a wind-tossed agitation of autumn hues—cerise velvet, a flutter of mauve chiffon, hair in ringlets above dazzles of rose and burning orange. Their mothers shrilled and raised admiring arms to the ceiling and the soulful dryads. Their fathers mumbled and wished the gleaming boards would give way to good stone-flagged floors where they could plant their feet wide apart and talk about things that interested them.

Lady Charlotte and her husband opened the dancing to music provided by a string sextet brought from Bury St. Edmunds. Mr. Darsham's stiffness of movement made their steps less fluid than they might have been, but added a rather fine solemnity. Lady Charlotte wore blue silk trimmed with silver, her thin neck filled out with a ruffle of silver lace, shining against the black and white sobriety of her husband's attire. As they spun with slow grace below the chandeliers, light danced from her hair in time with the flicker and retreat of her satin shoes.

The players' final chords were a prelude to a stir near the door. Old Mrs. Darsham made a regal entrance. Her son hurried to her side and escorted her to a chair below the minstrels' gallery. She studied Kate curiously in passing and asked a question, which Mr. Darsham stooped to answer; she produced an offhanded shrug before she settled herself disdainfully in her chair.

"Now it'll be the quadrille," said Verena gleefully. "You must show them!"

She had spent two afternoons teaching Kate certain dance steps. Some came naturally, some were baffling. Verena had been delighted to find herself in the role of teacher, with Kate as pupil. They laughed immoderately; and the more they laughed, the more smoothly the steps came.

Mr. Darsham bowed before Kate and his daughter.

"We need four couples, Miss Quantrill. I wonder if you would care to join us?"

Beside him, suddenly, was Matthew Rouse. It had to be admitted that he was impressive—taller than she had remembered, very slim and correct in his black suit with a gleaming gold chain across the waistcoat. Correct, yet with that devilish insolence always plucking at the corners of his eyes and lips.

"Miss Quantrill, you'd be doing me a great pleasure by setting off in my company."

So this was the partner selected for her!

There was no holding back. They went across the floor to form up with two more couples. And the music began, and she knew she must let it tell her feet what to do.

The men along the wall brightened as two footmen brought trays of bubbling glasses, but even after a few drinks, they were coaxed out onto the floor by their wives only with difficulty. Their daughters were the ones to flower in this hothouse atmosphere: many of them, home from school with colorful ambitions, were anxious to show their paces; and wives nodded and watched and schemed and felt that even if they were not entirely at home, this was the kind of home which was their due.

"You look so lovely," Verena said when Kate returned to her side. "So . . . so serene."

It was the last word Kate would have applied to herself, but with the next movement of her hand up to her black helmet of hair she found she was trying to play the part—poised and serene.

Matthew Rouse was coming toward her again. She tried to predict what he would say and what polite rebuff she could offer.

"May I ask your permission, Miss Quantrill, to dance with your attractive charge?"

Verena drew herself up to her full height, and before Kate could do more than nod surprised assent, was being led out onto the floor. Kate could not repress a laugh. And Matthew Rouse laughed back at her as he whirled Verena past.

Mr. Darsham had as partner a plump lady who stumbled repeatedly, each time to be reassured by his charming acceptance of blame. They danced with more abandon, and the tempo of the evening quickened, and Kate wished he could always look so warm and attentive and untroubled.

Lady Charlotte stood beside Mrs. Darsham, aloof and exquisite. None of the other men had the courage to ask her to dance.

Matthew Rouse returned. "And now, Miss Darsham, may I ask *you* for permission to dance with *your* charge?"

"It is gladly granted." Verena made an exaggerated curtsy.

Kate found Mr. Rouse's arm once more about her.

She half expected his inconsequential, glib chatter to commence in the first bar of the music. But for several measures he was silent. She tried to hold herself rigid and unyielding as they floated around the room together, but found it impossible. He was a most accomplished dancer, and was using his skill to put her at ease, to coax her into the music itself and let herself be carried up and along by it in a way she would not have thought possible.

When, just once, he laughed, there was no conceit in it—simply a quiet note of appreciation.

Kate said, "I fancy you attended a great many balls while you were in Europe."

"None. The community in which I worked in Holland was an austere one. Dancing was frowned upon."

"But not at home—your real home?"

They spun gracefully near the orchestra, and his cheek brushed hers. "By no means. They are great occasions, though they have their own brand of austerity. Very formal, our southern ladies."

"So you fled to Europe in search of less formal ladies?"

As though to punish her for the taunt, he began to urge her into a tight, remorseless circle. She found herself protesting and laughing at the same time.

"Better," he cried. "Much better. You should smile more often. I'd say you once did a great deal of smiling, Miss Kate."

"And still do, when there's a good cause."

They passed a few feet from Mr. Darsham, dancing with a nervous girl in bobbing ringlets. Kate tried to look distant. Somehow she had no wish for him to see her gay in someone else's company.

"You'd do well to find a good cause, then," said Matthew Rouse, "instead of following our host's every move with those haunted eyes of yours."

She tried to slow their giddy revolutions. "I think you go too far, Mr. Rouse."

Without slackening its tempo, the music changed subtly into a minor key. A plaintive melody sang out on a violin.

Matthew Rouse, his own voice darkening, said, "I am sorry. I should not have spoken like that. I have had experience myself of how such matters can hurt."

"You, Mr. Rouse? An affair of the heart?" She was glad to have the chance of matching his usual spry mockery. "I would hardly have guessed it of you."

"It was a sad business. A silly business."

"And you are quite recovered?"

"Let's say that I have no intention of pouring out my woes to you. They're petty enough, seen in the right perspective."

"Which is how you see them?"

They seemed for uncountable seconds to float in a pool of silence in the heart of the music. Then he said gravely, "We see only what we wish to see. Even when we know it's not there, or not like that at all. Don't you find that, Miss Kate, *don't* you?"

The last vigorous bars swept them to the end of the ballroom. He walked her back to Verena.

His tone was pert again, as if to cancel out that brief, strange melancholy. "At this very moment the lord of the manor assumes you will dance the next dance with him. And, of course, he has the right—and he *is* right."

They reached Verena. Mr. Darsham was indeed bearing down on them. His nod to Matthew was civil, no more. Humming with arch joviality, Matthew turned away.

Mr. Darsham had danced with a number of buxom ladies and their daughters, and Lady Charlotte had watched expressionlessly. If she was watching now, the picture must have been much the same as the others.

But Mr. Darsham had talked courteously to his other partners. With Kate he was silent. It was not the unexpectedly relaxed, companionable silence she had shared with Matthew Rouse when they began, but a silence as stiff as Mr. Darsham's arm, as painful as the grip of his fingers.

Until: "You can have little respect for me."

The music was unfaltering, yet she felt she had tripped over a misplaced beat. "What have I done?"

"It's what *I've* done. Asking you to be patient—and who am I to preach patience?"

She tried to let the music remind her of what Verena had taught her; but they were out of step, and he was not gracefully apologizing and correcting their movement as he had done with his other partners.

"I made a wrong decision," he was saying. "A foolish decision. Because of my own pride . . . self-righteousness . . ."

They passed Mrs. Darsham, stonily watching, and Verena, who waved as if it might be months before their next encounter.

"Five years," he said. "A death sentence."

She was dancing to the rhythm of his words rather than that of the musicians.

"It can't go on. I made the decision because I thought it was my duty. But love—Kate, is there no duty to love?" The melody carried them on to its climax, and ceased. "How do I undo it?"

There was applause all around them. Then the orchestra played a sustained chord. Kate released herself as unobtrusively as possible.

"Ladies and gentlemen . . ."

The door of the anteroom was thrown open, to reveal a huge buffet table.

At each end was a succulent capon. Down the center of the array stood three epergnes of fruit, and between them two hams. There were dishes of game pie and chopped lobster. Fruits, jellies, and custards stood in glasses like garish sentries between salads, galantines and mayonnaises, pastries and iced cakes.

Verena dutifully accompanied a footman to select a few delicacies for her grandmother, who remained seated in the emptying ballroom.

French windows had been opened onto the terrace. Kate was tempted by the breeze, and with a little nod to Mrs. Darsham, who paid no attention whatsoever, went a few steps out into the cool of the evening.

Silhouetted against the night sky at the end of the terrace stood a man and woman. He pointed across the garden and said something, and she laughed. They moved closer together.

The man was Matthew Rouse. The gay, unaffected laugh had been Lady Charlotte's.

It was the first time Kate had heard Lady Charlotte laugh since her return.

Chapter Eight

In the excitement of the reunion with her mother, Verena had made no further mention of the longed-for visit to her Aunt Alice. Now Lady Charlotte proposed that she should spend a couple of weeks of the late autumn there.

With the treat within her grasp, Verena looked uncertain. She wanted to go, but resented her mother's willingness to be rid of her so short a time after coming back.

"It *was* for me she came home, wasn't it?" she shrewdly asked Kate.

Kate could hardly tell her that this was just one of the theories being bandied about. Nobody knew the full story —nobody but Verena's father and mother. To blur the mounting grievance, Kate asked a lot of questions about this aunt she was so fond of, and Verena brightened and, in answering, began to look forward again to going.

Her parents' plans covered more than the holiday. They would both accompany Verena to Gloucestershire and then return via London, where Mr. Darsham had to do some research in the British Museum while Lady Charlotte interviewed a number of applicants for the post of resident governess.

"While Verena is away, Miss Quantrill, perhaps you too would care to have some time to yourself." Lady Charlotte was more animated, as if the mere idea of making a journey away from Senwich and including London in the itinerary had stimulated her imagination. "I'm sure you deserve it. If you'll leave an address, we'll let you know when your services are required again."

Leave an address! Did Lady Charlotte visualize her taking the waters at Malvern, or seeking lodgings in a noisy seaside town as a change from their own remote seaside home?

But at least, with time on her hands, she could accompany the boys to the great Herring Fair in Yarmouth.

It was an annual event which, like the herring, they had never been known to miss. Abel and John made sure of a clear day or two between voyages so that the whole family could go. This year there would be Sarah as well.

She went home, to find life there disquietingly different, out of true with the life she had been living at Darsham's Tower. She had a panicky feeling of being lost between two shifting, changing places to neither of which she really belonged.

After three days of helping Sarah—making sure that she fitted into Sarah's routine, did things Sarah's way, and did nothing which would upset what Sarah had now established—she realized that the dress she wished to wear to Yarmouth was still in her room at the Tower.

It was a way of passing an hour or two: a saunter up to the house, perhaps a stroll around the grounds, and a check on what other possessions she might have left behind.

She had set eyes on Mr. Darsham only once since the evening of the ball, and then from a distance as he set out toward whatever strange fascination he found on the heath. Now, entering the Tower, she was acutely aware of his absence. Of course, she had seen Verena's preparations for leaving, had known the three of them would be gone. But there was more to it than that. Even without such foreknowledge she would have sensed the emptiness—an emptiness like that of her own home when her father quit it at the end of his rare visits.

For a while she sat in her room, then went out into the silent corridor. Mrs. Jenkyn would be downstairs, Emberson would be there, the maids and footmen would all be living their own life, waiting for the master and Lady Charlotte to return and bring them out about their duties. Up here was stillness.

On impulse, Kate went up to the next floor.

She paused, then hurried up another flight, and another, fleeing from temptation—the temptation to explore those rooms where the Darshams slept, to see . . . but to see what? To see whether, in spite of the maids' tidying up after they had gone, there was any scrap of evidence, any emotional intimation somehow hanging on the air, that there was one room where they shared more than the cold formalities exhibited in their public faces? . . .

On the fourth landing she stopped and leaned on a window ledge. The village was partially masked by the church tower. Below, half a dozen men were digging along the seaward edge of the churchyard. From here they appeared very small, their progress slow. They had worked all summer, and one autumn tide might make a mockery of all their puny efforts.

"What are they *doing*?"

The nearest door had opened, and a woman with unkempt gray hair erupted, to thrust her nose against the windowpanes. She confirmed that what she saw was what she had seen from her own window, and said, "Digging. Always digging. And now he's got others at it."

It was not the prim dark shape seen every Sunday in church, and not the presiding dowager of the Harvest Ball; but it was nevertheless Mrs. Darsham.

Abruptly she changed her target. "And who are you? What are you doing up here?"

Kate began to explain. Mrs. Darsham watched her mouth as though commanding it to stop talking nonsense and tell the truth.

After a few sentences she interrupted, "I will not be kept standing here in this draft. Come in."

The room, its windows giving a slightly different view of the activity below, was choked with potted plants. They were crammed on the window ledges, on small tables, and suspended from brass chains. Mrs. Darsham sank into a buckle-back chair and nodded peremptorily at a cane-seated one facing it. Kate obeyed and sat down.

Behind the old lady's head was a large engraving of two golden retrievers nuzzling a dead pheasant, flanked by a painting of a bearded gentleman which must have been done some years before that in the ancestral gallery, but was still unmistakably Robert Darsham.

"You were at the ball," Mrs. Darsham challenged. "You were not introduced to me."

Kate took up her explanations again.

"Hum. I understood Flora Hartest was Verena's governess."

Her face was a seamed, muddy brown, marked with darker brown splotches. One moment her eyes would be piercing and aggressive; the next, a veil clouded them over. She wanted to know everything that was happening around her but could not concentrate long enough to grasp what she was told.

Kate slowly went over the distinction between her duties and Miss Hartest's.

She was again cut short. "It's high time you brought Verena up to tea with me. She really must learn to show some consideration. Isn't that one of the things you're supposed to teach her? Why, when I was a child . . ."

"When they come back, I'm sure she'd love to come to tea."

"Back—from where?"

"Verena is staying with one of her aunts."

"Alice, I'll be bound. Hum. Always fussed the child. Never had any of her own, of course; and she won't now."

Kate had considered mentioning Lady Charlotte's search for a new, resident governess, but it was not really her place to do so; and coming on top of the confusion about herself and Miss Hartest, it would surely bemuse the old lady completely.

"Well"—it was dismissive—"mind you bring her up to see me." And as Kate got up and went to the door: "Whoever you are. . . ."

They were to catch the early train to give them a good, full day at the Herring Fair. Daniel would drive them all to Sheverton and stable his horse and cart there.

"Safer than the *Mary Matilda*," he prodded his brothers. "Never get there in that till it was all over!"

When Kate got up, well before dawn, there was a sharp frost. She bustled about, making tea and a hot breakfast, having established the night before with Sarah that she was to be allowed to take on this chore.

As Daniel harnessed the chestnut, Matthew Rouse crossed the yard and raised his hat to Kate.

"Good morning, Miss Kate."

"You're up early," she said. "The ground'll be hard for your shovels at this hour."

"I'm coming to the station with you."

"Indeed?"

"Your brother kindly offered me a seat. I have a few days' business in Yarmouth. It couldn't have come at a happier time."

He stayed close to her as the cart lurched up to the door, and was quick to help her up. Boxes had been arranged as makeshift seats. They squeaked and shifted at each bump in the road, and as the cart gathered speed Abel and John began to shout at Daniel. "Reckon we're going to find out what it's like to be landsick . . . sea's a smoother highway than this, I'll swear . . . Sarah, you going to present your husband with twins before we reach Minnerden Corner?"

Matthew Rouse had settled beside Kate. She wore the cinnamon dress she had reclaimed from the Tower, with large buttoned cuffs and a satin tie. Her straw bonnet was trimmed with rusty red and black ribbon, and she had the agreeable feeling that she was looking her best. The feeling would have been even more enjoyable if it had not been so frankly, impudently shared by Mr. Rouse.

Then, to her surprise, he edged away from her and stood up. "Mrs. Quantrill, the camber of the road being such as it is"—he swayed perilously—"I guarantee you more comfort if you'll allow me to sit by your right side and take some of the shock. Between your husband and me, you'll bruise less easily."

His eyes crinkled in such diffident courtesy that Sarah had to smile. She wriggled closer to Abel, and from then on was wedged safely between the two of them, their feet braced against the lurching floor.

The young Mr. Rouse leaned forward from time to time

to speak to Abel, but his eyes strayed compulsively back to Kate at the end of every sentence.

He had an appointment in Yarmouth with an engineer from the fens who was in the district studying the local network of roads and waterways. "They report he has worked wonders with steam pumping engines. And that could be the answer to what we're faced with in Senwich."

"An engine to hold back the sea?" Abel was skeptical.

"Holding back the sea is but half our problem. It's what the sea leaves behind that does the lasting damage. The marshes hold the water, and that undermines the church and the village, and the Tower itself."

"The Tower's well above flood level."

"So Mr. Darsham keeps telling me. What he won't see is that his home's sitting on a sponge. Only when we've got steady drainage can we strengthen the foundations and be sure of them."

"And you reckon this steam pump of yours'd do it?"

"Could make a powerful start. Benefit the whole area. More grazing on the marshes. And security for that grazing."

Matthew Rouse warmed to his subject. Now when he glanced at Kate it was to invite her, like any of the rest of them, to share his enthusiasm.

They reached Sheverton and joined a crowd on the platform, most of them festively bound for Yarmouth.

Passengers were jammed six to a side on the wooden seats of the carriage. This time Kate and Abel flanked Sarah. They were showered with cinders each time they went under a bridge—"No worse'n Abel's pipe," Daniel commented—and the pink prettiness of Kate's parasol, which she tilted across Sarah's face, looked somewhat mottled by the time they reached Yarmouth.

The station there reeked of fish. Boxes were being

loaded onto trains as fast as wagons from the quayside could bring them in. There was a noisy, jostling two-way flow of people and vehicles—full loads surging toward the station, empty wagons clattering back, and a great mass of men, women, and children always in motion.

Offshore was a forest of masts. Dutch and French boats edged in between Scottish trawlers. There was a babel of tongues on the beach and in the streets. Merchants were distinguished by their spruce city attire. The fishermen were in dark blue jerseys, some wearing a golden ring in one ear. Sea boots clumped over the hard and the road-way. Scottish girls with brazen laughs stood over ranks of barrels, their oilskin aprons dripping with grease and glint-ing scales. Salted and smoked herring from a score of huts and houses went on their inexorable way to the station—herring which massed every year off the banks, dying in their tens of thousands, never failing to appear year after year, never learning.

Abel nudged John and indicated a lean, hawk-beaked man deep in conversation with two smack skippers. "That's the one." Among their reasons for coming to the fair was the chance of picking up a number of short-term contracts which could be fitted in around the commitment to Mr. Darsham. They moved toward him.

Kate walked around with Daniel and Sarah for a while, listening to the flamboyant promises of the cheapjacks and the laughter and abuse of the bargains that were made on every corner, by every reeking barrel. Sarah soon tired, and decided to sit down and watch the bustle from a distance.

Kate strolled away on her own.

Two men in an inn doorway guffawed and called after her. A fisher-girl with arms akimbo muttered something insulting, not quite under her breath.

There was laughter and good humor everywhere. But it was on a dangerous edge: the drunken good humor could soon turn bad, the jokes become quarrelsome. Many men who came here regarded a fight as an essential part of the day's entertainment.

Across a street, Kate saw Matthew Rouse. He had left them at the station, stepping out briskly in search of the address he had been given; but now he seemed at a loose end. She turned away, not desiring his company. In her hurry she blundered into a large man with a Scottish accent so thick she could hardly understand what he was blearily saying. But the language of his meaty hands was plain enough. She pushed one away, only to have the other clamp on her arm.

A hand from out of nowhere chopped across the man's wrist. With an oath he lashed out, but was too drunk to aim properly. Matthew hit him once, hard, and flung him back against the wall. A flailing arm made Kate duck; then Matthew had struck again, once, twice . . . and the man was sagging down the wall with a smear of vomit trickling from his slack mouth.

Half a dozen men who had been drifting toward the spot in hope of witnessing a good hand-to-hand bout were disappointed. Matthew guided Kate past them, dabbing his mouth against the knuckles of his right hand.

"We seem fated to meet, my sweet Kate."

"I'm not your sweet Kate."

"Not yet, no. Maybe fate can do something about that, too."

"You're as ready to talk nothings as you are to use your fists."

"Ingratitude!" he rebuked her.

"I'm sorry. I do thank you for coming to my rescue."

A group reeling out of a tavern engulfed them and then

staggered apart. One cannoned into Matthew, who slapped him on the shoulder; the man grumbled, they both laughed.

Like answering to like, said Kate to herself.

As though he had heard her, Matthew said, "You don't condemn your brothers, Miss Kate, for the hard life they live on the barges. Don't tell me you don't know what it's like, in some places along the coast? And as for me—well, I've learned in a hard school on the levees. And in Holland —worked with the Dutch, drunk with the Dutch . . ."

"Yet so recently you were telling me of the severity of life over there."

He caught her arm to hold her away from a cart wheel jarring into the curb. "Dancing is the devil's sport to them. But drink and fighting—ah, they're less easily resistible devilries."

He stood looking from side to side, taking in the whole scene, until Kate asked, "Did you lose your way?"

"In Holland? I was too circumspect."

"I meant here, looking for your steam engine man."

"Ah, I see. No, I found his hotel, after a false trail or two. But he's out, and not aiming to be back until the mid-afternoon." He gestured helplessly at the tide of humanity flowing up every alley and gushing out into every square. "Little point in searching for him."

"I'm sure you'll find some diversion for the rest of the day."

She was about to step from the curb. Buoyantly, but with a touch of humility, he said, "Will you show me the town, Miss Kate? For today I'll admit to being a foreigner."

A few minutes ago she had instinctively wished to avoid him. Now she found the prospect of his company not altogether disagreeable, provided she was the one to set the pace and call the tune—which was what he appeared to be suggesting.

"You'll have seen the pier, and the ferry. And Nelson's column, of course."

"There's no 'of course' about any of it."

"But you can't have missed the column. It's so huge!"

She turned to point it out, only to realize that the twist of a street cut off the vista.

"Down here."

She began to hurry him away. He said, "You'll have to lead me by the hand, I warn you." It was literally true. To avoid being thrust apart by the crowd, they had to walk arm in arm or, when the pavement was too narrow, grab for each other's hand. There was nothing forward in the pressure of his fingers; rather, he made an easy joke of it when they were jostled and separated, and he had to draw her back as in some mannered dance movement remembered from the Harvest Ball.

They browsed along the shop windows of King Street and the colorful figureheads of ships marshaled against the quays. They talked disjointedly, yet it made sense; chattered back at an organ-grinder's monkey; watched the antics of urchins wheedling coppers from passersby.

She led him down on to the sands and, trudging some way south, they found a deserted stretch which the tide of humanity had not yet reached. A red-and-blue ball, lost by some child and half-buried, struck against Matthew's toecap, and he kicked out. The ball came loose in a flurry of sand. Without thinking, Kate pounced. She kicked the ball toward the water, and Matthew raced after it, and the two of them drove it over the soft sand and onto the harder, wet surface along the edge of the sea.

Kate had not realized how turned in on herself she had become these last few months.

Her shoe stuck in the sand and was tugged from her foot. With a despairing wail she stopped, and limped back to collect it. The red-and-blue ball bounced a few feet away, and floated out on the ripples, bobbing tantalizingly in and then bobbing back out again.

As she went down on one knee to put her shoe on, Matthew stood staring out over the water. A barque rode the horizon, making its slow way out toward tomorrow's dawn. A tinge of sadness clouded his eyes.

"Where are you?" Kate teased. "Can't you keep your mind off work—floods and drains and ditches? Or are you getting restless? Wanting to sail away?"

"Not yet," he murmured. "Though it might be safer."

"Safer?"

"For me."

"I wasn't aware you were in any danger."

"The ice is breaking. I'd hoped it was solid enough to last my lifetime." Before she could find any possible answer, he grasped her hand, helped her to her feet, and shouted extravagantly, "One kiss from you, and I should thaw completely."

She drew away. "I thought for an instant you really were worried about something. I ought to have known it was all nonsense."

"If you think I speak too lightly, I assure you it's safer than the other."

"You're talking a great deal about safety."

"I once made the mistake of saying all I felt, and showing all I felt. A long way from here, and it seems an age ago. It's not a mistake I've ever wanted to repeat." He resumed his contemplation of the distant vessel and then, as though from some far horizon of his own, said, "You, too. Dear Kate. You should be wary of showing too much. And of giving too freely. Don't show how ready you are to give."

A wisp of cloud darkened the sun. Its shadow slid a chill down Kate's neck. Her voice trembled. "Whatever you fancy you've read in my demeanor, Mr. Rouse—anything, at any time at all—it's most probable you've been misreading."

"For your own sake . . ." His heel stabbed down, scuffing up sand. "I won't speak for myself. Not because I'm afraid of those old echoes—though I still am afraid—but because you're not ready to listen. Not to me, you're not. But, Kate"—he spread his arms imploringly—"won't you please look for yourself? He has already destroyed one human being. And if he were free, and crooked his little finger at you, God knows what more misery he might inflict. Even now, I swear there's no stupidity you wouldn't commit."

She began to stumble away through the powdery sand. The esplanade was a bright mirage, leagues of blinding desert away. The sun came out again, but she went on trembling as she ran.

He caught up with her.

"Kate, I'm sorry. But I can't bear to see you destroyed."

"Don't cheapen yourself," she gasped. "You've . . . said too much . . . already."

"I've spoiled our day, haven't I?"

She laughed hoarsely. When he tried to say something further, she burst out, "Please go your way. And let me go mine."

He fell away behind. When at last she floundered to the esplanade and looked back, he was a solitary figure, still a hundred yards apart from the main throng, standing and looking after her.

It took twenty minutes to find the rest of the family. Mercifully, Sarah was tired. She did not wish to stay late. John and Abel had concluded a satisfactory deal and were ready to head homeward whenever it suited the others.

They left Matthew Rouse to his own devices—to his discussions about steam pumps and drainage, or possibly, Kate told herself fiercely without quite knowing whether she wanted to believe it or not, to talk about other matters with the bawdy fisher-girls, hungry for whatever sport was offered when darkness ended the day's trading.

Chapter Nine

Migrant birds soared and swooped above the marshes, rehearsed their formations, and departed. The old men of Senwich watched the shiftings and uncertainties of restless wildfowl, and prophesied a bad month.

On beech hedges the leaves reddened, rustling a papery protest in the wind but refusing to be stripped away.

Shore and hard were piled high with fish boxes like a tideline of flotsam. Those men who were not out spratting were kept busy, with their wives and children, packing the boxes as each boat came in to discharge its catch. Daniel Quantrill's wagon shuttled between village and station, loading and unloading.

The beacon flame on top of Darsham's Folly blazed every night as a marker for homeward-bound fishermen, faintly echoed by the sour glare of a cheapjack's naphtha-lit stall in the marketplace.

Then came four nights when all the boats from the Wash to the Stour huddled in their harbors or whatever friendly harbor they could reach; when the boxes were stacked in sheds and smokehouses well back from high-tide level; when wind and water smashed breaches in the seawalls and invaded every creek and inlet.

Senwich groin was twisted out of true. A jetty collapsed, some of its timbers swirling out to sea like straws on the drag of the ebb, others scattering over the banks. A few yards from the house, Kate had to pick her way over tangles of driftwood, rusty bolts, and weed.

Most of Matthew Rouse's defenses were standing firm. She wondered if he had slept at all during those raging days and nights. Anytime she had looked out or ventured out, she had glimpsed him somewhere: watching every inroad of the sea, studying each rise and fall, spurring his men on to hump shingle up from the beach or dig emergency soakaways. Once or twice he had appeared on the windswept top of the Tower with Oliver Darsham to get an overall view of the scene, pounding the low battlements with his fist to emphasize a point.

The reinforced bank east of the church shook off waves and mud. One half-finished ditch crumbled, but there was another to divert a swift rivulet away from the village. Only in the shallow dip between the churchyard wall and Darsham's Folly was there any real encroachment. Walking above it on the Friday after the gale, Kate saw that the water, fed by an overflow from the creek, had clawed down more earth only a few yards from the dark hulk of the Darsham mausoleum.

She strode out over drier land toward the old cottage on an exposed spur of heath. Even from a distance she could see there was something wrong. Thatch had been torn from the roof, and the chimney had collapsed into one end of the building.

As she approached, the door opened. She waited for old Mrs. Grote to glare out and tell her to go away—her usual greeting to anyone who came near. Instead, Matthew Rouse appeared, carrying a small stone crock.

She had an impulse to pretend to be making in some other direction. But that would look clumsy.

He said, "Your house is safe, I was glad to see."

"In better shape than this one."

"I've been trying to persuade the old . . ." He checked himself and moved down the slope from the cottage. "Twice I've tried to get her out of there. But she wouldn't budge, even when the wind brought half her roof in."

"She's a stubborn old . . ." Kate, too, stopped, and laughed despite herself.

"Witch?" he prompted. "That what you were about to call her?"

"Nobody really believes that, of course, but . . ."

" 'But'! Yes, I can imagine."

Kate glanced inquiringly at the crock.

"Soup." He looked oddly defensive.

"You mean Mrs. Grote actually accepted soup from you?"

"Wasn't any trouble. I mean, us having soup for the men out working in that weather, it made no hardship taking some up to her as well."

"Not many people get past the door."

"*Somebody* had to. She wouldn't come out, and she couldn't make any food for herself: the grate got buried when that bit of roof came down, and she just moved herself and what she could salvage into the other room. An infernal nuisance, nothing else."

"Yes."

"Said she hadn't been away from home more than two

days together in all her eighty years, and she wasn't going to be driven out now."

"Yes."

He almost glared at her, as if she were accusing him of some absurd sentimentality, and strode away toward the church. Kate gave him a few minutes' start, then turned for home.

As she went down into a dip between bushes, she recognized, on the next shallow summit, Oliver Darsham. Like everyone else, he was out assessing the damage.

They met in a hollow at the foot of the slope, out of the wind and briefly out of sight of the village.

He said, "I must talk to you."

"Verena's coming home?" She could read in his face that it was not this at all. Putting off the moment when he would speak, she hurried on, "You want me to come back, to be ready for her, to take up where—"

"I want you back, Kate. Yes. Back in my house. But it has nothing to do with Verena. You know that."

"Sir?"

"I will not have you calling me 'sir.'" Whatever had been pent up in him for weeks, or months, was surging up on its own overwhelming tide. "No more, Kate. No longer."

"I have no right to call you anything else. And you . . ."

"And I? I've no right to call you 'Kate': is that what you were going to say?"

She tried to continue up the slope and come into sight of the village again, but he blocked her way.

"Kate, you must listen. I can bear it no longer. I've watched you from my window, I've fought with myself, but . . . I came to meet you because I must speak. And you must listen."

He would not let her pass. She was too close to him now—his mouth close to hers, the shadows below his eyes like sullen bruises.

"There's nothing you can say," she breathed. "You have no right."

"Right! Is that all I'm ever to hear from you? No right, no right. And what's so damnable is that it's true. I despise myself. No right to dance with you and make half-promises, and then avoid you. . . ."

"No right to watch me and seek me out."

"Kate," he said, "I love you."

The wind moaned around the fringes of the hollow, but it was not the wind which sang unendurably in her ears.

"You can't talk to me of . . . of . . ." She would not let herself say the word.

"Of love?" he said.

"It's a fancy. It has to be."

"No fancy, but the truth. And you, Kate—could you love me?"

"I am not listening. I will not listen."

"You will love me."

"How could I? How could I let myself?"

"So you have to make an effort not to?" His eyes burned into hers.

"No. No." She could only sob it over and over again. "Please, no. No."

His mouth descended like the mouth of some dark yet splendid beast of prey, falling on her in this sheltered hollow which had become a trap. His arm held her. She fought, and his grip tightened. His mouth was cruel; and the worst cruelty of all was the response he aroused in her. She tried to twist her head away, yet at the same time was clinging to him. She couldn't let go, and he knew it. When at last she pulled her lips away, his lips pursued them. And she wanted to abandon herself to the delirium, to be an animal under the stormy sky, to let the cold hollow of the heath hold them for a few shuddering minutes out of time . . . to let him claim the warm hollows of her body.

His fingers slackened. She stumbled on a tussock of grass, and collapsed against the slope.

He stood over her. "Kate. you shall listen."

She shook her head helplessly. "Please let me go." But she could not even get to her feet again.

"I will not let you go. Now or ever."

"You must not speak. You're married, you're—"

"You call that a marriage?" His cry was as hoarse as the whisper of his breath against her mouth had been. "No, I must speak. You *shall* know."

Kate's right hand lay against a tuft of velvety moss. Grass stirred against her cheek. She closed her eyes, but felt the earth reel, and opened them again.

Oliver Darsham said, "You're well aware—the whole county knows—that my wife left me for a young pup who flattered her vanity. He wasn't the first. There'd been passing fancies before. Insulting in their triviality. That was her main pleasure—spiting me."

"But why?"

"I've asked myself that often enough, heaven knows. It must be born in some women. A desire to tantalize— pretty flirtatiousness before marriage, a disease afterward. This time, with young Sanderson, it went too far. But," he said in a gust of hatred, "she came crawling back. She had to come back. For five years."

The chill of the ground seeped up through her bones.

"Do you understand, Kate?" he was asking. "For five years, and no more."

"No, I don't understand."

"I agreed," he said slowly and deliberately, "to take her

back until Verena reaches the age of eighteen. Until she has been presented and has come out. We shall take a house in London for the Season, Verena will be seen through the whole ritual, and then my duty will have been discharged. My wife found, rather belatedly, that she missed her daughter. I am allowing her to be with Verena as she grows up, since I think that is best for the child. But once Verena has come out, my wife leaves the house—and does not come back."

"But where will she go?"

"Where she pleases."

"Poor woman," said Kate involuntarily.

He was poised against the sky as though to swoop on her again, more savagely this time.

"You think I've been too harsh? She has taunted me, destroyed any hope of happiness between us, neglected her daughter when it suited her, and then craved for her. I could have left her to the aftertaste of her own folly. Now I'm realizing that that, in fact, is what I ought to have done."

"Sir—"

"No, I will not have you calling me 'sir.' You're not a servant. You're 'Kate.' And my name is 'Oliver.' Say it."

"Before the whole world? Before Verena . . . Lady Charlotte . . . your cousins?"

The taunt went home more painfully than she could have predicted. He flinched.

"Not yet, then." His hand went to his brow; he seemed to be trying to squeeze sense out of it. "Five years," he said wonderingly. "Five years from now, I promise . . ."

"And until then?"

"No, it's impossible. I can't wait that long. It was absurd . . . quixotic . . . mad. I can't wait, can't lie awake night after night for five years, longing for you, seeing you everywhere—with my eyes open or closed, always seeing you and wanting you. Kate . . ."

"I see."

Now she found it possible to scramble up. He put out a hand to her, and she took it and steadied herself, but would not let him draw her close again.

"What do you see?"

"I see that because your wife is nothing to you anymore, you're hungry for a mistress."

"No! Kate, no!"

"Then what?"

"I want you to marry me."

It was halfway between daydream and nightmare. She said, "But it's impossible. You know it's impossible. You have a wife; if she leaves after . . . after five years . . . she'll still be your wife; she—"

"Kate, trust me. Tell me you love me. . . ."

"No."

"You'll tell me. In the end." He tried to laugh, to make a joking boast of it as Matthew Rouse might have done, but it was not in his manner. "I shall not rest," he said, "until we're together."

"It's easy enough to make such vows, when you know you can't be held to them. You're safe: you're already bound, and anything you say to me is only a game. Not a game I care to play."

"You shall see," he declared. "I'll put an end to this charade. Soon. Very soon—somehow—I swear it."

Kate sprang to the rim of the hollow. Senwich seemed so near that it was a wonder the whole place had not overheard their conversation.

The path marked where heath ended and marsh began. Oliver walked beside her. When they had gone a few hundred yards, he stooped, picked up a sliver of flint, and examined it, then tossed it aside.

"You collect stones?" It was a banal politeness, setting the conversation back on safe ground.

"Only if they show signs of human workmanship. Craftsmen of prehistory. You've never been interested in archaeology, Kate?"

She laughed at the mere idea.

"Because the present has been intolerable," he said, "I've lived a great deal in the past."

She thought of those faces in the gallery, and unidentifiable shadows back to a time of flint tools and sinister burial mounds. Faces and shadows were equally incomprehensible.

Somebody was calling. In the gully between church and house Matthew Rouse stood, urgently beckoning Oliver Darsham to join him.

The laborers had uncovered what looked from a distance like the gray cranium of a huge skull. Standing above it, one saw that the grayness was that of knapped flint, and that in it were red flecks of old brickwork. The rounded surface must continue in both directions under the soil that had not yet been dug away.

Oliver Darsham bent over it.

"But it must be centuries old."

Matthew, his boots and trousers plastered with mud, knelt beside him. "But there are signs here"—he prodded —"and here . . . it's been strengthened in the not too distant past."

"That's impossible. I've never heard of this tunnel before. It *is* a tunnel?"

"Looks like it."

They both stood up, their heads turning to follow the line of the masonry. It was directly between the mausoleum in one direction, the Tower in the other.

"Smugglers?" Matthew hazarded.

"My family has survived many tribulations," said Oliver Darsham stiffly. "We never found it necessary to eke out our living by dealing in contraband."

"Have I your permission to break through the top?"

"You have. And perhaps you'll send one of the men for Hartest. If it connects with the churchyard, he should know about it."

Picks chipped carefully into the stonework until a large piece fell through. Bricks and flints were then picked away and heaped to one side, until the hole was wide enough to allow a man through. A lantern was brought. The Reverend Godfrey Hartest arrived, bewildered.

Matthew said, "I'll make sure it's safe."

Oliver made an instinctive gesture of protest. "Oliver": Kate realized that, in spite of her protestations, this was how she was beginning to think of him.

He was as excited as a little boy. What did he expect—a revelation of some lost treasure, some aspect of family history as yet unknown, some secret passage by which his ancestors reached the church in times of religious persecution?

Matthew lowered himself in. His head was still showing when his feet touched the ground. The lantern was handed down, and he had to stoop to peer along the tunnel. Crouching, he disappeared.

"All right." His voice echoed eerily from the hole. "It's pretty sound."

Without hesitation Oliver swung his legs over the edge and dropped. There was a sound of shuffling, a murmur of resonant voices.

"Sir Edwin," said Oliver suddenly, loud and incredulous.

Mr. Hartest blinked more rapidly than ever. "Sir Edwin? But he committed suicide. He was forbidden burial in consecrated ground."

Other exclamations were muffled as the two men below moved farther along what must indeed be an extensive tunnel.

Then there was a strange, strangled moan.

And silence.

Kate took a step toward the edge. The rector put out one arm to hold her back.

"What is it?" he called into the yawning gap.

After a moment Oliver reappeared. His face was ashen. Staring up, he was hideously like a pallid corpse awakening from the dead, waiting for the earth to yield it up again.

Mr. Hartest leaned over to give him a hand, while Matthew pushed from below. Oliver scrambled free, and crumpled to a heap on the grass. He held up both hands in supplication to the rector, then mutely pointed to the hole.

Matthew hauled himself out and rolled clear, after setting the lantern near the edge.

"Better take it," he said to Mr. Hartest. "Take it—and see for yourself."

Oliver let his head sag between his knees as though about to be sick. When Mr. Hartest had gingerly lowered himself into the tunnel, and then, after an age, clambered out again, Matthew said, "I think you'd better go with Mr. Darsham, sir. Talk it over with him . . . between yourselves."

The rector had to help Oliver to his feet. They turned toward the Tower. Then Oliver said, "Seal that up. Put it back as it was. And no one else is to go down there. You hear me? No one!"

Matthew protested, "But—"

"Seal it up! At once. And cover it over, and there's to be no further work on this spot."

He limped away. Mr. Hartest offered him an arm, but it was shaken off.

Kate stood beside Matthew. "What did he see? What was it, down there?"

"It's not for me to tell you."

"But what could have done that to him?"

Matthew's gaze was following Oliver as he plodded up the slope and beside the wall of Darsham's Folly to the gate. For once there was no attempt at a flippant veneer as he spoke.

"I wonder what it feels like to find out you died the day you were born."

"I don't understand."

"Neither do I. Nor, I guess, does he."

Chapter Ten

Mrs. Jenkyn said: "Shut himself away, like he'd got the plague. Like it was something he'd caught down in that place, whatever it was, and he won't let anyone near him."

The tunnel had been resealed, not by any makeshift cover but by a sound reconstruction of stone and brick to keep it watertight. Earth had been packed down again. No one walking above would be in danger of crashing through.

It put paid to Matthew Rouse's scheme for a deep drainage channel. Whether he tried to argue it out with his employer, putting forward suggestions for piping across the tunnel or any other method, Kate didn't know. All she or anyone else knew was that the workmen sealed the gap, tidied up, shored up the side of the gully on which they had been working, and were transferred to repairs on the bank by the jetty.

Verena came home from her stay with Aunt Alice. For some days she found it hard to settle to the familiar routine. And it was in every way the old, familiar routine. No governess had been engaged after all. "You ask me," said Mrs. Jenkyn sagely to Kate, "there was a bit of a set-to about having somebody else in the house. The master wanted things kept the way they were." So there was Miss Hartest as before; and Kate, as before, but spending less time out of doors now that winter was full upon them.

Lady Charlotte restored things, in fact, to their earliest pattern. She haughtily abolished Verena's visits with Kate to the rectory. "These dreadful winds—all the salt in the air—absolute havoc to the complexion." Miss Hartest's complexion, one supposed, was beyond redemption: she trudged up to the Tower again as she had done when Kate first came here.

Kate mentioned old Mrs. Darsham's request that Verena should sometimes take tea with her.

"Nonsense." Lady Charlotte's reaction was immediate. "One of her stupid whims. I doubt if she remembers it. I'm afraid, Miss Quantrill, that if you and Verena did go up to her room she'd deny ever having invited you."

There was a new confidence in her manner. She might be serving the sentence ordained by her husband, but in his absence she had no hesitation in running the prison according to her own dictates.

It was not merely an absence, but an abdication. What could he possibly have seen or experienced in that subterranean chamber?

Verena grumbled about not going to the rectory anymore. "It made such a change." But then she studied the weather, and was not too unhappy that Miss Hartest was the one who had to make the journey. It would have been different if there had been no piano here, but as it had been restored, she was content enough.

"Aunt Alice let me play for hours," she told Kate. And when they were alone together, she confided, "Uncle Stephen's a wonderful pianist. And plays the organ in the school chapel. Used to let me go along when he practiced."

"He lives by his music?"

"Oh, no. He's only a schoolmaster. Papa can't be bothered with him. But they're so nice, Miss Quantrill, truly they are."

"I'm sure they are."

"And I used to play for hours," said Verena blissfully.

One afternoon Kate heard her tackling a very ambitious piece which she had not heard before. The door was open, and Lady Charlotte stood there, also listening. Verena's fingers were taxed to their utmost. As far as Kate could tell, she played few wrong notes; but she did miss some from sheer fatigue.

"Far too stormy, my pet," said her mother at the end. "Not the kind of thing a young lady should attempt."

Kate half-expected Oliver to appear and denounce the fortissimo chords which had been clashing out through the open door. But from something Lady Charlotte said a few minutes later to Mrs. Jenkyn, it appeared that he had at last emerged and gone to London.

"On a different kind of research this time," said Lady Charlotte cryptically, more to herself than to Mrs. Jenkyn.

When he returned two days later, Dr. Cawdron was sent for at once. Kate and Verena, sitting by the window of the schoolroom, saw the doctor arrive.

Was it true, then, that he had really contracted some strange disease still lingering in that tunnel?

With an effort Kate forced her attention back to the knitting lesson she was giving Verena. It was typical of the girl that, lacking real proficiency, she should insist on undertaking something complicated. It was to be a Christmas present for her father—a fine wool jersey, not the heavy fisherman's type but one which he could wear under his topcoat when out exploring his prehistoric sites.

"It'll be a wonderful surprise," Kate encouraged her. "I know he'll be delighted."

"You think he will?" Verena had suffered too many rebuffs to be optimistic. Yet doggedly she forged on, concentrating on the work in hand, just to show that it could be done.

Kate wondered what was being said between Oliver and the doctor. And wondered about Verena and her father. If it all came true—*Be patient . . . I promise . . . I love you*—would he learn to love Verena also; could Verena play her part in coaxing him out into the warmth of life, out of his shell of disillusionment?

If it all came true . . .

There was still Lady Charlotte. Five years, he had said. But even if all of them served that full sentence, and Lady Charlotte went, there must surely be a divorce? Kate knew little about such procedures, but doubted if a marriage could be broken up simply because Oliver wished it. There was nobody she could ask. Miss Hartest would probably know—and be horrified by such questions.

"I've done it wrong," cried Verena. "I'm sure this isn't the way it's meant to go."

"You've dropped a stitch."

Kate took the needles and picked up the stitch. Verena bent over her task again, her tongue peeping fitfully between her lips.

How could anyone as vain as Lady Charlotte endure such a situation? Could she honor the stern terms on which she had been allowed to return; or was she, while the rest of the house slept, endeavoring to regain his love?

For a passionate man to have a beautiful woman like that near him, a woman who was his by right if he chose to exercise the right, was surely intolerable. Sooner or later, if she set her heart and soul and body to it, Lady Charlotte must succeed in winning him back.

Unless she had no wish to.

"Miss Quantrill, I've done it again." As Kate took the knitting from her, Verena whined, "Why didn't you stop me? You're supposed to be watching what I'm doing."

"Let's have a break for a few minutes," said Kate.

It was as Verena was about to resume work that they both saw a man running up the drive. It was Daniel. Kate leaned forward, puzzled. A few moments later Mrs. Jenkyn came to the schoolroom.

"Miss, you'd better come. Your brother's here, after the doctor."

Kate sprang up. "Sarah?"

"She's started."

"But it's not due for another two or three weeks."

"Well, it's gone and started. And the midwife's over the other side of Stowmarket, with her father—he's not expected to last the week."

Kate hurried downstairs. Daniel stood in the hall, smacking his right fist repeatedly into his left palm, glaring at the library door. It opened. Dr. Cawdron finished what he was saying into the room.

"Very well, sir. I'll dig out his notebooks. But I never heard him speak of any abnormal circumstances other than your . . . hm . . . slight malformation."

The doors closed. He turned querulously to Daniel. "Your wife? In some haste, isn't she? You're quite sure—"

"It's hurting dreadfully," said Daniel. "For God's sake, come."

Dr. Cawdron glanced at Kate. "I think it might be a help to have you along, Miss Quantrill."

"I shall have to ask—"

"Leave it to me, miss." Mrs. Jenkyn already had Kate's cloak for her. "I'll tell the mistress. You go along as fast as you can."

Sarah lay with her neck arching over the pillow, straining away from the next stab of pain. As each fresh spasm went through her, another runnel of sweat formed on her brow and trickled to the pillow or into her eyes.

Dr. Cawdron examined her, listened to her sharp protests of breath, and nodded as though this was all most enjoyable.

Over his shoulder he said to Daniel, "Will you run over to my surgery, please, and fetch the chlorine bottle. Mrs. Levitt will know where it is. Chlorine—right?"

Daniel hurried off.

Sarah began to sob in a faster rhythm.

"Will he get there in time?" Kate asked anxiously.

"There's plenty of time. And it gets him out of the way—makes him feel he's doing something to help."

When Daniel returned, the doctor washed in a chlorine solution. "I shall be glad if you too will disinfect your hands, Miss Quantrill."

Daniel was dismissed from the room.

"I think if you would take Mrs. Quantrill's hands . . . so . . . yes, splendid . . ."

Kate held, and watched, and became part of Sarah. She felt the same quickening pulse, and the same disappointment when an agonizing convulsion was not the final, triumphant thrust.

Dr. Cawdron was chatting unconcernedly. "Some of my colleagues prefer premature babies to be born in the infirmary. Don't agree. Still far too much infection. Come on, Mrs. Quantrill, we're nearly there. Good. Good. Puerperal fever, now. . . ."

Again a quickening. Sarah's gasps excited Kate far down, deep inside. There would come a time when she would lie like that herself, twisted and sweating and sprawled out, because of the son Oliver would have planted in her.

"Too many deaths in hospitals still. Mothers too ill to feed their children—sometimes not even knowing there's a child there. Don't be alarmed—we have made sure it won't happen here. Ah . . . yes, I think so . . ."

Oliver's son. Not this year, but next year, sometime. . . .

A smeared, glistening head appeared.

"Good," said Dr. Cawdron.

Let it be a boy, Kate prayed. A good-luck sign. If it's a boy, she said to herself, it means I shall marry Oliver and it will all come right somehow, and I shall present him with a boy. . . .

"A boy," said Cawdron.

Sarah sank back thankfully, then raised her head again to see the tiny scrap of a child which the doctor was holding. He gave it a gentle slap, a harder one, and there was a sudden indignant squeak.

"Good. Excellent. Sometimes have trouble with the early ones—lungs won't hold the air. This one's in good shape." He probed gently with his fingers, turned the child over. "Yes, looks like a fine specimen. Miss Quantrill, if you'll come around this side of the bed . . ."

His abrupt manner concealed a gentle dexterity. A quarter of an hour later mother and son were clean, refreshed, and quiet. There was a happy, dreamy stillness in the room.

"I think we may now let the father in," said Cawdron. "But I'm entrusting the child to your care, Miss Quantrill. Keep it well wrapped up. It would have profited from another couple of weeks in the warmth."

" 'It'?" said Kate indignantly. The tiny, wizened face had already become that of a real live person. She was sure, already, that it could never have been a girl's face.

"A boy!" said Daniel reverently.

"What else did you expect, in *your* family?" said Cawdron.

Kate spent the night at home. Next morning Abel and John returned from a voyage, made admiring and facetious noises over their nephew, and showed themselves as hungry as ever.

The household could not be left to run itself. Sarah declared that she could perfectly well organize it from her bed for a few days, but she was still weak, and it was obvious that Florence would be unable to cope on her own. Kate announced that she would stay on until Sarah was fully recovered.

There was an argument. Kate won.

She would have to go up to the Tower to tell them.

She let herself in at the side door as usual, and made her way around to the hall, where she could hear voices. The front door was open. Lady Charlotte, with a purple cape over her shoulders, was about to go out. She was laughing, close to hysteria.

"Who are you, then? Who was I fool enough to marry?"

"Whoever may have told you—"

"Does it make any difference who told me? It does not alter the facts."

"We don't *know* the facts."

They both saw Kate at the same moment; and Lady Charlotte, with a derisive pout at her husband, went out.

Oliver stood immobile, waiting for Kate to speak.

She said, "I must ask you to release me from my duties for a while. To stay at home for a while."

"Yes," he said numbly. "You have every justification, of course. I'm sorry."

It was not the sort of reply she had expected. "My sister-in-law—"

"What has your sister-in-law to do with it?"

Kate explained. He appeared to be listening but was taking little of it in. Before she had finished, while she was still promising that it was only a matter of a week or so, he said out of the blue, "You must forget every word I said to you that day . . . the day when . . ."

"Yes. I'm sure it's best. I quite understand."

She surprised both of them with the matter-of-fact curtness of her reply. And why, when she knew this was best and had known all along that everything that other day must have been a wild aberration, did she feel such an acute anguish?

Oliver, some feet away from her and making no move to come nearer, looked lost—lost in his own house.

"You . . . you said I had no right to speak. Now I see how true that is. I am a fraud, Kate. A grotesque fraud."

"You spoke impetuously. It is forgotten."

"No! That is not at all what I meant." His weight sank onto one leg planted askew, until she was afraid it would buckle under him. "Kate . . . I owe it to you to show why I cannot fulfill my promise."

"It is forgotten," she repeated.

"You must *see*."

He led her to the baize-lined door and held it open for her. A scared maid peeped out from the far end of the passage and dodged out of sight. Oliver took five or six steps along the passage and, producing a key from an inner pocket, opened a door.

Within, a lantern hung from a hook. He took it down and lit it, to reveal a steep flight of steps descending into dank shadow. Oliver led the way, forcing the shadows to retreat, but never entirely quelling them.

Kate stopped on the lowest of the stone steps. Somehow

to put a foot down onto the floor would be to commit herself to something from which it wouldn't be easy to escape.

The gloomy cellar was haunted. Of that she was positive. She had never before felt the chill breath of a ghost on her cheek, but now was convinced that a whole gibbering family of them waited in the shrouded corners. Faces formed and dissolved in the uncertain light.

Oliver said, "Over here." Beside a mesh of wine racks was the outline, sunk into the moist, green-smudged brickwork, of what might have been an old kitchen range, neatly boarded up. "I thought nothing of this until I calculated where the tunnel would reach the cellar, if it did reach this far." He selected another key. "And for years I thought nothing of this bunch of keys in my father's desk . . . until I discovered their purpose."

He raised the lantern so that its beam fell behind the edge of the uppermost plank. Awkwardly he inserted the key, and the whole wooden barrier swung into the cellar. Where the grate of the range ought to have been was a low, open doorway. Oliver swung the lantern to show, beyond the opening, an inner arch barred by an iron gate.

There was a key for this also. He opened it, and waited for Kate to pass him.

They were in the tunnel.

The roof and walls dripped slow, unpredictable droplets of moisture. A few shallow puddles had formed in the uneven flooring. Oliver's shadow fell over them and crawled up the wall, spreading and distorting as it went. He stooped over a stone coffin and held the lantern above its lid, waiting for Kate to come beside him.

Edward Darsham . . . and an identical coffin, raised on bulbous stone legs, immediately beyond it, bearing the name of Henry Marjoribanks Darsham.

Oliver said, "Victims of the plague. It was forbidden to

bring such bodies out of London. They ought to have been thrown into the plague pits with the rest."

"But they are here," she murmured.

"Yes. And over here, Sir Edwin—who took his own life. And"—the lantern swung, light flooded into another carved inscription—"the Lord Darsham who died on the block, and who should have been buried in quicklime."

The dark lines of his face seemed to grin wider with pride.

It was the Darsham clannishness again. Even those banished from the holy precincts of the family mausoleum for spiritual, health, or political reasons had found their way as close to its wall as was humanly possible. Family piety prevailed over all other obediences.

Oliver's hand began to shake, so that their shadows did a weird, trembling dance on the walls. Dejection claimed him again. He trod solemnly on, past three more coffins which he did not trouble to show Kate; and stopped at last, hard up against the shape of an iron-studded door at the far end of the tunnel.

The lantern rose again, this time above a pathetically small coffin.

Kate could not set one foot in front of the other. She stayed petrified, listening to the erratic plop and patter of water.

Oliver did not say a word, but he was demanding that she come to him.

A cold drop on her left ear startled her into life again. She covered the remaining distance, and looked down at the more recent plaque on the little box.

It read:

OLIVER ALEXANDER DARSHAM
born 12 January 1838
died 12 January 1838

Chapter Eleven

The refuse left by the storm had been cleared from the garden, but the slightest gust of wind still shook down further broken twigs, and a large branch had been loosed and dropped on the grass. Leaves heaped against the terrace, and the pergola of the small rose garden was leaning in on itself.

Matthew Rouse stooped through a gap torn in the hedge, testing with a tentative foot the slimy mess beyond the opening.

Lady Charlotte crossed the terrace and picked her way fastidiously through the debris.

Standing at the window, Kate, dry-throated, heard herself rasp, "But there was another child—a twin?"

"I have heard of identical twins," said Oliver. "Never of twins so identical as to be given the same names."

"That *was* the date of your birthday?"

"And the day of my death, it appears."

"You never knew of that tunnel before?"

"Never."

"Or of its . . . contents?"

He was obsessively brushing his hands together as if to rub away not merely the grime of the cellar and tunnel but some deeper, murkier stain.

"My father never mentioned its existence. And my mother . . ."

He paused.

Kate said, "You've asked her? After what you discovered, you must have asked her."

"I kept putting it off. I hardly dared. If there was some terrible secret, something kept from me, there must have been a good reason for that concealment. But it was no use: I had to know."

"And . . . ?"

"And she says I must have been having hallucinations, and there's only one Oliver Alexander Darsham—myself."

"Then how does she explain the coffin?"

"She doesn't. She doesn't believe it can be there, so it is simply not there. I begged her to go down and see for herself. To come with me. But she is scared of enclosed places—she lives high up in the house because she likes to be far above things. She refuses to see for herself, and refuses to hear what I say. And then she is so vague, of course. Her mind wanders, and when I try to pursue the questioning, she says"—he managed a morose smile—"she always knew no good would come of all that digging, and I must see a doctor."

"Which you have done."

"Not because I fear for my eyesight. Or for my reason, though for some dark hours I did so. No, I've asked Cawdron to go through his father's records for anything which may provide a clue as to who I am."

"If you're not Oliver Darsham . . ." She tried to grapple with the enigma which he himself, after days and nights of inner debate, was still unable to resolve.

"Then I'm nothing," he said.

"You are . . . yourself." It became terribly important that he should see this. "Wouldn't that be better than . . ."

"Than what?" He was beside her but miles away, not touching, making no effort to draw her into his arms as he had done out in the hollow, out under the freedom of the heavens. "Kate, I am nobody. I wanted you to see—to understand why I have nothing to offer you now."

"Nothing but yourself." She held out her hands so that he would grip them again. His arms remained limp at his sides. "You asked if I could love you. Then"—she tried to restore a vestige of a smile to those brooding features—"you told me I would have to love you, in the end."

"I had no right."

"Now *you're* the one to talk of right! If I were to love, it would be you as a man, not as a name—whether it be Darsham, or whatever it be."

"I have been brought up to believe myself a certain man. There have been traditions, a way of life—a thousand things to make me what I am. Kate, I cannot wipe them away and easily become somebody else."

"You are the same man you were a week ago, a month ago."

"I am assuredly not the same. And—oh, God, don't you see?—I must *know* who I am."

A feeble ray of wintry sunshine touched the paneling beside them. Outside, neither Lady Charlotte nor Matthew Rouse was any longer in view.

Kate said, "Sir—"

"I told you I would not let you call me . . ." Then he laughed wryly. "But what are you to call me? I'm not 'Oliver,' am I?"

"Were you christened in the church?" she asked suddenly.

"I have verified that an Oliver Alexander Darsham was christened, yes."

"In Senwich church?"

"Yes."

"On what date?"

"On the third of February, 1838."

"Then . . ."

But he was no longer listening. He stared past her, out of the window.

Lady Charlotte and Matthew emerged from the dilapidated pergola. Her head was coquettishly on one side. He bent toward her, nodding and smiling—exerting all that easy, endearing charm of his, thought Kate.

The man was a fool—under the eyes of those windows, under the eyes of Oliver Darsham, flirting with a woman whose fickleness had already brought pain and humiliation into this house.

"Of course!" It was the softest of whispers. "That's who told her. He's the one. And it's a great joke—you see what a joke they think it is?"

The two went around the corner of the Tower. Oliver stormed toward the hall and flung open the door.

There was no longer any sign of Lady Charlotte, but Matthew was in the middle of the drive, shading his eyes and apparently taking a rough bearing on the stump of the old mill at the end of the village, framed between the gateposts.

"Rouse—a word with you."

Matthew finished his scrutiny and came to the doorstep. "If we're to get the harbor reinforcement finished before the spring tides hit us—"

"You have finished now."

"By no means. I won't rest easy until—"

"I said you've finished, Rouse. I shall be glad if you will make arrangements to leave as soon as you can get your things together."

Matthew was stunned. "But the work's not complete. You took me on to make a good job of it, and that's what I aim to do."

"I shall pay your account," said Oliver, "and let there be an end to it—an end to all your occupations in this district."

"I fancy you owe me an explanation, sir."

"I fancy you're the one who owes some explanations, sir. But I shall be glad to waive them."

"Now, see here—"

"You will get off my land," roared Oliver.

"If you're worried about what we saw down there in that tunnel—"

"What we saw," cried Oliver, beside himself, "and what you gossiped about . . . what you had the impertinence to tell my wife—"

"I'll not stand for that." Matthew's voice was as savage as Oliver's.

"Who else? Who else would drip poison in her ear, encourage her to make a mock of me? You like to make an impression, Rouse—I've watched you, I found your little tricks amusing, for a while. My wife finds them far too amusing. She is too easily diverted."

The rage boiling up in Matthew was far more intense than the almost gay violence of his attack on the drunkard in Yarmouth. That had been brisk and impersonal. This was savage and very personal. But as his mouth and fists tightened, he glanced at Kate; and in deference to her he took a deep breath and said with a dignity she had to admire, "If that is what you think, sir—"

"It is what I am compelled to think."

"Then I should certainly not be happy working for you. I shall leave without delay." Matthew paused. "Before I go, may I draw up recommendations for the work remaining to be done?"

"Nothing further is required from you."

"You're making an almighty mistake." A vein throbbed in Matthew's forehead. "More than just one mistake."

He went.

In all this, Kate's original purpose in coming to the Tower had been lost sight of. Now she ventured, "I am needed at home."

"Yes?" It seemed of no consequence. "I can understand your not wishing to remain here."

"It's only because of Sarah. My sister-in-law. She has had a baby—a son."

"A son," he said remotely. "Yes, of course. Of course you must go to her. I will . . . tell my wife."

As though answering the touch of a spur, he went off without another word.

Perhaps, thought Kate as she walked dejectedly away, neither he nor Lady Charlotte would ever be happy without the other to torment. It was a disturbing, perverse thought: she could not imagine from where it had swum up into her mind.

The next morning Daniel took his pony and trap to the rectory. Matthew's luggage was not substantial enough to call for the slow, capacious wagon.

Kate was busy in the kitchen when she heard the trap returning down the lane. She looked at the clock: Daniel could not have got to Sheverton and back so soon. She was relieved to find that she had not been lost in a trance, misjudging the morning's work.

Daniel came in. "Mr. Rouse wishes to say good-bye to you."

Kate's sticky hands clutched instinctively at her apron. She waited for Matthew to appear at Daniel's shoulder.

"I've shown him into the parlor," said Daniel.

Hastily Kate washed her hands and untied her apron. Daniel watched with brotherly scorn. When she touched her hair and let out a sigh of irritation, he rumbled, "It's only to say good-bye. And with a train to catch, he'll have no time to look at you too closely."

Kate went into the parlor.

Matthew was contemplating the slope outside and the gleam of the creek, as though still formulating plans for the safety of Senwich. He turned and held out his hand.

"It's good of you to see me, Miss Kate. I didn't want to leave without having one more sight of you."

They shook hands. He smiled gravely, without his usual impudence.

"I hope you'll have a pleasant journey," she said.

He looked full into her eyes. "I don't take kindly to insults. You could say it's none of my concern what's said or done in Senwich after I've gone—but I hate the notion of you believing ill of me."

"I shall believe only what I remember of you personally," said Kate, inexplicably sad, almost wishing he could be his old brash self and would leave with his old swagger.

"I want you to know that Mr. Darsham's accusations were untrue. I kept my mouth shut about what I saw in the tunnel."

"It . . . it is no concern of mine."

"No? I think, Miss Kate, that everything about Mr. Darsham is very much your concern."

"My brother says you'll need to hurry if you're to catch your train."

He said, "You would not consider coming with me?"

Its quiet seriousness made it worse than if it had been delivered in his old, bantering manner.

"I was told you wished to say good-bye," she said.

"You don't take me seriously."

"I've no wish to."

"Let's not be serious, then. Come for the happiness of it."

What was so appalling was the stirring of an inner urge to do as he suggested: to turn her back on a place she knew too well, a way of life she knew too well; and above all to turn her back on the tangles which could never be straightened out. It must be in the blood, a wanderlust like her father's. To be done with Senwich and her home, which was the boys' home rather than hers, Sarah's now rather than hers; and done with Oliver Darsham, who was not Oliver Darsham.

But surely not to commit herself to this unreliable will-o'-the-wisp from an alien country?

When she did not reply, he said more bitterly, "Do I take it you're holding out for a better offer—from someone we both know?"

"If you think that by slandering someone else you will make me fonder of you, you're mistaken."

"Come with me, Kate. Let me show you what's out there, way over the rim of the world." He was trying to recapture the note of lightheartedness which now for some reason eluded him. "I'll dam rivers for you. Build a few castles if that's what you want. Carve a piece out of the world for you. You select it, I'll do the digging."

"You're very sure of yourself."

"If a man's not sure of himself, how can he expect

anyone else to be sure of him? He can't win a thing any other way."

"And you wish to win."

"Always."

"You always win? I find that alarming."

"I didn't say I always won. I said I always *wish* to win."

"And when you lose?"

"When I lose," said Matthew, "I learn. And try harder next time." He looked her up and down, capturing a picture to take away with him. "Trouble is, there are some things at which a man doesn't get another try. Too many mistakes at the start, he finds he's lost the game."

Daniel's feet scraped impatiently along the passage outside the door.

"A pleasant journey," said Kate again, with crisp finality.

"And . . . you'll not be coming with me?"

"You didn't truly expect me to, did you?"

"No," said Matthew, "I guess I didn't."

They shook hands once more, meaninglessly, and he left with Daniel.

She was taken unawares by a pang of loss. It was not that she wanted Matthew Rouse to stay on in Senwich or to persist in any illusions about her. And not that she could ever have gone with him, in spite of that ridiculous flicker of temptation. But his easygoing vigor had added a new color to the village. There had been those brief, unpremeditated occasions when she had found him easy to talk to and talk with. What they had said had not been what they were really talking about. And there was still so much left to be discussed, to be thrown to and fro and laughed over, in a way she would never achieve with . . .

With whom?

"With anyone else," she said aloud, forcing herself to keep it vague and inconclusive.

She ran to the window.

There was no sign of him. The trap would be well on its way by now. Daniel wasn't one to waste time when there was a train to catch.

And even if Matthew had still been visible and still within earshot, how could she call him back? What could she possibly have to say to him that would make it worth his while turning back?

He would soon find somebody more to his taste. A score of them, probably. And make the same shallow declarations to all of them.

His easy laugh had been absent when he said good-bye. But he would soon recover it, soon use it again on whoever crossed his path.

Christmas was upon them. A squad of saucepans rumbled and bubbled on the range. The oven was as crowded as the larder. A turkey rotated slowly on its bottlejack before the fire, shielded by the curve of a Dutch oven. Before being allowed to run off home for the afternoon of Christmas Day, the backhouse boy had to stoke the grate and fill the scuttles so full that he could barely carry them. He was in no great hurry to leave: food with the Quantrills, on this day especially, was better than he could hope to have with his own family.

The day before Christmas, Lady Charlotte had come down to the infant school, where the children were assembled for the occasion so that she might present half a sovereign and a book of moral tales each to the boy and girl with the best attendance record. There was a small gift for each of the tenants, and small baskets of food were delivered to the doors of the poorer families. Lady Charlotte made her stately circuit of the village with a fixed smile and then escaped back into the seclusion of Darsham's Tower.

On the day after Christmas, there was another visit from the Tower. The gig drew up outside the Quantrills' house. Verena got down and rapped three times with the rarely used brass knocker on the front door.

She had brought a present for Kate, and waited impatiently for Kate's gasp of delight as it was unwrapped.

"They'll suit you, won't they? There were some lighter ones, Papa said, but the darker shade goes better with your eyes."

The gift was an amber necklace and brooch, the hue of dark toffee. In the necklace, opaque and transparent stones alternated. The brooch, in a gold setting, had a secret inner glow, a tiny flame which dimmed when held away from the light but never quite went out.

"Thank you," Kate breathed. "But—"

"It's from me," said Verena. And added guilelessly, "Papa chose it."

"He . . . liked the jersey you knitted for him?"

"He liked it well enough." Verena hunched her shoulders in a shrug vividly reminiscent of Oliver. "He asked who helped me with it. And then he said yes, and nodded."

Kate fastened the clasp behind her neck and pinned the brooch high up on her green cotton dress. She studied the effect in the glass above the parlor mantelpiece.

"It's beautiful."

Verena hugged her. "You'll come back soon?" she said as they walked out to the gig.

"I don't know," said Kate.

"But you must. I've got no one to talk to."

"Your mother . . ."

Verena took up the reins. "My mother," she said expressionlessly.

Kate watched her go, confident now in her handling of the animal and the gig, yet in spite of that assurance a forlorn little figure.

In the evening, after baby Josiah had been settled in his cot and they had had an early supper, Sarah and the three brothers sat down to an hour or two of whist. Sarah offered Kate her seat, but Kate knew she would be unable to give the game her full attention. She was not consciously thinking of anything else: in fact, like someone with a heavy cold or someone sitting too long by the fire in a stuffy room, she was confusedly aware of things only through a haze which falsified distances and outlines. Home was unreal. Memories of Darsham's Folly, though so recent, were unreal.

She went out for a stroll to clear her head.

It was a still, cold evening. A waning moon silvered the rooftops. From one corner of the marketplace the lower arc of its halo was apparently balanced on a tip of the Tower battlements.

Kate stood for a long time on the hard, lulled by the hoarseness of the slow waves on the shingle. A lamp shone out between curtains in one cottage window. Otherwise the village might well have been deserted. It was not until she was walking back across the marketplace that brisk footsteps echoing up an alley told her she was not the last living being in Senwich.

Mrs. Jenkyn came out into the bleached light of the square.

"Miss Quantrill—I thought you were a ghost, so quiet over there!"

She had been spending an hour with her sister-in-law, a widow like herself and the only relation—and that only by marriage—she had in the neighborhood.

"Not looking too bright. Not too bright at all," she confided with the smug seriousness of one woman determined to outlive another.

They walked slowly and companionably out of the village and up the road toward the fork. The moon slid stealthily behind the Tower.

"You had a good Christmas?" Kate asked.

"Not what I'd call a good one. It was a sight too cheerless, for my liking."

"Mr. Darsham is still . . . not well?"

"There's no way of telling, with him. But he cast a gloom over everything this year, that I will say. We did our best to be merry below stairs, but the whole atmosphere of the place was against us." Mrs. Jenkyn shook her head. "He'll never be quite right, you know. Never." Then she said hurriedly, "But perhaps I shouldn't be saying things like that to you."

"Why specially not to me?"

"Well, I did wonder . . . You'll be coming back soon?"

"I'm not sure."

"I think you're needed. I think . . . but then, I reckon you're needed where you are. How's the little mite coming along?"

"He's flourishing," Kate assured her.

"Yes, Eliza says that. She's just been telling me how she's seen him out, and how she's sure he'll do well. Make sturdy bones, your family. And Mrs. Daniel's feeding him herself?"

"Of course."

"Yes, well, there it is, isn't it? Makes good bones," Mrs. Jenkyn confirmed. "Not like poor Mr. Oliver."

"His was a difficult birth?"

"Difficult from the very start. Such a to-ing and fro-ing there was that night." Mrs. Jenkyn, still in a mood inspired by the signs of mortality in her sister-in-law, recalled sad portents. "It never was easy for him, never what it ought to have been for him. Never thought he'd live. What with the mistress having that awful fever, and the boy no strength in him at all. . . . And then that slut of a wet nurse—a real go-come-flight, that one. No, miss"—Mrs. Jenkyn's head wagged contentedly—"with all their money, they can't always match the likes of your Daniel and that good wife of his."

They reached the fork. One side of the road was in deep shadow, a darkness which gave way to moonlight halfway down the lane to the creek.

Mrs. Jenkyn was saying, "I was glad of your company up the road, miss," and Kate was about to bid her good night, when the clatter of hooves erupted from between the gateposts a hundred yards away. The wild eyes of a horse gleamed momentarily in a sword flash of moonlight, then were blinkered into the shadows of the trees. Mrs. Jenkyn stood well back from the road. The horse and its rider thundered past Kate. A few seconds later the hooves left the road and were lost in the softer fringes of the heath.

"You saw?" marveled Mrs. Jenkyn. "You saw who it was?"

"Only that it was a man."

"It was Mr. Oliver."

"But surely he will not ride—"

"Hasn't ridden since he was thrown. Because of the pain. Yet that was Mr. Oliver, I'll swear to it."

Riding out, thought Kate, because of something more urgent and overpowering than the pain.

Mrs. Jenkyn was longing to be off up to the house to learn what had happened during her absence. They said quick good nights and went their separate ways.

Daniel went into Sheverton next morning. He returned in the afternoon all agog with news from a variety of sources.

Lady Charlotte had been seen riding like a mad thing under the moon, past the Kiln Farm and off in the direction of Chedstowe. Mr. Darsham had been seen in the vicinity awhile later, but heading west. Also, Mr. Darsham had been seen and heard in Sheverton, making inquiries at the railway station and at the hostler's, and then riding off in a towering rage. As far as anyone knew, Lady Charlotte had not gone off by train; at least, not from Sheverton—she could, of course, have ridden to a station farther up the line.

Going to join whom this time?

Kate thought of Matthew Rouse and his interest in Lady Charlotte, his too-ready sympathy for her; and of how Lady Charlotte's apathy sloughed off in his presence. She dismissed the idea. It wheedled its way back.

Late in the evening of that day a gelding with a broken leg was found in a gravel pit eight miles south of Senwich. It was identified as one of the Darsham stable, and with Mr. Darsham's permission was shot.

It was not until the dawn of another day that its rider was found. A fowler out on the marshes was working his way along a deep cut when he saw a dark huddle in the reeds. He waded closer, saw what it was, and fearfully heaved Lady Charlotte's head and shoulders up from beneath the surface of the water, and propped her sodden corpse as decently as possible against the steep bank.

Chapter Twelve

The coroner was a Chedstowe solicitor. He held his inquest in the Senwich schoolroom, seated at the teacher's desk while witnesses and the public—a handful of villagers who would later report the evidence in embroidered detail to those unable to attend—sat on a hastily assembled half-dozen chairs or squatted with splayed knees at the children's desks.

It was established that Lady Charlotte had ridden out of Darsham's Tower at nine o'clock on the evening of Boxing Day. Mr. Darsham frankly volunteered the information that he and his wife had had a long discussion about their daughter's education and future, and that it had grown acrimonious.

"She had been rather free with the wine that evening."

Whatever his feelings at the time, he was not censorious now: he was simply stating the regrettable facts.

When she cut the debate short by flouncing out in a temper, he had tried to follow.

"I had no wish for her to be roaming the countryside in that state of mind. The moon was up, but the light was unreliable, and with frost on the roads and hard ruts in the lanes, she could easily take a nasty spill."

Heads nodded solemnly in the schoolroom.

Mr. Darsham did not try to gloss over the existence of the family dispute. Stiff-lipped, he deplored his responsibility for continuing it to a point where his wife lost control of herself. But there was nothing to be done about it now.

His pursuit was unavailing. He soon lost her trail, and began to worry. Inquiries in Sheverton and on the road to Chedstowe led nowhere.

Whatever silent speculation there might be in the improvised courtroom, and however voluble that speculation might grow afterward—"Wasn't going to let her get away *this* time . . . hunted her down, I'll be bound . . . now, I'm not saying he did find her on his way back from Sheverton, but he *could* have done, and then who knows, eh?"— Mr. Darsham was treated with deference by the coroner and appeared all that one could have asked of him—a bereaved but dignified man, giving bleakly straightforward answers to questions and making no attempt to exculpate himself from whatever fault might have set the tragedy in motion.

There were few married men in the room who had not at one time and another skirmished with their wives over the children. Few such conflicts had ended with such a cruel twist as this.

The verdict was one of accidental death. The coroner respectfully tendered his condolences to the widower.

Lady Charlotte was laid to rest not in the Darsham vault but in a newly dug plot some yards away.

This prompted a buzz of comment. Had he hated her so much, then: though taking her back into his house, had he found it impossible to forgive; and right at the end, was he, in spite of his stiff concealment of emotion at the inquest, still incapable of forgiveness?

Kate sat by the creek on a thick oak bollard, her cloak drawn about her.

I'll put an end to this charade . . . soon . . . somehow . . . I swear it.

The words had kept her awake half the night after she heard of Lady Charlotte's death. They went on murmuring insidiously through her ragged dreams. Even in daylight they refused to be banished.

She sat with her back to the imperious Tower and its eternally watchful windows.

The red morning sun had paled as it climbed, and now hung in a haze of muddy yellow. The water, itself yellow, broke in a slow, creamy froth along the breakwater, seethed over it, and was sucked back. On the rise of the heath beyond, three Scots pines hung like tufted gibbets against the impenetrably leaden sky.

Oliver Darsham was free now.

But he was not Oliver Darsham.

Of course he would not approach her immediately. He would observe all the conventions.

She did not know which distressed her most—the thought of his coming to her, or of his never coming at all.

Just before noon she retraced her steps to the house and put potatoes on to boil. There was no real need for her to be here any longer, but Sarah accepted her help so that she herself might spend more time with the baby. And perhaps, Kate half-wondered, they were all shy of asking whether she was home for good or likely to leave again soon.

In church Mrs. Darsham's usual somberness was flanked by the full mourning of her son and granddaughter. After service the three of them stood by the porch accepting the condolences of a tenant who had been away at the time of the tragedy. As Kate passed, Mr. Darsham leaned toward his mother and murmured something quiet but insistent.

Kate had reached the lych-gate when she heard Verena calling after her. Looking back, she found the girl and her grandmother coming after her as fast as old Mrs. Darsham's shuffling feet would carry her.

Heads turned. The drifting groups beyond the churchyard wall slowed, and conversation was hushed in the hope of hearing what Mrs. Darsham had to say.

"When may we expect you to return to your duties, Miss Quantrill?"

"I have had a duty to my family, ma'am."

"Which has not yet been completed?"

"I wasn't sure whether . . . what other arrangements were being made."

"No other arrangements have been made. And I should have thought you the first to realize that the child needs you, after her recent bereavement."

Verena said, "Please, Miss Quantrill—you are going to come back, aren't you?"

"And this time," said Mrs. Darsham, "I shall expect to see you more frequently. You will bring Verena to tea. We must keep her mind occupied," she went on loudly, as though Verena were deaf or elsewhere. "No silly vapors, or any maudlin nonsense of that kind."

"If I'm needed—"

"I've already made that plain, girl."

Obviously it was settled. Kate felt that she ought to

argue, raise objections, put a better face on it. But the Darshams had settled it, as they settled most things in Senwich.

"I'll tell Papa." Verena hurried back up the path.

Mrs. Darsham let out a little snicker. "I was sure he would not let you go so easily." Before Kate could say a word, she crackled, "I'm no fool, you know, I'm nobody's fool. My window has as good a view as any other, and my eyesight's excellent. Excellent. No, I'm nobody's fool."

On the way home Kate told herself that she had not made any irrevocable decision. She would suit herself. She would make up her mind when and how it suited her.

But her mind had been made up for her. She announced her intention as soon as she crossed the threshold. It was easier with John and Abel away, and only Daniel and Sarah there.

"So you'll want your things taken back up to the Folly?" said Daniel. "At this rate I ought to quote you a special tariff—it comes cheaper on seasonal work than on individual journeys."

Sarah opened a drawer and fidgeted with the knives and forks. It was unlike her. She was in the habit of taking things out only when she needed them, putting them tidily back when she had finished, economizing on her movements; she was a neat housewife, not one to waste a moment or to have doubts about her utensils. Into the drawer she said, "You're sure you want to go back there?"

"It was understood from the start," said Kate, "that I was granted absence to help you over the first few weeks. I've been here too long."

"Not for us, pet. Tell them we can't do without you."

"I'll be more useful there than here. And I'll be earning my keep."

"Oh, Kate." Sarah swung around and leaned against the drawer. "Is that all?"

"What else should there be?"

"It's not that you're . . . letting yourself rush back into something you don't really want? Just to forget something else you did want?"

"I've no idea what you're talking about."

"We thought perhaps—"

"*You* thought," said Daniel gruffly. "I knew all along he was a wanderer, that one."

Kate's cheeks burned. "You've been making up wild tales about me and Mr. Rouse? Is that it? The sooner I'm out of here, the better."

"I shouldn't have . . ." Sarah was close to tears. "Please, Kate, I'm sorry. But just because of that, don't rush back to the Folly. Please. There's something wrong there. Something that'll do you no good."

"I did well enough before. And I'll make my own decisions now."

"No use arguing it," said Daniel, "when she's in that mood."

Kate prepared to return to the Tower, disclosing no faintest glimmer of her own doubts.

She had escaped once before, when Verena took a holiday; and returned; and escaped again because of Sarah's baby; and now was being drawn back once more.

It was an uneasy admission—that she should regard the interludes as escapes.

It was one thing to be a Darsham employee on the estate or on the docks, or at sea, with no personal involvement. Straightforward enough, probably, to have been one of the girls Oliver's father pursued—or, if not his father, at least the man whose name Oliver bore. Robert Darsham had enjoyed himself, the girls had presumably been entertained, he had paid up when there was any paying to be done, and no disturbing echoes were left.

For herself it was more intense. She had been singled

out. Oliver had taken her in, released her, taken it for granted that she would return, and beckoned her back when it pleased him.

She was giddily caught in a whirlpool. In each quickening swirl she had surrendered a fragment more of herself, like a ship breaking up, fighting its way out of the turbulence only to be sucked back and at last engulfed.

It would have been wiser to struggle clear when Matthew Rouse offered her the chance. Or when her brothers wanted to tow her away.

Wisdom seemed to have little to do with her feelings for Oliver.

Her room was dank and shivery, although the bed had been aired and a fire was burning cheerfully in the grate.

Mrs. Jenkyn came in, ostensibly to see if she was comfortable and if anything had been forgotten. After fussing unnecessarily about for a few minutes, darting covert little looks at Kate, she nodded her satisfaction and went to the door.

"Well, you're back, then," she summed up. "You're back, after all." Her hand on the knob, she nodded again. "I didn't think he'd wait long."

That night and the next Kate found it difficult to sleep. She was alone in a fathomless emptiness; yet it was an emptiness alive with sounds. The wind had a different note here from the sigh it made under the eaves at home. Boards creaked. Footsteps seemed to approach her door, so that she held her breath, waiting; and then there was silence, a gulf of silence into which another creak or unrecognizable murmur dropped at last.

She wondered if this house could ever be made a happy one. And whether she would be given the opportunity of making it happy—warm, happy, lived-in, like her own home and others she knew in the village.

Was that what Oliver would want of her? Could he be coaxed out of his dark seclusion to share the task with her? It made no sense otherwise.

Those first few days there was no sign of him. It was just as it had been before: she arrived, he disappeared.

Yet the atmosphere had subtly changed. She detected a new deference in the attitude of the maids, of the groom when she and Verena went out or returned in the trap, and even of Mrs. Jenkyn. They might all be putting her discreetly on trial as possible mistress of the house.

Miss Hartest, too, had changed, but in the opposite direction.

"Miss Quantrill, is there really any further need for you to share Verena's lessons? I would not wish to keep you from more interesting pursuits." Her earlier, prim hostility had flared into outright scorn. "You'll hardly need this knowledge now."

Verena's eyes widened. She looked apprehensively from her teacher to Kate. Kate wondered whether she read the same implication into Miss Hartest's remarks—that Kate had snared her prey, that Oliver was hers without the need for any further tuition.

"But I like having Miss Quantrill with me," Verena protested.

That same afternoon Kate obeyed Mrs. Darsham's order to bring Verena up to tea with her. She had taken the precaution of asking the maid to remind Mrs. Darsham of the arrangement an hour beforehand, and then going up again twenty minutes beforehand on the excuse of finding out what biscuits or cake Mrs. Darsham would prefer. So when Kate and Verena reached the room, they were expected.

"Tell me what you have been learning," said Mrs. Darsham bluntly, the moment Verena had sat down.

It was difficult to find a good answer to such a general

instruction, and Mrs. Darsham tut-tutted while Verena fumbled for something bright to say. But it soon became evident that the sound of Verena's voice was enough—it made little matter what lessons she described—and Mrs. Darsham was content to make snappy little comments now and then, or to interrupt with some little anecdote of her own which rarely finished.

Kate sensed that, in spite of their lack of real communication, they liked each other. On both sides it was a prickly, rueful liking—but it was there. She saw how readily they could become her allies, when she needed allies. There was only one thing missing—one person.

A second cup of tea was being poured from the silver pot when they all three heard, at the same moment, Oliver's footsteps. He was coming up the stairs two at a time, crossing the short stretch of landing; and then the door was thrown peremptorily open, and he strode in.

"Mother, what do you know about a man called Withersedge?"

Mrs. Darsham fluffed up like a pigeon and made a pettish little cooing sound not unlike a pigeon's. Then she said, "Miss Quantrill, we do not have a fourth cup, do we?"

Oliver loomed above her, then turned to Kate. "Miss Quantrill, I'm sorry to have burst in like this. And sorry I have been too much occupied to welcome you . . . back." She was sure that he had been on the verge of saying, "welcome you home." He put his hand apologetically on Mrs. Darsham's shoulder, but it was still Kate he was speaking to. "That bungler Cawdron has woken up at last. Found his father's notes. And there are several references to a Withersedge who was staying here when I was born."

"Notes?" said Mrs. Darsham plaintively. "And a man staying here, all those years ago? You do talk such nonsense nowadays."

Oliver sat down, forcing himself to patience. "Mother"
—there was an uncertain undertone, as if it had just occurred to him that he was not sure of his right to call her
this—"*do* you remember anyone called Withersedge?"

"Heavens, why should I?" Then the evasive, irritable
eyes brightened. "Mark you, I'm not one to forget people
easily. And there was somebody with that name . . . stayed
with us, yes, but then, so many people stayed with us.
When your father was alive, there was no telling . . ."

"No, of course not. But this Withersedge . . ."

"Never saw him again. He was gone by the time I
recovered."

"Recovered?"

"He was a doctor," Mrs. Darsham recalled trium-
phantly. "Dr. Withersedge."

Oliver sat on the edge of his chair, hardly daring to
breathe.

"He didn't practice while he was here, of course. Just
came to stay. Some friend of your father's. He was always
out walking—as bad as you are. Used to come back covered in mud. Used to lie down in it."

"Lie down in it?" It was an encouragement rather than
a question.

"He was an ornithologist. Thought of nothing else but
wild birds and where they came from and where they
went. Haven't thought of him for years. But"—she studied
Oliver with mounting suspicion—"whatever made you
bring his name up now?"

"He was a doctor, you say," Oliver prompted her
quietly.

"Doctors. Hum." She brooded. "All the same. Quite
impossible to trust any of them. When I think of Cawdron
—not this whippersnapper we have now, but his father, I
mean—*think* of him! Dashing off into a disease-ridden
hospital just when he should have been most careful about

me . . . and then coming back and giving me that dreadful fever. . . ." The eyes threatened to dim again. "Or did he give me that before? Utterly irresponsible, in any case. And as for . . ." She was losing her grip.

Oliver said, "Dr. Withersedge?"

"Who? Oh, that fellow. There was something about him going as a ship's surgeon."

"On one of our ships?"

"May have been. It was of no importance," said Mrs. Darsham grandly. "No importance whatsoever."

Verena was clearly longing to ask what this was all about, but in the presence of both her father and her grandmother she was too cowed to speak.

"New Zealand," said Mrs. Darsham. "I remember he talked about studying bird life in the Pacific, and something about New Zealand . . . hum . . . birds," she said vaguely. "As bad as you, forever grubbing about in the marsh." She shook her head, dismissing the eccentricities of menfolk in general.

Oliver waited, then accepted that this was all he could learn this afternoon. Perhaps it was all Mrs. Darsham would ever be able to offer on the subject.

He stood up.

"When you've finished, Miss Quantrill, I'd be obliged if you could spare me a few minutes. Perhaps you'll take a glass of wine with me in the library. Shall we say half-past six?"

He kissed Mrs. Darsham's brow. She was sharp and alert again, but aware not of the past but of the present. There was a malicious sparkle in her manner as she watched Oliver go, and then turned to Kate with an arch, knowing nod.

In her own room at fifteen minutes past six, Kate brushed stray wisps and knots of hair back into place, smoothed out the puckers in her gray cotton dress, and made herself sit perfectly still on the edge of the bed for a full five minutes before going down to the library.

A lamp burned on the desk, and another stood on a table close to Oliver's elbow. He came toward her as she closed the door, and without force and with no more than the touch of his hand on her arm, kissed her. It was a confident, unhurried kiss.

Had he sat in that chair rehearsing it all in his mind while she, perched on the edge of her bed, tried to control the trembling of her knees?

He poured her a glass of wine and indicated a chair facing his.

He said, "Kate, you must help me. There is no one else I can trust. And no one else I want to trust."

As he raised his glass to her, the lamplight kindled a deep ruby glow within the wine. They drank, and the glow seemed to be carried warmly and soothingly into her throat. In years to come they would sit facing each other along the dining table, with guests or without guests, and raise their glasses like this; and always she would prefer the intimate drink together, alone with him in the library.

He said, "I shall have no peace until I know who I am."

As he leaned forward, he shielded the light from her, so that color died in the wine. Her second taste of it had an oddly sour tinge.

One side of the skull shone yellow.

She must not sit here mute and stupid, offering him nothing. "It is still so important? You're still not resigned to being simply the man you have grown up to be—christened Oliver Darsham . . . and therefore Oliver Darsham?"

"I must *know*."

"Who is there to tell you?"

"Cawdron," he said. "That has to be where we begin. With his father's notes. Kate"—he had to talk it out with somebody, which was why she had been summoned to this lamplit room—"there are pages of references. Not all in one place, but scattered over a period. I must have all the relevant passages copied out so that I can see them as a whole. There has to be an answer there, somewhere."

"Dr. Cawdron—"

"Cawdron refuses to let the records out of his possession. Prattles on about medical etiquette—and what about medical etiquette at the time of my birth, dammit? Something decidedly unethical there, I'd say."

"It's all best left alone," said Kate.

"I want it settled. Cawdron has agreed—reluctantly, I'll grant you—that the passages relating to my father . . . I mean to say, passages relating to Robert Darsham and the birth of Oliver Darsham . . . should be copied out. But it must be done on the premises, he insists."

Kate understood. "You wish me to do it?"

He reached for her glass and refilled it. "I'm asking too much of you?"

"I don't know what you can expect to find, or what good it will do."

"This is the first scent I've had. If you copy those notes out, we can sit down—together—and see what they mean. And . . ."

So there was more to come. "Yes?" she said.

"I have been trying to trace other sources. But it's not easy for me. If I make too many inquiries in the village, I draw attention to myself. Until the whole truth is known, I do not care for there to be gossip. I must be the first to know. Then I can make the right decision."

"You're asking me to be a spy—to wheedle things out of people, but let them know nothing in return?"

"I need your help," he said. "I need it so much, Kate."

But not this kind of help, she wanted to say. Not enmeshing herself in his old obsessions, the legacy of a Darsham upbringing.

"I want you to be my wife," he said. "But not until you can be sure who I really am."

Rebellion flickered within her. He seemed to be offering marriage as a prize if she was a good girl and carried out a few tasks for him first.

"Either I know who you are now," she said, "or I shall never know."

"How could we build a marriage on such an uncertainty? A man has no right to ask a woman to share the aftermath of former misery. Or to marry a man who cannot even solve his own identity."

"If he loves her," she said, "he has no right *not* to ask."

"You would marry me just for what I am, now?"

"If I were sure."

"But there's the damnable thing. We can't be sure."

"Sure of ourselves," she said. "That's all that matters— or ought to matter."

He sank into contemplation of the ruby pool within his glass.

From somewhere far off Kate seemed to catch a sad wisp of laughter. *There's no stupidity you wouldn't commit.*

She wondered what following wind was carrying Matthew Rouse on his carefree way across the world while she and Oliver wrestled here with these old fevers. If only Oliver, too, could laugh. Take her in his arms and learn love today rather than the dark infatuations of yesterday.

But he was not ready and would never be ready until these uncertainties were cleansed. Must she bring him the truth as a dowry?

"Very well." It was forced out of her. "I'll copy out the notes for you. And I'll ask what questions it's safe to ask in the village."

"Kate. Whatever the truth may be, I'll bear it. Whoever I am, I shall love you. But," he cried, "I must *know*."

Chapter Thirteen

Old Dr. Cawdron had kept his records in tall leather-bound ledgers. Fees and scrawled calculations made a jumble of the left-hand pages, but he appeared to have derived some satisfaction from practicing a fine, flowing hand on the right-hand page. Some of the notes were cryptic, quite unintelligible after all these years; but they were invariably written out with painstaking neatness.

The volume laid in front of Kate had a musty, rather sickly sweet smell, and the pages were limp to the touch, unlike the crisp clean foolscap she had brought to make her copies.

Dr. Cawdron settled her in a cramped little room with little more than a chair and an old desk. He made no pretense of concealing his disapproval.

"Mr. Darsham has demanded absolute secrecy from me. I imagine the same applies to yourself." As Kate nodded, he said crossly, "If he lets many more into the secret, it can hardly be a secret much longer."

If this was meant as a slur on her discretion, Kate refused to be provoked.

"Absolute secrecy," the doctor repeated. "Yet he wishes to make free of other people's secrets." He tapped the page he had opened before Kate. "You do understand that you are to make notes only of references to Mr. Robert Darsham and the birth of his son? I have come across several other notes"—his little finger flicked strips of paper inserted into the pages—"but there may be more. I shall have to rely on you, Miss Quantrill, to put out of your mind anything else you may read."

"Of course," said Kate stiffly.

"Very well."

Reluctantly he left her alone with the book.

The smooth flow of the handwriting was misleading. There was little continuity in the actual notes. The late Dr. Cawdron had not kept separate pages for individual patients, nor had he made much distinction between recording treatment of the patients and making comments to himself, sometimes philosophical and sometimes apparently to jog his memory as he went along. How he ever found these entries when they were needed was a mystery.

There were some tidy but meaningless lines which must represent medical formulae, and other terms Kate could not understand. It was hard to guess whether any of them related to the Darsham case or not. She concentrated on extracting clear dates and references from the crowded pages, beginning with those marked by the present Dr. Cawdron.

On the tenth of January, 1838, his father recorded

being called to Mrs. Darsham. *Quite unnecessary*, he noted. *R. D. in worse fret than Mrs. D.* On the eleventh, however, it seemed that labor had really started.

The next few lines, though still neat, appeared to have been written in a hurry: "Chedstowe Infirmary. Smallpox. Notified Hankey and Bruce. Harbormaster diverting traffic Lowestoft and Yarmouth. Check Antwerp crews."

On the twelfth he noted tersely: "Mrs. Darsham son five pounds three ounces. R.D. delighted. Hope not premature (delight). Respiratory trouble."

There were some jottings about an old man with a broken leg and, on the following page, a mention which had nothing to do with the Darshams but seemed to Kate to belong somewhere in the sequence of events: "Chedstowe epidemic. Infirmary rota with Hamilton, Baker, Hankey."

There was no gap after this, not so much as a blank line; but there must have been a gap in time. The next entry bore the date of January fifteenth: "Mrs. D. puerperal fever. Wet nurse engaged in my absence. Supplies adequate. Withersedge still at Tower. Why Nurse Simons dismissed? Child has malformation of hip. Not noticed at delivery."

Kate turned over several more pages. She had a bewildered feeling of being on the fringe of events, seeing things only in snatches. It was true of too much of her life: on the fringe of her brothers' lives, of Oliver's life . . . brushing against Matthew Rouse, and retaining nothing but the disquieting memory of his laugh.

And this, even more disquieting—this assembly of fragments, which must have meant something once but could surely never mean anything clearly again.

The Darsham name jumped at her from the page again, after she had turned over one after another. It was three weeks later: "Recommend hospital treatment for O.D. hip. Mrs. D. adamant. Withersedge gone. R.D. failing."

She copied out some following paragraphs and was well on her way into another, writing mechanically, until she realized it dealt with someone quite different.

On the eleventh of March the name appeared again. A name she was beginning almost to hate. A rebellious prayer whispered at the back of her mind. Let Oliver Darsham prove not to be a Darsham. Let the two of them set out together from nowhere—both of them real, neither of them a figurehead.

Darsham. . . .

"Doubt that O.D. is child I delivered. Cannot tell R.D. now, on deathbed."

Finally, on the line below, there was just one word: "Withersedge?"

The name, a question mark . . . and no more.

Kate persevered, but there were no more notes to be made. The writing came to a stop with several blank pages still left in the book.

Dr. Cawdron came in. "Everything satisfactory, Miss Quantrill?"

She indicated the unmarked page which lay open before her.

He said, "My father died. In another smallpox outbreak, about a year after the child's birth."

The way he said "the child" showed that he was in full possession of Oliver's doubts and self-questionings.

Kate said, "You've no idea . . . you have no theories about what could have happened . . . about Mr. Darsham, and that other . . . other child?"

"I have my work cut out, Miss Quantrill, to keep the living alive. I do not propose to trouble my head about reviving the dead."

Kate gathered up her notes and went back to Darsham's Tower.

Oliver must have sat hour after hour, night after night, in that chair by the steady flame of that lamp, churning the unanswerable questions over and over in his mind. With Kate there now, he had an audience on which to try the sound of his bewilderment, as though the echoes might now answer more than he had been able to ask.

"Old Cawdron states that he attended my mother's confinement." The sheets of Kate's notes rustled in his hand. "He delivered me—delivered her child, that is. A son. Then he was called away."

"Even though Mrs. Darsham had had a difficult time, and the baby was in poor shape."

"Cawdron was conscientious in his own way," said Oliver scrupulously. "When Chedstowe Infirmary was founded on public donations, three doctors gave their services free. It was all that kept the place going. It was twenty years and more before they could afford a full-time matron. When there was an outbreak of smallpox—more than the place could cope with, really—Cawdron decided he had to be there. I don't blame him for that. He worked himself nearly to death; as I'm on the board of guardians, I have been able to make judicious inquiries which establish that beyond all doubt. A year later, it was literally the death of him."

"And Dr. Withersedge," Kate interposed, "looked after Mrs. Darsham while he was away."

"He must have done. And found a wet nurse when my mother contracted the fever."

"Mrs. Darsham said something about him bringing back the fever that made her so ill."

"Times are muddled in her mind. Cawdron was in the

infirmary when she *had* the fever. By the time he was back, she was recovering."

"To find that the original nurse had been dismissed. Who was Nurse Simons?"

"Someone engaged from London, I believe."

"And Dr. Withersedge wasn't satisfied with her?"

"That we shall never know." His fists clenched. As though about to hammer them against a brick wall until it yielded, he groaned, "But somebody must know. What sort of blunder did this Withersedge make, and how did he cover his tracks?"

"Mrs. Darsham was in no state to know what was going on. Your father—"

"Mr. Darsham," said Oliver tautly, "was longing for a son. He was not well himself, he was overexcited. But he knew that at last he'd had a son. He would be very unhappy if something went wrong."

"With the family doctor away, someone blundered!"

"Whoever I am," said Oliver, "I'm not that son."

"Is that why"—she had a flash of comprehension— "Lady Charlotte is not buried in the family vault?"

"If she was not married to a Darsham, she has no right to lie there."

He took this for granted. The family tradition was so staunch that even when he found he had never truly belonged to that tradition he still bowed to it.

Kate moved in her chair, and a ghostly reflection shivered in the glass doors of the nearest bookcase.

Oliver looked not at her but at her ghost. He said, "Do you believe I killed my wife?"

The figure in the glass slid wildly to one side. Kate gripped the arm of her chair. Until she had been asked outright, she had not dared even in her own imaginings to shape a definite yes or no.

She paused too long.

"I can see you don't think it altogether impossible," said Oliver.

"I . . . couldn't let myself believe any such dreadful thing."

"But you can't let yourself dismiss it." He turned from the transparent wraith and looked her full in the face. "Kate, you're not the only one. I have seen it in their eyes. Here in the house, and outside. And I disdain to give them an answer. But, Kate . . . you are one who must be told. Whatever other doubts you may have of me, I won't abide that one. I swear to you, I did not kill Charlotte."

She let herself slump back, drained of breath. She was dizzily thankful. He was telling the truth; there could not be the slightest doubt of it.

She murmured, "I'm sorry."

"For allowing yourself to consider the possibility? I would find it hard to blame you. And, heaven knows, I do bear some blame myself. We had a terrible argument that night." His hands came together on his knees, twisted, came palm uppermost. He stared bleakly down into them. "It was . . . sickening. So much spitefulness, such hatred. I am still disgusted—by myself, by the whole dreadful business."

"It's finished," said Kate.

He did not seem to hear her. "I had vowed I would abide by the rules—rules I had laid down myself—even when they tormented me, when the thought of *you* tormented me. But once she had learned what lay in that tunnel . . ."

"How did she learn?"

"From young Rouse, of course. Who else?"

"You are sure of that?"

"There could have been no one else. How many other

people know of its existence? And who else would have taken pleasure in presenting her with such a weapon to use against me?"

A log shifted in the fireplace, emitting a jet of sparks. Oliver went to balance it more securely with the tongs, and remained gazing into the flames.

"It was her night for revenge. She was always craving to be revenged—for slights which had never been offered, or disappointments all of her own making. We argued about Verena, but that was only an excuse. She derided everything I most respect. Called me a charlatan. Asked what right I had to dictate to her. Sneered, and shouted—said she would take the child away, I wasn't fit to be father of her daughter, she would proclaim to the world that I'd been made a fool of." The log spluttered again, and this time he stubbed it hard with his foot. "I said savage things to her, I know. I was beside myself. But she whipped me on. Such outbursts were all she ever lived for. And that night . . . she died for one."

Kate could not picture emotion snarling out from Lady Charlotte's pale, listless face. Yet that must be the picture by which Oliver was mesmerized in the fire.

"She would provoke a quarrel on any pretext," he said. "Then, when she began to lose it, she could not stay still. She would storm off and shut herself away in her room, or rage right out of the house. As she did that night. Riding like a maniac to ease her fury, or to lash it to a greater fury. I would never know which it was to be until she came back. That night"—he turned away from the fire—"she didn't come back."

"You went after her."

"I thought she was so far out of her mind that she might do something stupid."

"You married her," said Kate. "You . . ."

He came to her, took her hands, and drew her to her feet. He crushed her hands between his, and kissed them.

"A marriage does not have to be like that. I will show you. Kate, I will show you how it ought to be."

She freed her hands and put them lightly on his cheeks and drew his head down toward her until their lips met.

Then she hurried from the room. Not as Lady Charlotte would have hurried from it, in a frenzy, but in an absurd, exhilarating fear—fear of what her own emotions were capable of.

Miss Hartest curtly regretted that she must be away for two days and said she would be grateful—though making no more than a token display of such gratitude—if Miss Quantrill would keep Verena occupied. She suggested, with the merest hint that Miss Quantrill might unfortunately have as little grasp of the subject as her pupil, that they would profit from working on the next chapter of the arithmetic book which they regularly used.

Kate was conscious of a cowardly relief. Confined to the house, she would have to postpone the tricky task of stirring up and selecting fragments of gossip which might answer Oliver's insistent question.

At the same time, she could not wrest her attention away from the problem. It was far more baffling than the columns of figures she tried to work out with Verena.

The wet nurse, of course. That was surely the key to the whole situation.

At what stage had she been introduced to the house? If the baby had died, or was known to be dying, why call for a wet nurse at all? As a desperate measure which failed?

Had she already weaned her own child, or brought it with her?

Kate intimated to Mrs. Jenkyn that she would not say no to an invitation to tea in the housekeeper's room again.

Mrs. Jenkyn was delighted. Perhaps she regarded it as a sign that in years to come she could expect to be Kate's favored confidante.

Over tea and toasted tea cakes they discussed the weather, the likelihood of spring gale damage, and the pity of having to keep Verena indoors for days on end. Kate tactfully let Mrs. Jenkyn take the next step, introducing Oliver into the conversation with the observation that he, too, seemed to have shut himself away lately—"I shouldn't say it, miss, but it was a blessing, really, a good riddance, I say, but there, it must have shaken him up notwithstanding"—and he had not been seen out on those strange walks and diggings of his.

"Perhaps when he rode after her—it was the first time he'd been on a horse for years, wasn't it?—he hurt himself. He may find it more difficult to get about."

"You'd be a better judge of that than me," said Mrs. Jenkyn obliquely.

Awed by her own cunning in steering the subject the way she wished it to go, Kate said, "Even as a child he showed himself in some pain?"

Mrs. Jenkyn welcomed the opportunity to reminisce. And it was easy enough, at one juncture, for Kate to say casually, "Did you ever know anyone called Withersedge, who was staying here about the time Mr. Darsham was born?"

"Withersedge—staying in the house, you mean?"

"I think so."

Mrs. Jenkyn pondered. "There was so much to-ing and fro-ing," she said at last, as she had said once before. Then she brightened. "Now I think on, there was somebody here, yes. I wouldn't remember the name, not after all this time. But there was some friend of the master's. Yes . . . because we did wonder why he didn't pack up and go at a time like that, instead of hanging about. But he did leave soon after, I think. Why, miss—what makes you ask?"

Kate tried to shrug it off and yet keep the topic alive. "Mr. Darsham mentioned him as a friend of his father's, and I was sure I knew the name somewhere, and it worries me. You know how these things nag at one."

"I do indeed. Silly little things you can't forget and can't quite remember—keep you awake sometimes, don't they?" Abruptly Mrs. Jenkyn said, "Come to think of it, I have a notion he was the one who fetched that little baggage into the house."

"Who?" asked Kate, more airily than ever.

"The wet nurse. Yes, he must have been the one. Because Dr. Cawdron had had to go off to the infirmary because of that outbreak, whatever it was. And the other nurse left, just like that. Yes, that's right." Memory flooded gleefully back. "Off she went, and that man—what did you say his name was . . . ?"

"Withersedge."

"Mr. Withersedge, then. He brought that girl in."

"From the village?"

"Not her. Not one of us," said Mrs. Jenkyn with the fierce patriotism of a Lincolnshire woman married into Senwich. "From Castleyard, it was."

Kate took a deep breath. "Was she feeding her own baby at the time? I mean, did she bring it with her?"

"That I couldn't say, miss. Precious little we saw of her. She was kept upstairs like one of the family."

"She could have left her own child at home."

"Could have done. She was here for Mr. Oliver, and when he was all right, then off she went. And just as well, for when we *did* see her, there never was such airs and graces."

"You don't remember her name?"

"That I do," said Mrs. Jenkyn. "Never give her a

thought all these years, but I'd not be likely to forget it. Prudence. That's what it was." She sniffed. "And a more unlikely name you'd never think up. Prudence Botting," she concluded, proud of the detail she could sum up.

Castleyard lay south of the heath, a scattered hamlet of tenant cottages serving a manorial estate on one side and two eight-horse farms on the other. There were some sheep-walk fields, a windmill, and a turkey farm. The sea was only four miles to the east, but its winds touched no more than the treetops above the hollow.

The Botting family survived in Castleyard in the person of an elderly Miss Botting. Her cottage by the duck pond was pointed out to Kate without hesitation by the first man she asked.

She was a gnarled little woman with rheumatic fingers twisted like the branches of a bare, petrified oak. Her voice was croaky but uncompromising.

"Prudence? What's everyone coming here asking about *her* for?"

"Everyone?" said Kate, startled.

"There was another lady here asking about her."

"When was this?"

"A few days back. Could have been a week, I suppose."

"But what did she want to know?"

"What do *you* want to know?" demanded Miss Botting.

"Someone is anxious to trace her." Kate had tried this over and settled for it on the way here. "It's in connection with help she gave a family in Senwich many years ago."

"Not quite what that other one said." The old woman eyed her up and down, then edged to one side. "Come you in, then."

The door opened into a tiny room which could not have been dusted for many months. There was little space between a walnut sofa, its upholstery oozing horsehair, and the table and sideboard. Wedged between the door and the sideboard was a mahogany stool covered with a frayed, faded tapestry. A cluster of stuffed birds stared beadily out from a dusty glass bell on the sideboard.

Miss Botting's beaked nose and glinting eyes would have been perfectly at home in the bell. She said, "I reckon she's in some kind of trouble, then?"

"It's simply that we have some information for her, when we can find her."

"That's going to take some doing."

"Prudence was your sister—a younger sister?"

"Not her."

"Your niece?"

"She were a Woolnough. It was my nephew, my Billy." A tear was poised in a wrinkle below her eye. "After all I did for him, and all I told him, he has to go and marry the likes of her."

When nothing more was forthcoming, Kate prompted, "They lived with you?"

"That they did not. I wouldn't have had that one in my house. That drabble-tailed hussy—oh, no, she stayed on with her father, and him so drunk half the time he wouldn't notice what went on under his nose while my poor Billy was away."

"Away?"

"In the navy. And what she didn't get up to while his back was turned, poor lad." Miss Botting seemed to be absorbed by the strands of cobweb across one window-pane. "Though he'll be getting on for sixty now, I reckon. She were a lot younger'n him—but she won't be so young now."

Kate tried boldly, "When they had their baby . . ."

"Oh, that. Yes." Miss Botting grunted.

"When she went to work in Senwich, she took the baby with her?"

The old woman fidgeted. "I don't see it's nobody's business. All this ferreting about." But old hatred got the better of discretion. "Oh, she took it, all right."

"And when she brought it back . . ."

"She didn't bring no baby back here."

"But . . ."

"Said she'd left it with friends. Friends! What kind of friend had *she* got? Left it, she said, while she got packed up ready to leave. Comes back here as brazen as you like, with a new dress and coat and Lord knows what else besides, and says she'll set up a proper place for Billy. And off she goes."

"But didn't she ever tell you or Billy . . . ?"

"He was away then, at sea. I don't know what she told him, or where he went to when he got back. She took good care not to let me know."

"But the baby?" Kate persisted.

"Got rid of it, if you ask me." Miss Botting leaned forward, one claw against her yellow beak. "I'm not saying there was anything wrong with it. But I'm not saying there wasn't. We get a tidy few of 'em around here, you know—some with web feet, with a curse on 'em, because of what comes out of the sea over there. No"—her head pecked down and up, down and up—"it couldn't have been quite as it ought to be, that one, not right enough for her to show Billy when he came home."

"You saw it yourself, before Mrs. Botting took it . . . him . . . ?"

"Oh, it was a him, all right. But I only saw it the once. The way she rushed off with it. But it didn't look right to me. No, not right. Twisted, I'd say."

"And you never heard from them again?"

"Just the once. Oh, it was years. I got a letter from Billy. A letter," said Miss Botting, still marveling. "Said he was out of the navy, and setting up in an inn. And she'd gone off, but he was going to get her back. More fool him."

"And that was all?"

"Never another word. I got a girl to write for me, but there was never an answer."

"Do you still have the letter?"

Miss Botting's jaw began to shake. Any moment now she was going to jib again at the inquisition. It was hard to blame her.

Kate said, "If there was an address on it . . ."

"I'm not going to tell everyone who comes ferreting about here."

"You mean you've told somebody else?"

"That one who was here the other day. How many more of you?"

"I assure you I know nothing about this other lady."

"Well, that's funny, isn't it? All these years, nothing; and now everyone wants to know about that Prudence."

"What did *she* want to know?"

"I don't see what that's got to do with you, any more'n the rest of it. First there was her, making out it was something to do with parish registers or something, and making me feel I'd done some wrong somewhere, instead of me being the one who was wronged. Just left here, and not a word. And now . . ."

"You did show her the address." Kate made it sound reproachful.

"She had a way with her."

"And I haven't?"

"You want that address, you'd better ask her. Comes from up your way. Oh, I've got a fair idea who she is. Parish registers and all. Yes, well, maybe that's so. With that brother of hers."

"She had a brother with her?"

"Not this time she hadn't. But I've seen 'em here before, every once in a while. When our vicar's away, and that one comes down to preach, and she's always with him."

Stunned, Kate prepared to leave. The old woman was in a hurry now to get her off the premises. There was nothing more to be learned here.

But there was a lot to be learned from Miss Hartest. Jogging back toward Senwich, Kate wondered helplessly what questions she dare ask—and what could possibly have drawn Miss Hartest into this in the first place.

Chapter Fourteen

Oliver was away, sitting for three days on the bench in Sheverton. Kate had no chance to report to him before confronting Flora Hartest. She had to make her own decision how—and whether—to attack.

In fact, it was Miss Hartest who took the initiative.

The two of them were in the schoolroom. Verena had gone to the lavatory and was, as usual, taking her time over it. Without warning, Miss Hartest said, "Did Miss Botting give you Billy's address?"

Kate gasped.

"I take it that that was what you were seeking?" Miss Hartest went on with crisp complacency. "You deduced that the solution to the mystery must lie with the wet nurse. Or was it Oliver who deduced it, and sent you to carry on the more embarrassing part of the inquiry?"

"How do you . . . what makes you think I went . . . ?"

"As my brother's helper, Miss Quantrill, I am used to interpreting Senwich people and their ways. When one knows their individual foibles"—she allowed herself a more open disdain than Kate had ever heard from her before—"most of them are pathetically transparent. When you left Verena with me yesterday, you were very flustered. And I gather you asked the groom how long it would take you to drive to Castleyard. And—"

"You have been spying on me!"

"I simply allowed the man to talk. But you haven't answered my question. Did you get Billy's address?" When Kate did not answer, she smiled. "I can see you were less persuasive than I was. Never mind, Miss Quantrill: we all have different . . . talents."

Kate prayed for Verena to come back. Not so that she might dodge any further interrogation, but so that she might gather her forces and decide how best to deal with Miss Hartest.

"I can save you the trouble of tracking Billy down," Miss Hartest continued. "It would be stupid to condemn you to following the same trail all over again. Two wearying days I had of it recently."

"So that was why you were away."

"It was. And now I know where Billy Botting is."

"And Prudence?" Kate was unable to resist asking.

"Apparently not with him. But we shall see."

"We?"

"I suggest that we allow Verena a day to herself to practice the pianoforte. We place her in Mrs. Jenkyn's care, and you accompany me to London. I would not wish to venture alone into the places it may be necessary to go. And I think you, too, would prefer a companion."

"Why do you not take Mr. Hartest?"

"My brother is far too unworldly. Besides," added Miss

Hartest, "I think you should be present to see for yourself."

"To see what?"

"Whatever there is to be seen. And heard."

A dozen doubts and questions tumbled now into Kate's mind. Before she could utter any of them, Verena came back.

To catch the early train, they had to leave Senwich when the sun was little more than a flush of orange in the reluctantly awakening sky. Frost lay on roofs and fields to leeward, but not where the salt wind struck. There was a spidery latticework of branches against the shimmer of the creek.

Kate wore her cloak over a warm woolen dress. Miss Hartest, she found when they reached the train, had a severe gray cotton dress under her coat. Her whole demeanor was of gray steeliness. Without troubling to consult Kate, she bought two first-class return tickets. As the stationmaster ushered them to a compartment and held the door open, she nodded distantly in a way reminiscent of Lady Charlotte.

When the train clanked and hissed out of Sheverton station and began to gather speed along the embankment, Miss Hartest settled herself comfortably.

"Now," she said in the tone she often used when catechizing Verena in the schoolroom, "one point I have been unable to establish. Who engaged the girl as wet nurse—who knew of her, so far away?"

Withersedge, thought Kate: the bird-watcher roaming the countryside, perhaps eating at the local inn and noticing and remembering the pregnant girl when he needed her—when, left with Mrs. Darsham and the dying child, he very much needed a substitute for that long-awaited son whose death could bring all the Darsham fury down on whoever let him die. But she did not say it aloud. Miss Hartest had not been privy to Dr. Cawdron's records. Neither the doctor nor Oliver would have wished Kate to make her a gift of Withersedge's existence.

She said, "Perhaps there was no one in Senwich suckling at the time."

"That seems logical." Miss Hartest mused over the passing landscape, then turned her gaze piercingly on Kate. "But I have the impression that you know more than you are saying. Would it not be helpful to pool our information?"

"We both know the girl was Prudence Botting," Kate hedged. "That, surely, is the main thing."

"Agreed. But if today's journey proves fruitless, and we have to think further . . . what can you contribute, Miss Quantrill?"

Kate shook her head, and tried to emulate her companion's remote stare out of the window. She could tell that Miss Hartest was still watching her, and still suspicious of her.

"How much has Oliver asked you to do on his behalf?" came the sharp question. "And what does he intend to do with what he learns?"

"I am sure he will do what is best," said Kate.

"Best for whom?"

Kate was saved from replying as the train slowed and stopped at a station. An elderly lady and gentleman got in. They both looked apprehensive as the train shuddered and jolted into motion again. The lady surreptitiously groped for her husband's hand and held it tight.

Flora Hartest remained looking challengingly at Kate for a long minute, then took a small book of sermons from her reticule and began reading in spite of the swaying and shaking of the carriage.

A thin rain spattered the windows. In a blurred field a

boy picked stones, his tattered collar drawn up around his throat. A church on a distant rise formed a pivot around which the railway line curved slowly until it swung off above a river and into another station.

Kate glanced covertly at her traveling companion. The reasons for Miss Hartest's scarcely veiled scorn in the schoolroom recently were plain. Since she knew that Oliver Darsham was no Darsham at all, what concern were the Darsham history and tradition for him or Kate—or of his ambitions, whatever they might be, for Kate?

Come to that, what was Miss Hartest's concern with it; what had set her off into her thorough inquiries into Oliver's true identity?

The fields gave way to straggling ridges of houses, and thickened into groves of chimneys. A smoky chasm closed in on the train and guided it to a platform under a vast arch of echoing roof.

Outside, Kate was horrified by the turmoil of horse buses and shouting cabbies.

Miss Hartest raised an imperious hand, and a hansom clopped to a halt. "The Salutation, Southwark," she said.

The cabby appraised her dubiously. "You're sure that's what you mean, lady?"

"Quite sure."

"The old Salutation?" he tried nobly. "Down on the wharf?"

"If it is in Southwark, and is called the Salutation, then that is where we wish to be taken."

The man raised red-veined eyes toward heaven and argued no further. Kate found it comforting to have someone as confident as Miss Hartest beside her in this tumultuous city, yet was disturbed by her newfound arrogance.

The hansom battled its way through conflicting currents of traffic, across a bridge below which thronged the masts of another busy traffic, and along crooked lanes until it came out perilously close to the edge of a cobbled quay.

"You're sure you want to get down here?"

A tavern sign creaked above their heads as they descended. Miss Hartest paid the cabby and added a fourpenny tip to the fare. He studied the coins for a moment, studied Miss Hartest's unyielding countenance, and decided not to comment. As he was about to flick his whip at the nag, she said, "We shall wish to leave in half an hour. That should be ample time. If not, I will tell you when you arrive."

"Now, look, missis . . . how do I know where I'm goin' t' be half an hour from now?"

"I trust you are going to be here."

The cabby growled something inaudible, cracked his whip more vigorously than he had intended, and swore as the horse lurched forward. The wheels spun on the cobbles, and then the hansom disappeared up the narrow street down which it had come.

A couple of grubby-faced, barefoot lads looked at the two women and sniggered. An old slattern with no shoes, but with slippers whose soles were pulling away from the uppers, veered away from them and plunged into the dark open doorway of the inn.

Miss Hartest followed her, with Kate close on her heels.

Their eyes adjusted to the gloom. Deeply stained settles shaped themselves against the walls. Kate narrowly missed colliding with a long table made of four roughly hewn planks. A titter came from one corner.

Miss Hartest marched up to the bar counter.

A tall man in a grubby jersey, his trousers tucked into sea boots, turned with a tankard of ale in his hand and bumped into her. A curse trembled on his lips. Then, with an unexpectedly pleasant smile, he said, "I'll be asking

your pardon, ma'am." Miss Hartest favored him with a
brief inclination of the head. There was another titter from
the shadows. The man glared in that direction, and there
was instant silence.

Miss Hartest faced the landlord.

He was a man in his late fifties or early sixties, with a
bulbous nose and only a few remaining wisps of hair
straggling across a red-blotched scalp. He did not wait for
his visitors to speak, but growled, "If you've come to
throw your tracts all over the place, you'd best be taking
'em elsewhere. We ain't got no time for that sort of thing
in here."

Miss Hartest said, "You are Mr. William Botting?"

"No reason why I shouldn't be."

"Originally from the parish of Castleyard?"

The man put two grimy palms on the counter and
leaned on them. "What's this about?"

The drinkers on the benches and in the chairs by the
window were quite still, as though part of the furniture.
Everybody listened hopefully. Kate did not risk so much
as a glance over her shoulder.

"We would like to speak to you in private," said Miss
Hartest.

"I've asked you—what's it about?"

"About your wife."

An ugly laugh twisted from Botting's throat. "And since
when have I had a wife?"

"That's one of the things we'd like to ask."

"*Her?* Haven't set eyes on her this ten year or more.
What's happened—she made trouble for herself somewhere?"

"And about your child," said Miss Hartest. "If you
could spare us a moment . . ."

"The girls? So it's them. Offed it long ago, both of 'em,
and now you're going to tell me they went the same way

as their Mum. There's nothing to tell: I could ha' told *you*."

"I'm referring to your son."

There was an even stranger silence. Kate was suddenly sure they had made a terrible mistake. The man's ghastly, distorted face told her there was something wrong.

"A son?" he whispered at last.

"I think you know what I'm talking about," said Miss Hartest implacably.

"You'd . . . reckon you'd better come into the parlor." As Botting's voice thickened, echoes of his home county seeped into it. He let out a yell. "Nellie, come out here, will you?"

A woman edged past them, grumbling, as they went through a door beside the counter and were shown into a room with creaking wickerwork chairs. Curtains and the tablecloth retained the smell of paraffin from a large lamp with a smeared glass.

Botting nodded to the chairs. Kate and Miss Hartest sat down, but he remained standing.

"Who are you, and what's all this about a son?"

"We are from Senwich," said Miss Hartest. "You remember Senwich?"

"Went there a time or two. I don't recollect much."

"Your wife spent a short time there as a wet nurse."

"If she did, that's the first I ever heard of it." He rubbed his knuckles along his stubbly chin. "Besides, how could she be a wet nurse if she wasn't . . . if she hadn't already . . . ?"

Kate's unease intensified. She said, "Miss Hartest, I think Mr. Botting may not know the full—"

Miss Hartest brushed her aside and continued on the lines she must have settled in her own mind before ever reaching this squalid back parlor. "Where is that child? What happened to him?"

"We never had but the two girls. And them after we left Castleyard and came down here."

"There *must* have been a son. Mr. Botting, are you telling me you never knew about him?"

"And don't reckon much on the story now."

"Mr. Botting, I'm appealing for your help. A ticklish legal and moral question has arisen with a family in the area which can be resolved only when we know precisely what happened thirty-six years ago. I implore you: please tell me frankly what you know about the arrangement your wife came to regarding your child."

"I don't know a thing about it. I swear it."

Kate intervened. "Miss Hartest, we do know that Mr. Botting was away at sea at the time."

Flora Hartest seemed to be on the verge of brushing this aside, too. Before she could do so, Kate added, "That's what I heard from old Miss Botting. I imagine she told you the same."

"Old Miss . . ." Billy Botting stared from one to the other. "You mean old Aunt Meg's still alive? Why, the old . . . so *she's* the one who put you up to whatever it is? Never could keep a still tongue in her head. Always looking for some mischief to brew." Then he gave a rueful snort, and finished sheepishly, "Though mebbe I should ha' listened to her on one or two things."

Miss Hartest had been nudged onto a new track. She said, "Mr. Botting, when you joined your ship in 1837, did you know before leaving that your wife was pregnant?"

"That I didn't."

"And when you returned, she said nothing about the child?"

"Nothing. Now, let's have this straight, miss. Are you telling me there was a little 'un?"

"In view of your wife's ability to act as wet nurse . . ."

"But what happened to it?"

"You were not party to any . . . financial arrangement?"

"Just a minute. Just a minute, now. She done well for herself while I was away, that I do remember. Told me how hard she'd been working, to save up and make us a home. Being lucky, she said. Only she didn't fancy us going on living in Castleyard any longer."

"And you did not query the source of her savings?"

His sly look told its own story. Billy Botting was not the man to question too deeply the origin of any comforts when they were offered to him. An attractive young woman with a glib tongue would not find it too difficult to wheedle him into submission.

He said, "But it was a boy. You said it was a boy. Was he . . . did he . . . live?"

"We have reason to think so."

"*Think* so?" The bleared face worked agonizingly. "You mean I've had a son, he could have been with me all this time, we could have . . . we . . . ." The rheumy eyes gleamed with easy tears. "That slut—she sold my son? Is that what you're saying?"

"I wouldn't wish to say precisely that, Mr. Botting, but—"

"Where *is* he?"

Kate had a grotesque vision of Oliver confronted by this human wreck. And she knew with frightening certainty that once the truth was laid before him, Oliver would insist on bringing it about, on coming face to face with his father.

Botting's hand scrubbed incessantly at his chin. With a touch of his earlier slyness he said, "Doing well, is he? A good boy, doing well for himself?"

"If what we surmise is correct, yes, he is doing well."

"Wouldn't do him no harm, would it, to give a thought to his poor old father, slaving away here."

Miss Hartest said icily, "But you say you can give no

positive corroboration of your wife's arrangement with . . . with her employers at the time."

"I wasn't there. You know I wasn't there."

Kate felt sorry for the man. He was floundering in a morass, groping for firm ground.

Miss Hartest got up. It was a signal for their departure.

"I'll be seeing my boy?" Botting sought some solid assurance out of the confusion. "You come here and tell me there's a boy, and you say I ought to be able to say yes or no, when it's the first time I ever heard of him, and . . ."

He gave up, baffled.

Miss Hartest said, matter-of-fact rather than sympathetic, "I think we shall need to be in touch again."

The door opened without the formality of a knock. The girl Botting had called Nellie put her head around it.

"There's a cab outside. Said he was told to be here."

Miss Hartest led the way. They caught a homeward train with fifteen minutes to spare. There were already other passengers in the compartment, so it was impossible to discuss the interview.

Kate put her head back and closed her eyes.

Prudence Botting had certainly had a child. She had taken it with her to Darsham's Tower when supposedly engaged to suckle Robert Darsham's son. "Supposedly" . . . because the real Oliver Darsham had not outlived his first day. Dr. Withersedge, in a panic, had hastily dismissed the nurse who could have identified the real baby, and announced the employment of Prudence as wet nurse. No one in the Tower apart from Withersedge knew that she had brought her own baby with her; and when she left, it did not leave with her. Her husband's aunt never saw the child again; and Billy Botting himself was not even aware that he had fathered a son.

Mrs. Darsham, ill with the fever, would know nothing

of the substitution. When she recovered, the baby boy was presented to her as her own.

Prudence was lavishly paid and went away.

There was something missing. Kate rubbed her eyes, stinging with dust and tiredness. The story was solid enough, all too convincing; but somewhere there was an awkward fact she had forgotten to fit into place.

It would have to wait. Her only duty now was to report to Oliver and let him make what he would of it.

When they were two stations from Sheverton, the compartment emptied. The carriage was not clear of the platform before Miss Hartest said, "It is clear, is it not?"

"I think so," said Kate cautiously.

"But there can be no doubt about it. I had my suspicions from the start—from the moment my brother told me of that coffin in the tunnel. I said to Charlotte—"

"*You* told Lady Charlotte!"

So it had not been Matthew Rouse, ignominiously dismissed on a false suspicion.

Flora Hartest colored slightly. "I was not aware, of course, that Oliver had chosen not to confide in her." She went on more imperiously than ever, "Obviously old Dr. Cawdron was terrified of Robert Darsham, and foisted onto him the son of a sailor and a village slut rather than confess that his own son had died. Cawdron must have had to pay handsomely from his own pocket. And yet . . ." Now she faltered; stared again, hard, at Kate. "Miss Quantrill, you are still holding something back. Do *you* know who placed that coffin in the tunnel? And why? One would not have expected Cawdron . . ."

Kate barely repressed an exclamation. The missing piece of jigsaw slotted into place.

The keys! She knew about Withersedge, and she knew this other thing which Miss Hartest could not know: the existence of those keys which Oliver had found in his father's desk.

It was wildly improbable that Withersedge, a mere visitor to the house, should have known of those keys and of the secret tunnel, should have extracted them from Robert Darsham's desk, personally laid the dead baby to rest near the family vault, and replaced the keys.

There was only one other explanation. Descending from the train under the flickering lamps of Sheverton station, she was too dazed to accept it and yet too dazed to argue it away.

The jigsaw was complete but incredible. Let Oliver himself interpret the picture it presented.

As though plucking her thoughts out of the air, and carrying them on, Miss Hartest said, "Cousin Oliver—or whoever he may be—must be told."

"Of course."

"As soon as he returns from dispensing justice"—it was enunciated with great relish—"he must turn his mind to the rights and wrongs of his own case."

They collected the Hartest gig from the hostelry where it had been stabled this morning, and set out across the dark heath toward Senwich. It was bitterly cold, and the wind was rising. Kate drew her cloak tightly about her.

"As Oliver's chosen emissary," said Miss Hartest, "I imagine he will wish you to be present when I explain what we have discovered."

A few lights in the village twinkled a welcome, but Kate's heart was heavy. It was not simply the cold which numbed her senses.

She ought to have stayed in Sheverton tonight, sought out Oliver, and told him, however incoherently, what Miss Hartest proposed to put before him. But Miss Hartest would hardly have countenanced that, guessing what would be in her mind.

High up in the Tower a brighter light marked Mrs. Darsham's window. The gig slowed on the corner, turning toward the gateposts where the stone beasts crouched, seemingly ready to spring when it reached them.

Down the slope, the door of the Darsham Arms opened and a man stood framed against the yellow glow. The set of his head and his mock salute as he went in were instantly recognizable.

Matthew Rouse was back in Senwich.

Chapter Fifteen

The ripples gathered force, chocolaty with churned-up sand and backed by a slow, sinister swell.

"Don't go much on the look o' that," said old Hodmedod.

A splintered hatch from some long-drowned ship bumped and twisted against the end of the groin, slowly and then more desperately jarring itself to pieces.

Kate had left Miss Hartest and Verena together in the schoolroom. She could not have borne to sit there and make a show of sharing Verena's lessons, with Miss Hartest sardonically measuring her up from time to time. She strolled in a reverie to the edge of the hard.

Matthew stood some yards down the shore, appraising the defenses and shaking his head over the scoured shingle. She heard him say, "Add a strong easterly to the next few tides, and we may not withstand the pressure."

Crunching back up the beach from the man he had spoken to, he saw Kate. The lines about his eyes crinkled, just as she could have predicted they would.

"Miss Kate. It's good to see you again."

She was disturbed by her own pleasure in seeing him; and yet, it was as if they had been chatting together only yesterday.

She said stiffly, "I didn't know Mr. Darsham had re-engaged you."

"He hasn't. I'm here on my own authority, staying at the inn."

"He'll be none too pleased."

He smiled grimly. "My work was abandoned too soon. I had to come and check, whether Mr. Darsham wants me here or not. I shall soon be going back to the States."

"I . . . I thought you had already gone."

"I've been making the most of some weeks in the fen country. But way out there in the middle of Whittlesey Mere—and that's quite an achievement, that reclamation, believe me—right out there I got to feeling in my bones that there was danger here. I had to come back."

"I thought you were an engineer, Mr. Rouse. Not a seer. Very modern and scientific."

"Any engineer who can't feel every stress and strain in his own bones," said Matthew, "is no true engineer."

As though in obedient demonstration, the harbor groin rasped and let out two sharp crunches like the creaking of a rheumatic knee.

Matthew winced.

"We've had storms before," said Kate. "We live with them. I expect we can stand up to another one."

"Can you? And another, and another one after that? Do none of you understand?"

Wheels grated over the cobbles. Abel was pushing a handcart toward the chandler's. John came out of an alley behind him. They saw Kate and saw who was with her. Abel waved, and said something to his brother; and the two of them grinned complacently.

"They're not setting off into that?" Matthew jerked a thumb at the sullen horizon.

Kate was incapable of answering. She was furious with the boys; they had talked about her and Matthew Rouse before, and now they would be at it again.

Close beside her, he said, "It wasn't only Senwich and its storm warnings that brought me back."

Turning her head, she caught the faint rise of the wind and the change in its pitch. But it did not stifle what Matthew was saying.

"I missed the sound of your voice. I'd guessed it would be bad—but I'd no notion just how bad it would be."

"Mr. Rouse, I won't listen."

"That's what I said. To myself. I wouldn't listen. Wasn't going to strain to hear you, over all that distance. But it was no use. I had to come back, so I'd be near enough—seeing you out walking, and knowing I'd hear your voice, even if not so very often. Even if I'm not allowed to touch, Kate . . . dear Kate. Just to see you. Hear you."

Over the ridge of heath, just visible above the roofs of Senwich, a carriage made the turn and disappeared behind the cottages. She followed its progress in her mind: the descent, the slight rise, the junction of road and lane, and the final turn toward the gates.

It could only be Oliver, home from Sheverton.

Matthew laughed ruefully. "You still won't hear *me*, though, will you?"

Flora Hartest told the story against a faint background of inappropriately lilting music. Verena was playing the piano while they, the three of them, sat shut away in the library.

When the account was ended, Oliver made no move. His right hand remained curled over the end of the chair arm. His eyes and mouth were stoical, impassive.

At last he mutely consulted Kate—seeking only confirmation of what had been said, not her love or sympathy.

"So"—it was unnaturally calm—"I am the son of a village slut and a feebleminded sailor."

Miss Hartest made no attempt to soften or deny it.

"When you were born," said Kate, "they were both young and in good health. Whatever may have happened to them later, they were worthy enough . . . sound enough . . . then."

"Worthy?" he said remotely.

"If there is any disgrace in it," said Miss Hartest, allowing herself to be magnanimous, "it is Dr. Cawdron's. We are hardly going to raise a scandal over that, after so long."

"No," said Oliver. "Not Cawdron. The decision was my father's. I mean, it was Robert Darsham's."

"Nonsense. He was the last person to have—"

"Cawdron was away at the time. Called away to Chedstowe. A Dr. Withersedge deputized for him—a friend of old Robert's. And Robert sent that friend to find a substitute son and smuggle him into the house."

Miss Hartest shook her head in arrant disbelief.

"The keys." Kate had known intuitively that Oliver would say this. "The keys to the tunnel were in his desk."

"But couldn't someone . . . this other man . . . ?"

"Withersedge? Found the keys, provided the coffin, had the nameplate engraved . . . and buried it as closely as possible to the vault in the churchyard? I think not. It was old Robert."

"Foisting an impostor on the world?"

"Rather than let the line die out."

"There were others to keep the line going."

"Mr. Darsham's daughters?" said Kate, out of her depth.

Both of them looked pityingly at her. On this at least they were in accord.

Miss Hartest said, "I still can't accept that. Not of old Robert, from all I've heard of him. But one thing I know. Whatever else may be in doubt, one thing is certain: Godfrey is the closest male relation—the legitimate heir."

Kate understood, and wondered why it had taken her so long. This was the force behind Flora Hartest's dedication to the quest for Billy Botting, his lost wife, and the child sold off by Prudence. The Reverend Godfrey had true Darsham blood in his veins. He had a claim to Darsham's Tower. And his sister saw herself there at his side, as she had always been at his side, only now with most of the advantages she had so far lacked. Men, she had once said to Kate, married for beauty or for money. If she could not be beautiful, at least as the lady of Darsham's Tower she could offer the other bait.

"Robert Darsham," said Oliver, "felt it so important that there should be a son to follow him that he arranged for me to be taken into his household rather than have no son at all."

"Godfrey had not been born then. If he had known about Godfrey, if he had lived long enough . . ."

"You believe he might have disowned me? Do I have the right to make any such assumption?"

"You have no rights to anything," said Miss Hartest.

"Cousin Flora—"

"No right, even, to call me that."

Kate could not believe that the haughty, determined Oliver would let a woman like this—until so recently a poor cousin whom he condescended to employ when it suited him—beat him into submission. But the uncertainty which had been gnawing at him since the discovery of the coffin must have bitten more deeply than she had guessed. He bowed his head. It was surrender. He said, "We must discuss arrangements to make sure that Godfrey can take his rightful place."

"I'm glad we agree."

Kate could bear it no longer. "But what about all the work you've put into the family business?" she implored Oliver. "Building it up, doing so much for Ipswich, for the crews, for . . . for a . . . Can Mr. Hartest," she cried, "ever hope to do as much?"

"The question is not one of money," said Flora Hartest. "It is entirely a moral one."

The tone of voice was familiar. It must have been passed down through generations and reached out even to the remoter branches of the family. Flora Hartest was undoubtedly an authentic Darsham.

Oliver said, "Your brother must marry, of course."

"Yes."

"And give up the cloth."

"You will have to put that to him."

"It would hardly be fitting for an earl of Blackshore to be—"

"There *are* no earls of Blackshore anymore!" Kate protested.

"There will be." To Oliver it was as real and important as it had ever been. He acknowledged her existence again with a distant, sad smile. "I had hoped I might be the one. Or . . . my son."

"Does it matter?" Kate was shamefully close to angry tears. "Does it *matter*?"

The sound of the piano grew stormier. Verena was enjoying herself thumping out chords with more vigor than accuracy.

Oliver was released from the spell. He pushed himself up from his chair and strode to the door.

"Stop that damned row. Do you hear me? Stop it at once."

An unresolved chord hung on the air. Between Oliver's arm and his side Kate caught a glimpse of Verena coming out, frightened, into the hall.

Miss Hartest said, "Perhaps you'll be kind enough to take Verena for a walk, Miss Quantrill. As you will appreciate, Oliver and I have confidential family matters to discuss."

Oliver did not contradict her. He stood aside to let Kate pass.

The fitful, blustery wind had settled to a steady blow from the southeast. Verena and Kate had to walk with their heads down, clutching their bonnets to their heads.

"How could they send me out when it's like this?" Verena lamented.

It was certainly no day for carefree walking. But neither Oliver nor Miss Hartest would have noticed if there were a hailstorm out of doors. Kate drew Verena into the shelter of a row of cottages, then turned toward the lane. They might just as well sit by the fire and beg a cup of tea from Sarah.

Halfway down the slope, Verena tugged at her arm.

"Miss Quantrill, isn't that your father?"

Kate raised her eyes into the wind. Then she held out her arms, and Captain Josiah stumped toward her and lifted her off the ground, and Verena was laughing as happily as either of them.

"So there's one of you about," he roared, when he had squeezed her almost senseless and set her down again. "Thought I'd never find a living soul."

"Sarah's not at home?"

"Not a sign of her."

"She must be in the village. And Daniel will be off with a load somewhere."

"And the boys?" Since Daniel's marriage, the habit had grown of calling only the other two "the boys."

Kate looked down at the creek. "You can only just have missed them. They were still here this morning."

"Gone off in that?" Captain Josiah studied the sea mistrustfully. "It's bad. And won't get any better for a while."

He offered Kate one arm and Verena the other, and they ambled toward the house.

"It was a rough passage. Worst I've known it in the bay. Carrying two passengers, and one was sick two whole days."

Verena shuddered. Kate said, "And the trade? It's going to work out well . . . or . . . ?"

"Remains to be seen. But the trade's there. It's got to be said, it's there, fair enough. And a lot of competition. It could be Mr. Darsham's right to commit himself to it now, before they set up too many of their own companies at the other end."

He stooped slightly under the lintel. Verena sighed her gratification at the warm breath from the damped-down fire, and began to pluck her gloves off, finger by finger.

Kate reached for the kettle.

"Funny," reflected Captain Josiah. "It was the younger fellow was so ill on the voyage. The other one was so thin, all skin and bones, you'd never have thought he'd live to see England. But he was going to come back, he said, and have a few last years of it after all that time down under. Knew these parts pretty well." He paced about the room as though, like his passenger, he wanted to see what changes had been made in familiar scenes. "Never did quite make out how he got to know 'em, though. Fond of talking, he was, but all about birds. Once he was started on that, there was no stopping him. But never much else."

Sarah's head went past the window, the baby's head close against her shoulder. Captain Josiah went to open the door, and they came in.

"Name of Withersedge." He finished off that conversation shipshape before starting on Sarah and his grandson.

Kate dropped the lid of the kettle, and the baby began to howl.

Chapter Sixteen

"Withersedge?" said Oliver. "You're quite sure?"

"You can check it on my passenger list, sir."

"Of course not. If you are sure . . ." Oliver could not remain still. He had perched on the arm of his usual chair, leaned with his head against the mantelpiece, and now was at his desk, striking it lightly again and again with his knuckles. "Withersedge," he breathed. "And an ornithologist, you say?"

"Always on about wild birds, sir. I think he'd even have welcomed an albatross, if we'd been unlucky enough to pick one up."

"Now. You think he proposes to settle in this neighborhood?"

"Not so close as all that," said Captain Josiah. "But in the county, yes, I'd say. He talked of a place on the

Deben, or just maybe along the Stour, in from the estuary. So long as he can watch his birds, he'll be content."

"I shall find him."

Captain Josiah glanced worriedly at his daughter in hope of enlightenment. But Kate was watching Oliver's every move—the slackening and tightening not just of his fists, but the corners of his mouth, his whole body. She was growing frightened—frightened of him and for him. His dreams and daydreams belonged in a different world from hers. And his awakenings had somehow been more cruel. Was he now inviting another discomfiture? If he found Withersedge and found it was the same man, what could he expect from him—release, or an added burden?

"I know most of the agents he is likely to approach in Ipswich," he said. "If he is seeking a house, a cottage . . ."

"A cottage, the way he was talking," said Captain Josiah.

"If he buys property, I shall trace him." Oliver took out his watch and flipped the cover open. "I shall leave for Ipswich at once. I shall have it settled, once and for all."

Kate said, "Surely he can do no more than confirm what we already know?"

"What we have surmised," Oliver corrected. "And I must meet him face to face. I must have it from his own lips."

The last nail in his own coffin, thought Kate despairingly. Did he really have to ensure that the very last nail should be placed so accurately, and so decisively hammered down?

Oliver rang for his valet. Kate said she would show her father out, and went to the door with him.

He was shy of her. "Been some strange things since you came to work here," he said awkwardly.

"Mr. Darsham's a law to himself."

"Yes." Once he would have chuckled admiration. Now

he rubbed his jaw and grunted two or three times, changing his mind about what to say. "You reckon it's been worth it for you?"

Mrs. Jenkyn was crossing the hall. In a low voice, Kate, opening the door to the wind, said, "It hasn't come to what I expected."

"Girl, if you want to leave . . ."

"I don't know what I want," she said, "yet."

Tied in some insidious way to Oliver, she knew she had to wait, as anxious as he was for the final stroke of the pen at the foot of the page.

The last nail in his coffin. The image haunted her.

The unrelenting southeasterly piled up water toward the Scottish coast. A motley assortment of ships took shelter in the bay. Some made their way up river and moored. A couple of wherries tacked into the creek and stayed there. There were two French smacks, blown off their fishing grounds, and a Dutchman hove to under the promontory. The Darsham Arms was doing brisk business.

In spite of the blustering winds, few Senwich folk could bear to stay indoors. The women were continually coming out for a look at the lowering sky. The men congregated on the hard or in the bar of the inn and reminisced and predicted; and waited.

"If that do turn . . ."

The unfinished threat was an echo chasing through every nook and cranny of the village. It reached even the Folly, relayed by the baker to the coachman and on into the servants' hall. Verena picked up a whisper of it, and timorously asked Kate, "What will happen to us, then, if it does turn?"

"If it's no worse than that blow we had five years ago," said Kate reassuringly, "we won't come to much harm. We're safer here than a lot of places."

She set herself to distract the child by relating one of Captain Josiah's lengthier and more outrageously vivid stories of the Bay of Biscay and many longitudes east. Miss Hartest had abandoned any further teaching; such menial tasks were, apparently, beneath her dignity. Kate, as she talked, was mentally sketching out ways of keeping Verena occupied until Oliver returned from Ipswich. After that there would be changes, had to be changes. She could no more predict the direction they would take than she could predict the direction of the storm winds tonight or tomorrow.

Mrs. Jenkyn came to announce that Mr. Rouse was at the door.

"In a fine state, I can tell you. Wants to see the master. I've told him he's away, but he won't take no for an answer."

"I don't imagine he will take it from me, either."

"I thought that as you know him, miss . . ."

Kate went down to the hall.

Matthew watched her descent down the curve of stair below the stained-glass window, its colors muted against the outer grayness.

As she reached the bottom step, she said, "Mr. Darsham is away."

"Has he sent you personally to get rid of me?"

"He is not here."

"That could be just a polite excuse—and I don't find it polite. I have to see him. He *has* to let me take some emergency measures out there. Whatever mistaken notions he may have about me—"

"I know they were mistaken," said Kate quietly. "That has been established."

He, too, was quiet for a moment. "I'm glad to hear that. Very glad." Then he said, "But I still have to see him, to make him understand—"

"He is not here," Kate repeated.

He was ready to go on arguing, but saw in her face that it was the truth.

"My God. Have you any idea how bad this is liable to get?"

The door of the small drawing room was open. He looked through it, and without waiting to be invited, went in and stood by the window. He was one with the rest of them, staring out, calculating, unable to turn away from what threatened.

He said, "He'll be mighty lucky to find anything here when he gets back." He narrowed his eyes as though the wind were beating at them even in here. "How could he have gone away at a time like this?"

"He had important business."

"More important than his home . . . his village? What kind of man does that make him?"

Kate remembered the fanaticism in Oliver's face as he left, and dared not answer.

Matthew forced himself to turn away from the window. He looked down thoughtfully at his distorted reflection in the polished lid of the piano, then said, "There's something I have to say to you, too. If Mr. Darsham will not hear me, then you shall hear me."

"I know nothing of Mr. Darsham's business, or his estate."

"I'm not proposing to discuss them."

"If you've come to speak more ill of—"

"I'll speak against nobody, Kate. From now on I speak only for myself." He waited, tight-lipped, as if to give her the chance of refusing to listen. But she was frighteningly aware that she wanted to hear him; and frightened that, once he had spoken, she would be unable to blot out what might be said. He went on, "I regret what I allowed myself to say in the past. Jealousy . . . it's a lingering poison.

There was more left in my heart than I care to think. Waiting for something it could work on. I'm not proud of it."

"Why should you choose to be jealous of anyone here?"

"Jealousy's never a matter of choice." He hesitated again. "What I brought here was . . . a contamination from the past." Then he began to speak more resolutely. "Back home we have quite a tradition of beautiful young ladies. We're very proud of our Southern belles, and they're mighty proud of themselves. A very special breed."

"I wonder you could bear to leave."

Her levity fell flat on her own ears. And it failed to deter Matthew. "The prize of them all was Isabel. Isabel Jervis. We all wanted her, and she basked in knowing it. But I was the one she chose." He was still contemplating the piano lid, but the reflections he saw were not of the room or the slanted outline of the window. "She had auburn hair, very long. So deep and rich that it made her cheeks and shoulders honey-colored. Eyes like a sleepy wildcat's. And her voice—you've never heard that Southern purr, Miss Kate?"

It was a question expecting no answer.

"Once in a while," he mused, "I suppose I must have seen that Isabel was just not there at all. She was so bright and so superb, and yet maybe there was no such person. I can say it now, but I couldn't then. She was as much a piece of engineering, an artifice, man-made . . . or, rather, woman-made . . ."

He faltered, baffled by his own memories.

And this dislike which Kate felt for a woman she had never seen, and never heard of until today—was this a canker of jealousy as irrational and contemptible as his own?

"You couldn't not be taken by her," he went on. "No

man could pretend. And I saw no reason why I should have to. She was going to be my wife, that was how it ought to be, and all our friends thought that was how it was going to be. So I told her everything she wanted to hear. Because she *demanded* to be told. It was the way things had to be for her—having her praises sung over and over again until they got to be true. And then, when there was no more that any man could dream up to say to her, she had doubts. Began talking herself into something else, and encouraging other people to talk her into something else."

"Something else," said Kate, "or somebody else?"

"So you do hear what I'm saying!" Inside the room and outside, the silence was unnerving. Seconds were somehow not ticking away but collecting, mute and overpowering. Matthew said, "Isabel has always had to possess. Toys, clothes, horses . . . men. Once she's got what she wants, it's of no more value. And while she waits for another excitement to turn up, she smashes the old toy piece by piece, and throws the pieces away."

"You were . . . thrown aside?"

"I had a friend, Sheldon Rutherford. A good friend. We knew some rough times together, and some fine ones. He was big and powerful, and a worker; but gentle with it. He thought Isabel was beautiful, and he was glad for me. But Isabel didn't care for there to be anyone else in my life. She took against Sheldon. And then, when I spoke my mind to her about it, out of sheer anger she took *to* him. He had no time to think. She didn't give him the time. He married her."

"You called him a friend?"

"I regret his loss," said Matthew somberly, "more than hers. I never could bring myself to blame him. She had that way with her. I told you: anything she decided to want, she had to have." Again he hesitated, checking every word against his memory. "There's no self-pity in this. Not anymore. If I'm sorry for anyone, it's the two of them."

"I don't understand how that can be."

"I'm sorry for her, because she'll never be satisfied. And even more sorry for Sheldon. And for whoever comes after him."

"Isn't that being too cynical?"

"It was happening," he said, "before I left. It was happening within six months of their marriage. She started in to break him. He just didn't understand. She was bored, and she took him to pieces, and then she was even more bored. She began inviting me over to their place for dinner, or happened to meet me at a ball or subscription concert, or even by chance—by chance, that's how she made it out to be—in the street. And she let me understand she'd made a terrible mistake, and it ought to have been me all along. That was when I got to feeling really sick. Sick enough to get right out and take the offer of coming to Europe for a while. Maybe it helped Sheldon. Or maybe I didn't honestly give Sheldon a thought. Could have been sheer cowardice."

"I've never thought of you as a coward."

"I don't much care to think of myself that way." A flash of his old smile broke through, and Kate wished a hundred problems could have been blown away so that she could freely return that smile. "But what else would you call it? I let something go very cold inside me, so I'd have said some part of me died. And I told myself it was very comfortable. And safe. Not taking anyone too seriously. Not staying anywhere too long, or with one person. But now I've met you, Kate; and it's not that easy anymore. Even if I don't stand a chance, I'd surely be a coward not to tell you."

Her heartbeats seemed crazily to be beating in her head. "Why *are* you telling me so much?"

"To be done with it, once and for all. Free of it. So there's nothing you have to wonder about afterward— after I've asked you to marry me."

"You can't," she whispered. "It's another of your flirtations. Not taking anyone too seriously. Not—"

"Kate. Will you marry me?"

"You've said you were safer . . . happier . . ."

"I didn't say happier."

"But after one taste of such a hurt, you can really fancy getting married now?"

"I do."

"And it is," she said. "That's what it is—a fancy."

"You despise me for what I've just told you?"

"No. But I think . . ."

She had to stop, because she truly did not know what she thought.

He put his hands on her shoulders. "I don't have any big promises to make. Except that I love you and I shall go on loving you. Not much luxury, Kate. In my work I'm liable to be always on the move. But somewhere in you there's something that says yes to that kind of life—I *know* there is, I know it, it keeps answering me . . . and you keep trying to shout it down."

She was angry with him for being so right. He did know, it was there, that wanderlust in her bones.

Absurd that she should feel so safe when he held her like this. Safe from the house and its ghosts. When he said, "Well, Kate?" and released her and stood back, the shadows crowded in again. Oliver himself loomed closer.

She realized with mounting terror that she didn't want him close. She wanted never to fall under that spell again.

Dusk hazed the garden and deepened the shadows in the recesses of the room.

"Kate . . ."

There was a dull bang which rattled the window. They both reacted to it in a split-second, recognizing it, fearing it. Another bang . . . and a sputter of light in the distant sky.

Somewhere out there a ship was in distress.

There was an odd silence. The wind itself might have caught its breath, waiting to hear if there was another rocket. Then it began to blow again, but was not the same.

"If that do turn . . ."

It had turned.

The sudden swing of the gale to the northeast let loose the water which had been building up against the Scottish coast. Released, then goaded on by this new master, it raced and boiled down the eastern shores of England.

The dismasted brigantine which had sent up its rockets off Senwich was caught in the tide whip. Its steering gear obviously damaged by the falling mast, it spun out of control; and every man on Senwich beach knew what would happen to it. The shoal a mile out was plain enough in daylight, with its fluffy collar of surf. Every mariner up these coasts knew how to avoid it easily day or night. And if by some carelessness one struck it at low water, the tide would carry one off again in due course. But not a tide like this. Not with the screaming thrust of a wind like this.

The brigantine struck, and for a moment seemed quite steady. The remains of its spars and tangled rigging were stark against the twilight.

Then an exultant wave crashed down on its bows and slewed it around.

"She's over!"

The stern reared up, and the ship heeled over. Still it was propped up by the shoal, struggling to right itself like a man braced against the wind with one foot doggedly pushing against the solid earth. But the sands of the shoal were not solid enough.

"Old Crusty's will do it . . . only one . . . can't *leave* them . . ."

Kate found that she was clinging to Matthew's arm. They were wracked by their own helplessness. The snatches of words, the conflict of shouts and orders, came from a group of fishermen dragging the biggest of the local longshore boats down to the seething water's edge.

"They'll not risk putting out in that?" said Matthew.

Oars for six men were tossed in. "Come along, then, all of you." As six of the fittest clambered in, others man-handled the boat off the roaring shingle into the surf. The oars dipped, but were flung clear as waves smashed in and tipped the boat up contemptuously, so that it tottered like the crudest plank seesaw. In the raging dusk the boat was a dark shape turning broadside on and coming back, lifted up to a height that threatened the destruction of shore and men below it. Then it slid down and scraped up a few yards of shingle, settling and tilting into the stones.

The men on shore dashed at it again to heave it out on the racing ebb. It bucked over the waves, but again the oars could get no grip; and back it came, its starboard gunwale tearing and splintering.

"We'll never do it."

"Mad," said Matthew. "They're mad."

"Can't leave them . . ."

The note of the wind fell like a falling phrase in a sentimental tune, then jeeringly shrieked up in a new crescendo.

There were a sigh and a howl from the beach.

"Look . . . on her weather side!"

In the uncertain light a shadow like a scudding cloud was bearing down on the doomed brigantine. Spray blurred the outlines. But as it came around with a flapping of torn shreds of sail, trying to line up on the harbor entrance, Kate recognized it.

"John and Abel—but they ought to have made Maldon by now."

"They must have had to turn back." Matthew's words were torn away by the wind. Everything now was at the mercy of that wind; and it knew no mercy.

The bows of the *Mary Matilda* plunged deep into a wave, and spray exploded far above the topmast. From where the onlookers stood, the barge seemed to be sucked rather than driven toward the shoal. The floundering brigantine was like a spider, waiting for its smaller prey.

"God," said Matthew. "Oh, God." It was a curse, not a prayer.

Sky and sea were darkening into one cold hell, broken only by splinters of cloud and the white saliva of greedy waves. The brigantine slumped. The barge was lifted and borne down upon it.

Kate strained to see, but her eyes ached, and looking out into the wind brought only a flailing agony across her face. She bowed her head, tried to fight her way closer to the water, but Matthew held her back.

Somebody was bellowing away behind her. But the gale was stronger than their voices, and the improvised lifeboat, lying crippled on the shore, would never respond.

"They can't go out," said Matthew. "It would be suicide."

"John," she wept. "John . . . Abel . . ."

The *Mary Matilda* was tossed against the brigantine. From here the shock of the impact was inaudible, but Kate felt it as surely as though she had been crushed between the two vessels. They appeared almost to be wrestling. The barge's lee board had fouled the tumbled rigging of the larger ship. They rocked to and fro at the mercy of each rush of water; then the board was torn away, and the barge reeled over the shoal, driving toward the turmoil of the harbor entrance. No man could have steered it straight in this fury. As the stricken watchers on the shore were driven back by more devastating waves, they saw the shape of the boat on a crest, lost it again in a trough, then saw it again as it shuddered around and plunged nearer still to the harbor. Its sprit had come down now, and it was rolling so heavily that it seemed fated to capsize at any second.

Matthew pulled away from Kate. She turned, to see him stumbling across the stones below the harbor wall. He was waving another man on. Two others stared, then followed. They scrambled up onto the path, crouching against the wind that promised to hurl them off into the water beyond.

Almost on hands and knees, pulling himself forward by the oak uprights of the groin, Matthew began to crawl toward the battered head of the pier.

"No!" Kate shouted after him. But her voice was contemptuously whisked away, as meaningless to him as it had been to Abel and John.

The men on the groin were dark, slow-moving slugs. The *Mary Matilda* was coming in too fast. They would never reach the end before she struck.

And if they did reach it, the collision could well dislodge them.

The only light left was an eerie sheen over the sea. It had the pallor of reflected moonlight, but there was no moon. It threw into relief the ragged outlines of the barge as it reared, bucked like a horse about to leap a fence, and flopped with its bows crunching between two of the posts of the groin. The bowsprit snapped and tugged shreds of rigging over the port side. As the water fell momentarily away below, the whole craft hung suspended.

A figure clawed up the tilting deck. John or Abel—there was no way of distinguishing—desperately threw a rope over. Matthew got to his feet and began to run crazily around the oak stanchions.

The rope curled and smacked against the groin a good ten feet away. The two brothers were huddled side by side now, hauling it back in fast, ready to throw it and ready to jump the moment they had the opportunity.

Water boiled up beneath the hull again, and the barge was wrenched free. From the way its bows went sickeningly down, it was obvious that it was filling fast.

The rip of the tide dragged it along the groin. Men went flat on their faces and held on. The *Mary Matilda* lurched away, shedding spars and a length of bulwark . . . was scooped up by a wave . . . was thrown again at the groin.

It seemed to run straight into the men clinging there. Then one of the brothers threw himself overboard and made a grab for the nearest massive wooden leg. His fingers slithered down the slime of the post. Another shape tottered on the gunwale. And sprang.

Matthew, in advance of the others, grabbed at him. Their arms interlocked. Matthew's head went over the edge. The two of them were hanging for an age. It seemed they would never move, could never force themselves up to safety.

The barge was pulled back, and tossed a third savage time into the battered timbers.

Matthew and whoever was linked with him had hauled themselves up on the crosspiece. The other brother was sliding very gently down. As the *Mary Matilda* struck for the last time, the end of the groin appeared to dissolve into the water. The sound of its collapse was so enormous that it was like the mightiest wave of all, smacking into the beach and reverberating from the row of cottages along the hard.

The tiny clinging figure was wiped off into the foam.

Two men leaned perilously out, looking down, making one move toward a descent . . . then, as the piers shook more terribly, abandoning it.

Slowly they all made their way back to solid ground.

Chapter Seventeen

Overnight the wind abated, summoned up its energies again, and by daybreak was urging the waves farther and farther inland. Families in cottages along the creek moved their belongings into upstairs rooms—when they had any upstairs rooms. The wreck on the shoal tugged and strained, shedding hatches, planking, and dead bodies as though it might lighten itself sufficiently to be free. Another attempt was made to get a boat out to it, to look for any survivors; but again it was beaten back.

What was left of the *Mary Matilda* was rammed into the angle of the bank and the landward end of the groin.

Kate sat all night beside Abel's bed, while he shivered and jerked like a man in the throes of the ague. At first light she saw from the window the drifts of water being thrust up from the creek, to stream back and then renew the assault.

Captain Josiah would not leave the beach. He paced far up the bay and back, tensing at the sight of every log and cask and tangle of weed thrown up by the sea. Two corpses fell face down into the teeming shallows, probably from the brigantine. It was Captain Josiah who insisted on turning them over, to study their faces and then to shake his head and stand up again.

There was a chance that John might be found trapped in the groin below the surface, when there were calm and daylight once more. Or that he might just possibly have been carried around the end of the wreckage and on down the coast.

But Captain Josiah refused to leave this stretch of the bay. Sarah came out with a mug of hot broth and pleaded with him to come home. If there were anything to report, everyone knew where they lived.

He drank the broth in a few gulps, though it must have scalded his mouth and throat, and handed the mug back to her. She returned to the house alone.

At ten o'clock in the morning another body came bobbing in on a deep swell, vanished into the heart of a wave, and then was tossed brutally up the shingle, a few hundred yards from where Captain Josiah stood. The back of the head was a hideous pulp. One of the older fishermen reached the corpse first and tried to wave Captain Josiah off.

"Let me. I'll tell you."

But his hand fell away from the sodden, streaming shoulder; and it was Captain Josiah who gently turned John over and looked into his face.

He stayed on his knees beside his son for a full fifteen minutes. Nobody else ventured near. If his eyes were wet, and if a salty runnel trickled down the side of his nose to his lips, no man would ever allow that it had been anything but the spray of the storm.

Matthew stood by the stableyard gate with Kate and Daniel. His boots and breeches were caked with mud. A few yards from the gate, the lane was already a quagmire. He looked toward the pillar of Darsham's Folly and said, "Murderer!"

"The sea's always been a killer," said Daniel.

"Not the sea. That man up there—only he's not even there, is he? More pressing engagements. If I'd been allowed to go on with my work here, if I'd been allowed to strengthen that groin, if . . ." His hand thumped down on the top bar of the gate. "Now we must save what we can. I'd be obliged by the use of your wagon. There's furniture to be moved to safety, and we have very little time."

Daniel asked no questions. He crossed the yard to the stable, and they heard a whinnying greeting and his deep, soothing murmur.

"You think some families should be moved?" Kate asked.

"The center of the village will hold. The inn ought to be safe. It will be cut off for a time, but it will stand. But the outlying cottages—those up the shore, along the creek, and a few below the level of the hard—they must be emptied. Are there any other carts we could press into service?"

Captain Josiah had come out of the house. He joined them and said, "There's the old dray Spence uses. And Ladd's sack cart, if that's any use."

"Everything can be of use. If you'd take command, Captain . . ."

"No, sir. You're the master here. Tell me what you

want and who you want, and where things have to go, and I'll see to it."

There was the jingle of harness from the stableyard. Daniel's usual leisurely pace had quickened.

"And I would suggest," said Matthew, "that we start with this house."

"This one?"

Kate and her father turned automatically to look at their home. It was so real and solid and safe.

But the overflow from the creek was no longer draining back. The deepening pool below the windows was no longer a pool: it had become part of the sea, ruffled by the gale and building up its own conflict of greedy waves.

Captain Josiah said, "We'll deal with other folk first."

"If you're under my orders, sir, you'll deal with this house first."

The two men weighed each other up. Then Captain Josiah saluted brusquely and turned to his daughter.

"You'd better get inside, girl, and decide what has to go. Not a scrap more than the things we can't do without. Sarah'll know what's best for the baby, and leave the kitchen to her. Abel wrapped up warmly. And . . ."

"Yes, Father." She knew what he could not bring himself to say. John, still not decently laid out, was still not to be allowed to rest.

As she went indoors, her father and Matthew were making swift plans. A minute or two later she heard Daniel's wagon roll out, pause by them, and then rumble off up the lane. Her father's voice ceased. He had probably gone with Daniel.

She found Sarah and told her what was to be done. They would pile all the stuff to be taken away by the kitchen door. It was a wide door, and Daniel could back the wagon up to it for loading; or perhaps Matthew was sending something smaller for them, and allocating Daniel to the whole group of cottages below the hard.

She went into John's room and stood helplessly by his bedside. She wanted to bathe his shattered face yet again, to refashion it patiently until it was whole again, and then to hear him speak to her again.

"He's in no need of you now," said Matthew gently, from behind her. "It's the living you have to think of."

She swung around. The ceiling was a shimmer of ripples reflected from the water outside.

"The sea!" It screamed out of her. "I hate it . . . hate it!"

"It does no good to hate it."

"Does anything do any good? All the work, all the . . . the . . . No, it's useless. You can never win."

"You'll never win against the sea," he agreed, still gentle. "But a man can take pride in giving it a good fight."

Now she could hear the suck and plop of the water below the window.

"You'll be wanting to get on," said Matthew. "I've arranged for two carts. One of them old Downey's. For your brother. You won't want him just piled in with everything else."

"Thank you."

"I'll be off, then. I've got to get them out of Darsham's Folly."

"But that's well above flood level. If the inn is safe, then surely the Tower . . ."

"One side of it is far from safe. The garden is already subsiding. A few hours of heavy seas, and we could be down to the foundations. The whole wall could come down. Worse, perhaps."

"But they won't leave."

"They will have to."

"On whose authority?"

"The authority of good sound sense. Perhaps," said Matthew with rueful respect, "I shall have to call on your father to add his voice to mine. I fancy it carries more weight."

He left.

It was a dismal business, deciding what to save and what to abandon. She told herself that in the end it would all prove a waste of time: the storm would die down, the water would recede at the last moment, and their belongings would be undamaged. But in the meantime she had to make up her mind, and make it up quickly, as to what was essential. Several times she caught herself staring at an old picture, a stool, a shelf of much-thumbed books, or a tapestry fire screen, unable to decide whether to be ruthless or not. She had to force herself, when in doubt, to plump for ruthlessness.

The innkeeper was glad to offer them the spacious, dry loft above his stables. There was room to lay mattresses out and to stack up their belongings, lifted straight from the cart through the double flaps. But he would not hear of John lying there with them. In spite of the crowd packed into the inn, he closed the tiny back room and insisted that the body should lie peacefully there.

Some cottagers would not seek shelter with neighbors or in the inn. They dragged their bundles up to the first ridge of the heath, and huddled below the patchy trees. They could not believe that they had been driven from their homes, but were even less prepared to believe that in such an emergency anywhere else could be safer than their own houses. If they must move, they would sit well above danger level and wait, cold and wretched, for the inundation of the entire village.

Walking away from the Darsham Arms, she saw the

coach from the Tower rocking toward the marketplace.
Curious as to its passengers, she followed it into the
square. Mrs. Jenkyn was coming out of her sister-in-law's
cottage.

"Oh, it's you, miss."

"Are you all right, Mrs. Jenkyn?"

"I hope that father of yours knows what he's doing,
ordering us about like this."

"He has persuaded you all to leave, then?"

"Having a bit of trouble with Mrs. Darsham." Even at a
time like this it was impossible not to share a grin. "I've
been sent to pick up a few of my things I left here, and
then I'm to accompany Miss Verena to Sheverton. And
Mrs. Darsham, when they've talked her around."

"Sheverton?"

"There's none too much spare room in the village. As
we've got the carriage, Mr. Rouse says we're to make our
way to one of the inns over there. The way things are,"
said Mrs. Jenkyn with grudging approval, "it could be
there's some sense in that."

"Give Verena my love. I'll see all of you when you get
back."

"When we get back." Mrs. Jenkyn nodded. "Though
what the master's going to say about all this . . ."

By early afternoon there were rebellious mutterings.
The ebb tide was pulling the sea back. Shore and river-
bank were littered with rubbish, and mud choked the lane
to the creek and smeared the marketplace and the hard;
but it would all wash away, it would all return to normal.
One family returned to its cottage and told Matthew
Rouse to give his orders to those who were foolish enough
to listen. This was their home, and here they would stay.

But high tide was not until eleven o'clock that night.

Another dusk brought no promise of respite. The wind

did not slacken for an instant, and the sea was a jubilant, rampaging maniac.

Kate was sitting with Sarah and young Josiah when Matthew came to her.

"I have only just been told that Mrs. Darsham refused at the last moment to leave the Tower. The coach has gone, but she's still there."

"Alone?"

"Absolutely on her own. She just has to be brought out."

"If Mrs. Darsham says she will not leave, she will not."

"She *has* to. Before it's too late."

Kate said, "You are really convinced of the danger?"

"In conditions like these, I am sure of nothing. But yes, I do believe the danger to be very grave. Your father would not have helped me so readily if he did not share this view."

"Very well. I will go and see Mrs. Darsham."

Sarah caught at her arm as she got up. "No, Kate."

"No," said Matthew. "Not you. I'll not allow that."

"If you accept my father's help, you'll accept mine."

"I'd rather that stubborn old woman died than—"

"I see you really do believe in the danger."

Kate took up her cloak and went down to the innyard. Matthew pursued her.

"After this is settled, you'll come with me—away from here? Be done with all this?"

"You can't ask me. Please, not now."

"Now above all times."

"There's my brother. Abel will need me for a while. He and John were so close. He . . . there's so much . . . so much to do."

"Yes." He pulled her to him, and kissed her, and shook her in an anger of love. "So much to do. I will stay, then—force them to let me salvage what there is to salvage. Somehow I will *make* them listen. And you will do what you have to do. But after that—after that, Kate?"

"After that there may be time to talk," she said, her cheek cold against his. "There's none now."

She floundered off through the mud which had been trampled into the village from every side. The lane was so slippery that three times she nearly lost her footing and had to clutch at a fence or a branch which stung her fingers.

The trees up the drive bent and howled in the wind. The door was almost snatched from her hand as she let herself into the house, and when she had forced it shut, that same wind moaned and whined beneath it like a mad dog ravening to get in.

There were no lights in the hall. Kate waited until her eyes had adjusted themselves to the spreading twilight, then went up the stairs. Mingled with the buffeting wind were what seemed to be shifts and creaks and groans of protest from the very bones of the house itself.

She climbed one flight in near-darkness, and had to stop by a window on the landing to regain her confidence. Far below, a lantern bobbed like a will-o'-the-wisp through the village.

She went on and upward until she saw a thin line of light under Mrs. Darsham's door.

Mrs. Darsham's greeting was uncompromising. "It is high time somebody took the trouble to come up. The girls have not refilled the lamps. I wish them attended to immediately."

Two candles in floral china candlesticks guttered on a table at her elbow, and there were two more in sconces on either side of Robert Darsham's portrait.

"Mrs. Darsham, everybody else has left," said Kate.

"They had no right to do so."

"You really must come with me. It's not safe to stay here any longer."

"What rubbish. Those two men ought to be ashamed of themselves, spreading alarm in that fashion. And now you." The querulous eyes were pinpricks of light as she leaned toward Kate. "What have you done with Verena? Why are you not with the child?"

"She has gone. And I've come to fetch you."

"You'll do no such thing."

A faint tremor ran through the floor beneath Kate's feet. She said, "Don't you feel it? The whole building is in danger."

"It always moves in the wind," said Mrs. Darsham comfortably.

"Please, Mrs. Darsham . . ."

"My son is the head of this household. I shall leave when he tells me to do so, not before."

"But he may not get back in time."

"Time?" said Mrs. Darsham. "There is all the time in the world."

It was unthinkable that Kate should drag her bodily from the chair and drive her like a stubborn animal down the stairs.

She tried again. "By high tide half the village will be gone."

"Highly improbable. But if there is some distress, I hope arrangements have been made for hot soup to be distributed?"

One of the candle flames swayed spasmodically in a draft and went out. With a job of her finger Mrs. Darsham indicated that Kate should relight it.

"I will not leave without you," said Kate.

"I will thank you not to address me in that way, miss."

"Mrs. Darsham, don't you understand the worry you will cause? If anything happens, Verena . . . Mr. Darsham . . ."

"I intend to have a serious talk about this whole affair with my son when he returns."

"For the sake of your family . . . your friends . . ."

"Hum." Then Mrs. Darsham's head was cocked suddenly to one side. Whatever the fogging and clearing of her eyesight and memory, there was nothing wrong with her hearing. She said, "Is that him?"

Very faintly Kate heard the hiss of wheels as they left the road and struck the drive. There was a click and tap of hooves, slowing. Silence. It might have been a trick of the unpredictable wind.

But she said, "That must be the carriage, back from Sheverton. It has been sent to fetch you. Please come down."

Mrs. Darsham reached for one of the candlesticks and held it out. "Take this. Go down and see who it is. If it is my son, tell him I wish to see him immediately."

Oliver stood below one of the wall lamps in the hall, reaching up to light it with a wax vesta. As Kate made her slow descent, shielding the agitated flame of her candle behind a cupped palm, he came to the foot of the stairs to wait for her. Behind him, leaning on a polished hawthorn stick, was an elderly man who remained planted in the center of the floor.

Kate said, "The servants have gone."

"So I have heard. So my daughter told me when I found her and the carriage in Sheverton. By what right that insolent creature Rouse . . ." But as she reached the last step, his face changed, his mood changed; he laughed, he opened his arms as though inviting her to fall into them. She stopped. Suddenly she could not bear the thought of being touched by him. "Kate!" he cried. "At least *you* have not left. *You* shall be the first to hear what I've brought."

She said, "Your mother asks that you should go up to her immediately."

"My mother? No, she is not my mother. But," said Oliver exultantly, "Robert Darsham was my father."

Chapter Eighteen

In the library, Oliver set a lamp on his desk. "As you will see"—his features were a saturnine glow above the lamp glass—"I found Dr. Withersedge."

The old man wore a tweed suit with a waistcoat buttoned tightly up to his stiff wing collar, over which pouchy folds of his neck sagged and wrinkled. His lower teeth were gone, and his mouth curved up in a tremulous bow toward his nose. When he lowered himself into a chair, he still clung to his stick, drawing it slowly around between his knees and resting his clasped hands on it. In spite of the deliberation of his movements, his eyes were clear and shrewd, his whole manner meditative rather than vague.

"I have brought him back with me to tell Cousin Flora the full story," said Oliver. "And to tell you."

"We mustn't stay here. You must go up and persuade Mrs. Darsham—"

"Nothing can happen to Darsham's Tower, Kate. Not now!"

He splashed wine liberally into three glasses, set one beside the doctor, and handed one to Kate. Then he perched on the corner of his desk, oblivious to the banshee wailing about the house.

"It was Dr. Withersedge who brought Prudence Botting here," he explained. "We were right in surmising that much. But we were wrong in one or two details. It was not simply that he had noticed her while passing through Castleyard—not simply a happy coincidence. He was *sent* there. Sent," said Oliver, "by my father."

Withersedge released one quavering hand to claim his glass. He looked up at Oliver, and his arched lips sketched a thin old smile. There was a great gap between the child he had brought to Darsham's Folly and this grown man before him.

"Young Botting was not my father." Oliver must have been over it many times with the doctor on their journey here, but had not yet lost the wonder of it.

Dr. Withersedge said in a reedy little chuckle, "If he had been, it would have been a matter of some medical interest. Botting had been away at sea for considerably more than a year before you were born."

"You see?" Oliver crowed at Kate.

She saw. The roving Robert Darsham, so discreet in his own village and so amorous elsewhere, had taken his pleasure with Prudence Botting while her husband was away at sea and had fathered a son on her. That son was now perched by the lamp on the desk, saying, "Tell Miss Quantrill the whole story, Withersedge—tell her."

"Prudence's boy was born a few days before Mrs. Darsham produced Robert's other son," said the doctor. "That was the main reason for my staying here. Robert was a rake, but a considerate one. He wanted to be sure that Prudence received adequate attention, from an old friend he could trust." His head, almost as bleached as the watchful skull, wagged to and fro. "I must confess I was apprehensive. My interest was always more in ornithology than in the complexities of the human frame. When I went off as ship's surgeon, it was mainly to study wildlife in the antipodes. My father was a doctor—no very assiduous one. He paid for me to become a gentleman, and in his spare time taught me to be a physician. I don't know which has been the greater failure."

"You brought me to the Tower," Oliver prompted him impatiently.

"Yes. Yes, quite. When Dr. Cawdron was called away to the Chedstowe epidemic, he left me in charge. That same night Mrs. Darsham's baby died, and Mrs. Darsham sank into a fever. Robert was desperate. He had to have a son. He turned to me. I was to dismiss the nurse at once, before she discovered what had happened. She was very indignant, I remember—couldn't understand it—but Robert paid her handsomely, so that she would not ask too many questions. We packed her off, and I went to bring Prudence and her child to the Tower. Once she was safely installed, I helped to bury one Oliver—Robert said he would have a suitable plaque engraved in London, when he was next there—and I helped to keep the other Oliver alive. The names had been chosen long before the birth. When Mrs. Darsham recovered, she found herself still with an Oliver Alexander."

Oliver shifted his position. The awkward thrust of his hip drew Withersedge's attention.

"A sickly child." He might have been talking dispassionately of some other case. "I was not conscious of the seriousness of the malformation, and I did not stay long enough to offer any advice. Not that my advice would have been worth a great deal, I fear. A sickly child," he repeated, nodding up at Oliver, "like your mother. A pretty girl, but poor bones. Poor diet—bread and cheese, a few turnips, and a hunk of fat bacon on a Sunday if they were lucky."

"I am here," said Oliver. "I'm alive."

"Yes."

And Prudence, thought Kate, was only too glad to hand over her baby to its real father, accept his money, and depart. Even if her husband had asked a few questions about the money when he returned, they would be less tricky to answer than questions about a child that he would have known could not be his.

"So I'm of good Blackshore stock," laughed Oliver, "and of good peasant stock. What could be finer?"

Withersedge continued to study him, obviously fascinated by what the weakling child had turned into.

"If a peasant girl produces sons"—Oliver raised his glass as if in a toast to her memory—"better her than some pretty piece of porcelain as a wife . . . eh, Doctor?"

From the hall outside came a faint flurry of draft and a gentle thud which Kate recognized as the sound of the baize-covered door swinging shut. It was followed by a diffident tap at the library door.

"I thought everyone had gone?" Then Oliver called, "Come in."

The door opened and the coachman stood there.

"Of course. Cockerill. What is it?"

"Sir, the water from the creek's starting to come over the road."

"And after high tide," said Oliver pleasantly, "it will start to go down again."

"I don't like the look of that road, sir. It's all sinking,

like. The carriage will still just about get through, but we mustn't leave it too late."

"We shall remain here until the water subsides. I shall have things to say to the staff when they return."

Kate said, "It really is bad this time. Worse than you know. My brother . . ." To say it loud nearly choked her. "My brother John has been killed. There'll be others."

"I'm sorry to hear it." Oliver's cool offhandedness robbed her of breath. "Fortunately," he said dismissively, "he's not the only son in your family."

Dr. Withersedge pressed down with both hands on his stick and pushed himself upright.

"In view of what I have heard, Mr. Darsham—"

"What you have heard is rubbish."

"I got to know these flats when I was younger. I know how swiftly disaster can strike. Dunwich, Slaughden, old Senwich that used to be . . ."

Kate found her tongue. "It would be wrong to leave Mrs. Darsham up there any longer."

The coachman stood in the doorway, surly, willing his employer to change his decision.

Oliver slid from the desk. "Very well. Doctor, if you will go with Cockerill, he will settle you comfortably in the carriage. Miss Quantrill and I will go up to fetch my mother." He winked knowingly. "My mother: I think that for her sake we must keep up the pretense, don't you?"

Withersedge's stick tapped heavily out across the hall. Oliver took up a smaller lamp, lit it, and followed with Kate.

"Cockerill."

"Sir?"

The coachman stopped, and Oliver caught up with him. He said something in an undertone. Cockerill looked startled; his lower lip dropped; he was about to make some sort of protest. Oliver snapped something, and Cockerill

turned away and went to open the door for Dr. Withersedge to go through.

"Oh, and . . . Doctor."

"Yes?"

"Cockerill will find you accommodation and let me
know. Perhaps you'll be kind enough to come back tomorrow."

"Certainly."

"We still have Flora Hartest to tell," said Oliver gleefully, taking Kate's arm and leading her toward the stairs.
"Poor Cousin Flora—doomed to discover that she is still
my cousin!"

He raised the lamp above his head, so that shadows
dripped like mud down the wall as they began to climb.

On the second landing Oliver stopped. He looked along
to where the pool of light from the lamp faded into the
carpeting. Gently he urged Kate forward.

"No." She held back. His hand tightened on her wrist.
"Mrs. Darsham . . . she's up two more . . . not this way. . . ."

"Come and see where we shall live."

Before she could speak, she heard an unmistakable
sound below. Hooves and wheels resounded along the side
of the house, dwindling fast.

She remembered the coachman's expression.

"You've sent the carriage away!"

"It's not the weather for an excursion. You and I have
more important things to do."

The madness of it robbed her of all strength. Her knees
shook. Oliver had dragged her boisterously along the corridor before she could begin to strike at him and try to
brace herself against the carpet.

He kicked open a door, laughing, and held the lamp
high.

"This will all be yours, Kate. All yours."

She staggered into the room, and he slammed the door

shut behind them. The lamp swayed in his hand, so that the room itself seemed to rock. Kate's head swam. She groped for support, and found only Oliver's arm. He was still laughing.

"We can't stay here," she cried.

"But that is just what we shall do. You belong here, Kate. Here with me. And here we stay."

Silk wallpaper gave off deep emerald echoes. In one corner was a tall wardrobe of inlaid mahogany, and under the window a pretty, slim-legged dressing table. The side curtains of the bed were drawn back, and in the warm draft of the lamp chimney a satin valance began to wave gently along its frilled length.

The room was as cold as death.

"It shall all be yours." Oliver made a sudden move toward the wardrobe, leaving Kate by the bed, which gave off the faintest of lost perfumes.

He opened the doors of the wardrobe and stood back, and again he was laughing.

Colors jostled within, like a crowded flowerbed at dusk. Kate caught the glint of a lilac ballgown, and of a rose-pink afternoon dress she remembered Lady Charlotte wearing.

"I have not yet had time to dispose of all this." Oliver reached for the nearest drawer in the dressing table and tugged it open. "I could scarcely send it all after her *this* time!"

He came back toward Kate. She shrank away, brushing against the hangings of the bed. He shook his head tolerantly, as though humoring her.

"I will send Verena to live with her aunt. She and Alice always get on well together. It will be company for both of them. And then we start afresh. If you want anything altered—in here . . . or here . . ."

Although he was treating it as a lighthearted moment,

he took care to come between her and the door, driving her toward another door, lifting the lamp so that her shadow splayed out before her.

There was a small, intimate dressing room beyond, without windows. Where one might have expected a window was a painting of a naked nymph drowsing above a woodland pool.

Kate turned to plead with Oliver. They must fetch his mother—the woman he was still to call mother—and must go.

He prowled around her in a steady, frightening circle, his eyes full of joy.

Kate said, "I have to tell you. Matthew Rouse has asked me to marry him."

Oliver let out a bellow of laughter. "Damned impertinence! That gives me yet another reason for kicking him off my land."

"I must get away. My brother is dead, the sea . . . everything . . . I must go away, as far away as it's possible to go."

"You will marry me," said Oliver.

His head swooped toward hers. It was no pleasantry, no game. She dodged, stumbled, and threw herself at the door. The knob slid between her fingers, she wrenched it open, and found herself in yet another bedroom, black and silver in the light over her shoulder.

She had chosen the wrong door. She was even deeper into this private maze of his.

"Don't run, Kate. If you run, I shall follow you. I don't want to have to follow you the way I followed Charlotte."

"Followed her?" Kate whispered.

He could not stay still. Talking, declaiming, freed by Dr. Withersedge of the intolerable burden which had threatened to crush him, he strode back through the dressing room and then came back again as Kate groped at a curtained door in the gloom and found it led only to a cupboard.

"You imagine I would allow her to flout me just like that? To dance off with her paltry, pathetic lover and make a jest of it . . . of *me*? I knew she would soon miss the life I had given her. Comforts are dull and everyday until you are without them. I waited . . . and then I followed. But none of it matters now."

Kate stood quite still. "Still I should like to know."

"None of it matters."

"It might—to me."

"You will not run from me," he said.

"Why did she run?"

"Because she was a fool," he said with a sudden gout of venom. "Spoiled, hysterical . . . petty . . . unworthy."

"Unworthy?"

"Of the Darsham name. Her own name went back only a few centuries. Petty," he repeated. "Shallow. It will be so different with you, Kate. *You* will set up no petty pretensions against me, will you?"

"You followed her . . ."

"From the moment she and that pup of hers left this house, I had them watched. It was too predictable. No quality to it—no style in the worthless creature. I knew her enjoyment would wane when he was thrown out of his regiment."

"You arranged that?" asked Kate quietly.

"I did not lack influence. Thrown out of his regiment and onto his own resources, he soon showed his true caliber. The resources remained small."

Kate began very warily to edge toward the door that he was blocking. If he kept pacing, kept jerking himself to and fro in his paroxysm of triumph, there would sooner or later come a moment when she could plunge past him and find the right door out of this nightmare.

Oliver stiffened and looked suspiciously at her.

She said, "You were influential there, too—in ensuring his resources remained small?"

"He was strangely unable to find a suitable position. Before very long they had to live on Charlotte's money. There was little of it, and she was never lavish with it. A sad situation."

"Yes. Sad."

"It was no great surprise when she chose to come home."

There could have been pitifully little question of choice in it. Oliver had played her on a line, tormented her, netted her, exhausted her, won her back without ever truly wanting her back.

He was ranting on, but Kate ceased to hear. His voice was only another note in the wind, adding to the discord of voices out of every tortured plank and panel in Darsham's Folly. Lady Charlotte was still here—in this very room—still sobbing, still smarting under the lash of his arrogance. Pride had driven him on and driven her down. Now Kate knew, beyond all doubt, who had been guilty. His derision rasped through the haunted room, fell away again; and she knew that, however petulant and flighty Lady Charlotte had been, she had not deserved to be the victim of such persecution. Driven to hysteria, she had been driven into another man's arms. Dragged back and allowed to go on living here under the most humiliating terms, she had once again been reduced to hysteria and then goaded out onto a last mad ride.

Had he been frightened, at the last minute, of what he had done—gone in pursuit of her to make sure she went well and truly to her death, or to recapture her yet again before she once again held him up to ridicule?

The intervening doorway was clear. She went quickly through it.

His free arm encircled her and pinned her against the doorjamb, twisted her away again, and thrust her gasping against the bed.

She cried out, knowing it had to be true: "I am going to marry Matthew Rouse." Even in this maelstrom of horror she felt a surge of pure joy. It was Matthew, had to be Matthew. "I am going to marry him. Marry Matthew Rouse."

"You'll marry me, Kate, and bear my sons. I am a Darsham, and you shall be a Darsham, and we'll start afresh, that's how it must be." Once more he set the lamp down, freeing his hands to reach for her. "I love you, Kate. I have the right to say it now. And you—you have no right not to say it. Tell me, Kate. Tell me."

What ought to have been poetry, what she had once half-dreamed would be poetry, became obscenity. Love was not love but vainglory. He wanted a brood mare, not a woman. His desire for Kate was only the implacable urge to produce a son. Words of sweetness were soured into foul, insane babblings.

"No," she shouted. "I'm going to marry Matthew."

His laughter cracked like a sob. As he tried to seize her, the whole floor vibrated. Then it was still, but the tremor was enough to strike through even Oliver's crazed rapture. For an instant he was uncertain. In that instant Kate reached the door and began to run toward the stairs.

"Kate!"

Like a tantalizing echo from far away she heard it in another voice. Matthew's voice. "Kate!" And it went on. "Kate, are you here? Kate!"

It was clearer at the head of the stairs.

"Kate, where *are* you?"

She heard a scream that must have been her own. An answer without words. And the rush and stumble of her own feet down the stairs.

On the next landing she risked a glance back. She could just see Oliver, one hand on the banister at the turn of the staircase. He looked as though he might plunge bodily down on her. But he was looking upward, not down.

The noise must have brought Mrs. Darsham to her door.

Faintly she called something.

Matthew yelled at the top of his voice, "All of you—come down! The whole place is ready to go. Come on *down!*"

"Oliver"—Mrs. Darsham's irritable whine was somehow amplified down the shaft—"is the beacon lit? We always light the beacon. On a night like this . . ."

"Come *down!*" Matthew was bellowing.

Kate's hand slid down the rail; she scurried down the last flight.

Matthew stood in the hall with a lantern raised high in one hand. In the other he held what might have been a huge pike snatched from the suit of armor, or a staff of some kind. As he swung the lantern around to be sure it was Kate, she saw that the staff was a large crowbar.

"I saw the carriage," he said as she reached him. "The coachman told me you had been left behind. And now the road's impassable. The garden has sunk, the house is standing on the edge of a trench . . . and it won't stand much longer."

He turned toward the door to the servants' corridor, jerking his head to make her follow.

"We can't leave them up there."

"If they're mad enough . . ." Matthew put his head back and made one more attempt. "Mr. Darsham—will you bring Mrs. Darsham down now . . . *now?* Through the tunnel."

"The tunnel?" Kate gasped.

The house shifted. It was not merely a shudder before

the wind, but a grinding shift of the entire building. Above
the stairs, the stained-glass window cracked down its full
length. The two halves fell inward with infinite slowness,
and then St. Cecilia splintered to fragments against the
baluster rail.

Matthew wasted no more time. He raised the crowbar
as though prepared to drive Kate before him with it if she
objected. She pulled at the baize-covered door. It was
stuck. The uneasy shifting of the house had warped the
frame. Kate put all her weight to it, and was through, and
held it open for Matthew.

"Take the lantern," he commanded.

They hurried to an open doorway which she remembered; and she remembered the dark, steep flight of steps
within.

"But Oliver? Mrs. Darsham?"

"I won't risk your life. I'll spend not another second on
that man's madness."

She guided their way down to the cellar. Water
streamed down one wall with the steady hiss of a weir. Its
icy grip closed around Kate's ankles.

"We can't go through the tunnel. We can't!"

"It's the only way out."

"But with it coming in like that—"

"There is no other way." Matthew thrust his face close
to hers and shouted, "No other way out. Do you understand?"

The wooden flap concealing the doorway to the tunnel
had been wrenched away, its lock smashed and splintered
from the far side by Matthew's crowbar.

"The tunnel is sounder than this cellar." He waved her
on. "Don't be frightened, Kate. You should know the Darshams by now: they made their ancestors' burial chamber
a whole lot more secure than what they built for the
living."

Kate ducked her head and went through the low arch. Then her feet would carry her no farther. The sound of water plopping and trickling from the roof ahead was ten times louder than when Oliver had brought her down here.

"No," she said. "I can't."

She turned back.

Matthew barred her way.

"Kate, it will hold. We'll get through—trust me. But if we wait too long, it will flood from this end. Now, *go!*"

She twisted and crouched even lower, and stumbled on with her eyes half-shut. Water cascaded down into her hair and rattled on the hood of the lantern. "Yes," Matthew was urging her from behind. "Go on, go on."

Her knee grazed against a stone coffin.

The thought of drowning here, surrounded by the Darsham dead, slowed her in terror and then drove her on in even greater terror.

Above, there came the shock of some minor earthquake, and a fragment of stone fell and grazed her arm; and the water trickling from the roof became a sudden savage downpour . . . and then relented. Some wave must have raced up the gully, clawing away earth and smacking ferociously down upon the stone and brickwork. It receded. There would be another. Kate could almost feel the rhythm that would be set up, the succession of shocks that would bring it all down about her ears.

She made a last lunge forward, and knew when the light of the lantern fell on one tiny coffin that she had reached the end.

There was a ragged gap in the wall ahead. Her feet scuffed and scrabbled over a scattering of bricks which had collapsed to the tunnel floor when Matthew smashed his way through. Beyond was a faint light, a flickering glow, against which the barred gate of the Darsham mausoleum hung half-open.

Only a yard or two now; yet it was almost too much. Kate gripped the edge of the gap and tried to pull herself up, groping for a foothold on the loose bricks.

Matthew came behind her and lifted her bodily.

She was through. She got up from her knees and ran, still with her head down, out into the roar of wind which was flailing the churchyard. It caught her. She would be blown away. Then it was Matthew who had caught her, holding her close.

"My dearest. Kate, oh, my dearest Kate."

She burrowed her head hard into his shoulder, away from the cruel cold and the storm wind and the madness of the Darshams—away from all fear.

She heard him say, "Mad. Yes, mad."

It took the greatest effort of all to lift her head away from its haven and look up into the sky.

The glow which had beckoned her across the vault was red and smoky against the blackness of the night. It rose and fell, flared and dipped.

They were trying to keep the beacon alight on top of the Tower.

"They always light the beacon"—it was her last tribute, almost in Mrs. Darsham's own last words—"always light it in bad weather."

"But what help can it be in this? What use do they think . . . ?"

"They have always done it."

Oil in the cresset flared and sputtered, plucked at by the wind and torn away. Two silhouettes moved in front of it, then disappeared.

And the silhouette of the Tower itself seemed to shake. Clouds reeled down on it, oily smoke swirled about the battlements. Then the beacon flame seemed to divide and fall. Burning tongues plunged down through the darkness, down to oblivion. Suddenly the shape of the Tower was no longer there against sky and skyline.

The storm roared. The ground trembled, and the sea launched its final attack on the ravaged flesh and sinews of the ruin.

Beneath Kate's feet was firm ground. Matthew's arm about her was firm. She was safe.

"Kate." It was all he said, and all she needed to hear, over and over again. "My dearest Kate."

It would take years for the waves to finish their work. Years to pick over the bones, shred away all that was recognizable, and gradually drag this corner of Senwich out to join old, long-lost Senwich in the depths of the bay. But finished, remorselessly, the work would be. One day there would be nothing left of Darsham's Folly but a whisper of wind off the sea, a shred of talk in a village inn, or a blurred memory in the mind of a sailor voyaging out across the wider, freer world.